The FOA Refe

MW00904427

Outside Plant Fiber Optics

And Study Guide To
FOA Certification

Jim Hayes

The Fiber Optic Association, Inc.
The Professional Society Of Fiber Optics
www.TheFOA.org

The FOA Reference Guide To Outside Plant Fiber Optics And Study Guide To FOA Certification

The Fiber Optic Association, Inc.

1119 S. Mission Road #355, Fallbrook, CA 92028
Telephone: 1-760-451-3655 Fax 1-781-207-2421
Email: info@thefoa.org   http://www.TheFOA.org

Updated February 2014.

CFOT© is a registered trademark of The Fiber Optic Association, Inc., US Patent and Trademark Office Reg. No. 3,572,190.

ISBN 1450559670

Table of Contents

Preface..vii

Chapter 1
Introduction..9
What is "Fiber Optics"?..9
Which Fiber Optics? 11
Fiber, Copper or Wireless ?..13
Standards Facilitate Fiber Applications 13
Two Important Issues When Working With Fiber 14

Chapter 2
Fiber Optic Jargon..19
What Is Fiber Optics?...19
The Metric System..19
Fiber 20
Fiber Optic Cable...21
Outside Plant Installations 22
Termination and Splicing 22
Fiber Performance Specifications..23
Tools 24
Fiber Optic Test Equipment 25

Chapter 3
Fiber Optic Communications 29
Why use fiber?...29
Fiber Optic Communication Networks 30
Designing Fiber Optic Networks 35

Chapter 4
Fiber Optic Transmission Systems And Components............................39
Fiber Optic Data Links 39
Sources for Fiber Optic Transmitters...40
Detectors for Fiber Optic Receivers 43
Specialty Fiber Optic Transmission Components...................................43
Data Link Performance And Link Power Budget 47

Chapter 5
Optical Fiber...53
What is Optical Fiber? 53
Fiber Types...54
Fiber Specifications 58

Chapter 6
Fiber Optic Cable..**71**
Fiber Optic Cable Design 71
Fiber Optic Cable Types 74
Choosing a Cable Design...80
Choosing Cables 83

Chapter 7
Splices and Connectors...**87**
Splices or Connectors? 87
Performance Specifications..88
Splicing Optical Fibers...90
Connectors 96
Termination Procedures...101

Chapter 8
Fiber Optic Testing **111**
Fiber Optic Tests.. 111
Visual Inspection 112
Optical Power 114
Optical Loss or Insertion Loss 118
OTDR testing..128
Testing Long Haul, High Speed Fiber Optic Networks 135
Other Testing 139

Chapter 9
Fiber Optic Network Design **145**
What Is Fiber Optic Network Design? 145
Cabling Design 148
Choosing Transmission Equipment 150
Planning The Route 152
Choosing Components...154
Cable Plant Link Loss Budget Analysis 160
Project Documentation 164
Planning for the Installation 165
Planning for Restoration 170
Managing A Fiber Optic Project...172

Chapter 10
Fiber Optic Network Installation **177**
Preparing For Installation 177
Installation Checklist...180
Preparing For Outside Plant Installations 182
Pulling and Placing Cable..183

Preparing For Premises Fiber Optic Installations 193
Equipping Installation Personnel 196
Training and Safety 199
Installing Fiber Optic Cable 207
Termination and Splicing 212
Testing the Installed Fiber Optic Cable Plant 215
Administration, Management, and Documentation 216

Appendix A
KSAs for CFOT + CFospT **221**

Appendix B
Fiber To The Home **225**

Appendix C
Additional References For Training and Study **239**

Appendix D
Definitions of Terms **241**

Index **249**

Preface

The purpose of this book is to provide a reference guide to those involved with outside plant fiber optic networks, either in design, installation, use, maintenance or troubleshooting, or those teaching the personnel who will work with it. This book is also the reference guide for FOA Outside Plant Certification. With a subject so broad, it's impossible to cover every aspect of the topic in depth. What will be covered in this book is the basics of fiber optic applications for communications systems that utilize outside plant fiber optic cable as a transmission medium.

The Fiber Optic Association, Inc., the nonprofit international professional society of fiber optics, has become one of the principal sources of technical information, training curriculum and certifications for the cabling industry. As technology has driven the rate of technical change ever faster, it has become a challenge to provide printed reference books that are not hopelessly out of date. Instead, many readers turn to the Internet for more up-to-date technical information.

The information on the Internet, however, is often biased toward commercial interests or application points of view, even that on supposedly non-commercial websites, and anonymous sources must be assumed to be untrustworthy or have a commercial agenda. The FOA is focused on education of technicians, not selling products, and we think it's important that every tech knows as much as possible about fiber optic technology without bias so they can deal successfully with design and installation in all types of applications.

The FOA created its Online Reference Guide (www.foaguide.org) to provide a more up-to-date and unbiased reference for those seeking information on cabling and fiber optic technology, components, applications and installation. It's success confirms the assumption that many users prefer the Internet for technical information.

With this book, we address the needs for those who prefer printed books or who must have them to meet academic requirements. However, the production of this book is done by "publishing on demand," where the book is not printed until ordered, and only after accessing the latest version electronically. Thus this edition meets the needs of those who prefer printed references without burdening them with trying to determine what material is already obsolete.

For those who want this printed version but also want access to the web for color graphics, self-study programs with automatic self-testing or links to even more technical information, we have go to the FOA Online Reference Guide website to find additional information on the sections covered in this book.
If you have feedback on the book, feel free to email comments or questions to the FOA at info@thefoa.org.

FOA Training Curriculum
The FOA provides training curriculum for those schools and trainers who have courses offering FOA certifications. FOA curriculum materials include instructor's guides, presentation slides, lab manuals, etc. Contact the FOA for the availability of appropriate curriculum packages for FOA certifications.

Other FOA Publications
The FOA Reference Guide to Fiber Optics
The FOA Reference Guide to Premises Cabling
The FOA Online Reference Guide (www.foaguide.org)

A note of appreciation
The material has been produced and reviewed by a number of contributors whom we wish to thank for their work in contributing, creating and reviewing the materials included here: Bob Ballard, Joe Botha, Craig Bowden, Duane Clayton, Tom Collins, Pat Dobbins, Darryl Dykstra, Craig Getchel, Bill Graham, Arnie Harris, Karen Hayes, Michael Hayes, John Highhouse, Ron Leger, Terry O'Malley, Eric Pearson, Bill Pruett, Jim Underwood and many, many more.

This information is provided by The Fiber Optic Association, Inc. as a benefit to those interested in designing, manufacturing, selling, installing or using fiber optic communications systems or networks. It is intended to be used as a overview and/or basic guidelines and in no way should be considered to be complete or comprehensive. These guidelines are strictly the opinion of the FOA and the reader is expected to use them as a basis for learning, reference and creating their own documentation, project specifications, etc. Those working with fiber optics in the classroom, laboratory or field should follow all safety rules carefully. The FOA assumes no liability for the use of any of this material.

Chapter 1
Introduction

Objectives: From this chapter you should learn:
What does "fiber optics" mean
How fiber was developed and used in communications
The difference between "outside plant" and "premises" fiber optics
Some advantages of fiber optics
What standards cover fiber optics
How to work with fiber safely

What is "Fiber Optics"?

Fiber optics refers to the technology of transmitting light down thin strands of highly transparent optical fibers, usually glass but sometimes plastic, using modulated light for signal transmission. Fiber optics is used in communications, lighting, medicine, optical inspection and to make sensors. The FOA is primarily interested in communications fiber optics and this book will focus on those applications.

A Brief History
Fiber optic communications began during the 1970s in R&D labs around the world (Corning, Bell Labs, ITT UK, etc.) and was first installed commercially in Dorset, England by STC and Chicago, IL, USA in 1976 by AT&T. By the early 1980s, the first fiber optic telecommunications networks connected the major cities on each coast of the USA and began being installed throughout the world.
By the mid-80s, with the introduction of the first singlemode fibers, fiber's bandwidth and distance capabilities made it significantly less expensive than other communications media and it began replacing all the telco copper, microwave and satellite long distance links. In the 90s, transoceanic fiber optic cables had replaced satellites between most continents. Now fiber has become cost effective for direct connection to the home.
CATV discovered fiber in the mid-1990s and used it first to enhance the reliability of their networks, a big problem. Not long afterwards, CATV system operators discovered they could offer phone and Internet service on that same fiber and greatly enlarged their markets.
The Internet was first transmitted over phone lines which by the late 1980s

were mostly fiber. But as Internet traffic grew with the advent of the web and everyone using email, it soon surpassed voice in traffic volume and found the phone system, optimized for voice transmission, highly inefficient for large amounts of digital data. The Internet with its unique transmission protocols became independent from the phone network, although it often used fibers in the same cables.

As cell phones became better and less expensive, creating a gigantic market for personal communications and portable data access, their backbones were built on fiber optics. Frequency allocations for wireless systems were limited so cellular backhaul used fiber to connect to worldwide phone networks.

Cities started using fiber optics early in the game, connecting schools, data networks from city agencies and public safety organizations first. Intelligent highway systems led to connecting "smart" traffic light into networks that could optimize traffic flow. When worries about terrorism led to the installation of many surveillance cameras around cities, the distance from cameras to monitoring stations was long enough that connecting them on fiber was much less expensive. Today some even offer direct fiber connections to their residents or businesses.

Computer networks (LANs) started using fiber about the same time as the telcos, in the late 1970s. Industrial links were among the first applications as the noise immunity of fiber and its distance capability make it ideal for the factory floor. Connecting graphics displays and mainframe storage links, the predecessors of today's fiber SANs (storage area networks) in data centers, came next. Today fiber is used in most corporate LANs as backbones, connections to desktops for engineering and graphics workstations and many wireless access points.

Utilities also have become big users of fiber. Practically every pipeline or electrical line has fiber running parallel to it or even inside the wires in the case of high voltage electrical distribution lines. Fiber provides communications over the routes and sometimes even includes sensors that keep track of the performance and problems. The electrical utilities are developing "smart grids" to make their power distribution more efficient and these networks depend on fiber for connections.

Other applications developed too: aircraft, ship and automobile data busses, CCTV for security, building automation systems, industrial networks and machinery, even links for consumer digital stereo!

Today fiber optics is either the dominant medium or a logical choice for every communication system. Costs have been reduced so much that fiber to the home is now cost effective, especially since it can offer services (entertainment as well as communications) that no other medium offers.

Which Fiber Optics?

Whenever you read an article or talk to someone about fiber optics, it's important to know which fiber optics they mean. All fiber optics is not the same. We're only concerned with communications fiber optics, but it's also used for lighting, inspection in medical and nondestructive testing and making sensors for physical measurements.

In communications, we distinguish between applications of fiber optics that differ in design and installation: "outside plant" fiber optics means outside buildings, as used in telephone networks, CATV, metropolitan networks, utilities, etc. and "premises" fiber optics as found in buildings and campuses. Just like "wire" which can mean lots of different things – electrical power, security, HVAC, CCTV, LAN or telephone - fiber optics is not all the same. And this can be a big source of confusion to the novice. Lets define our terms.

Outside Plant

Telephone companies, CATV and the Internet all use fiber optics, virtually all of which is outside buildings and is generally referred to as outside plant (OSP). OSP fiber optic cables hang from poles, are buried underground, pulled or blown through conduit or is even submerged underwater. Most of it goes relatively long distances, although OSP links may extend from a few hundred feet to hundreds or thousands of miles.

OSP installations can be placed into four broad categories, defined by how the cable is installed. Underground cables are pulled in ducts buried under the ground, usually in larger ducts with innerducts carrying one cable each. Direct buried cables are also underground, but rugged cables are buried without conduit, often installed with a plow that digs and places the cable at one time. Aerial cables are strung on poles, with the method of support determining the types of cables. Some are lashed to metallic messenger cables, some have metallic support elements built into a "figure 8" shaped cable, some are self-supporting. There are even high voltage power lines that have fibers in the center. Submarine cables are the primary means of international communications today. They are extremely rugged cables that are placed using special cable laying ships. We often refer to underwater cables as submarine cables too, but they are not as rugged as transoceanic submarine cables.

Outside plant cables are most always singlemode fiber for its distance and bandwidth capabilities – and the fact that these attributes make it much less expensive than copper cable or most radio frequency systems - and these cables often have very high fiber counts, up to 288 fibers or more. Cable designs are optimized for the application: cables in conduit optimized for pulling tension and resisting moisture, buried cables optimized for resisting moisture and rodent damage, aerial optimized for continuous tension and extreme weather and undersea cables optimized for resisting moisture penetration. All OSP cables have protection from damage by moisture, either with gel or dry tape or powder that absorbs and blocks moisture. Buried cables will have a layer of armor to prevent crushing and rodent penetration. Installation requires special equipment like cable pullers or plows, and even trailers to carry giant spools of cable.

Long distances mean cables are spliced together, since cables are not manufactured in lengths longer than about 4-5 km (2.5-3 miles), and most splices are by fusion splicing. Connectors (generally SC or LC styles) on factory made pigtails are spliced onto the end of the cable. After installation, every fiber and every splice is tested with an OTDR as well as an optical loss test set.

Outside plant installation requires lots of heavy equipment. The installer usually has a temperature controlled van or trailer for splicing and/or a bucket truck. Cable plows and pullers are common. Directional boring equipment may be used to place cables under roads or other obstacles without disturbing the surface. OSP installers have invested in fusion splicers, OTDRs and other equipment that can be quite expensive. Most outside plant telephone installs are done by the telco themselves, while there are a number of specialized installers who do telephone, CATV, utility and municipal work.

Premises Cabling

By contrast, premises cabling- cabling installed in a building or campus - involves shorter lengths, rarely longer than a few hundred meters or feet, typically with fewer fibers per cable. The fiber is mostly multimode, except for the user planning for the future who installs a hybrid cable with both multimode and singlemode fibers for future high bandwidth applications. All premises cables must be rated for fire retardance to meet building and electrical codes.

Splicing is rare in premises applications where connectors are used for more flexibility in future moves, adds and changes. Cables between buildings can be bought with double jackets, PE for outside plant protection over PVC for building applications requiring flame retardant cable jackets, so cables can be run continuously between buildings. Today's connectors often have low loss, and patch panels give more flexibility for moves, adds and changes.

Most connectors are SC or ST style with LCs becoming more popular with high speed systems. Termination is by installing connectors directly on the ends of the fibers, primarily using adhesive or sometimes prepolished splice techniques. Testing is done by a source and meter, but every installer should have a flashlight type tracer to check fiber continuity and connection. OTDRs have limited use in premises cabling due to their limited distance resolution. Unlike the outside plant technician, the premises cable installer (who is often also installing the power cable and Cat 5/6 for LANs too!) probably has a relatively small investment in tools and test equipment. There are thousands of cabling installers who do fiber optic work. They've found out it isn't "rocket science," and their small initial investment in training, tools and test equipment is rapidly paid back.

The Installers
Installers tend to specialize and few installers do both outside plant and premises cabling. The companies that do are usually very large and often have separate divisions doing each with different personnel. Most contractors do nothing but premises cabling.

Fiber, Copper or Wireless ?

The biggest advantage of optical fiber is the fact it is the most cost effective means of transporting information. Fiber can transport more information longer distances in less time than any other communications medium. The bandwidth and distance capability of fiber means that fewer cables are needed, fewer repeaters, less power and less maintenance. In addition, fiber is unaffected by the interference of electromagnetic radiation which makes it possible to transmit information and data with less noise and less error. Fiber is lighter than copper wires which makes it popular for aircraft and automotive applications.
Wireless was used as a long distance medium until fiber became available, but wireless is limited by available transmission frequencies so it was dropped as a long distance medium. While local wireless has grown exponentially, it uses fiber as a backbone and connection to the international phone system. These advantages makes the use of optical fiber the most logical choice in data transmission.
Twenty five years ago, fiber was just being introduced. It was expensive and required PhD's from Bell Labs to install it while copper wire was easy to install. Today most communications cabling installers do fiber and wireless as well as copper installations.
Because fiber is so powerful, at today's network speeds fiber has lots of headroom and users can look to the future of ten to one hundred gigabit speeds with confidence. Some telcos still use DSL over copper today but it's very limited in bandwidth over typical subscriber connection lengths and many older copper wires will not support DSL speeds, leading to many services providers converting to fiber to the home.

Standards Facilitate Fiber Applications

The adoption of any technology depends on having workable standards to insure product compatibility. Most of what we call standards are voluntary standards created by industry groups. Standards are not "codes" or actual laws that you must follow to be in compliance with local ordinances but sensible guidelines to ensure proper operation of communications systems. Standards are often developed by groups within each country, like EIA/TIA or IEEE in the US, but are increasingly becoming international under the auspices of ISO and IEC.

A listing of the EIA/TIA and ISO/IEC standards is on the website of The Fiber Optic Association. Information on the EIA/TIA standards can be found on the website of most of the suppliers of structured cabling hardware.

Two Important Issues When Working With Fiber

Safety When Working With Fiber Optics

The first rule for safety in fiber optic installation is to wear proper eye protection. Some people think that eye damage from working with lasers would be the big concern in fiber optic installations. The reality is that high power lasers burning holes in metal or burning warts off your finger have little relevance to your typical fiber optic installation. Optical sources used in fiber optics are generally of much lower power levels, with the exception of high power telco DWDM or CATV systems. Most fiber optic systems transmit in the infrared wavelengths where it is not visible to the human eye, so if it is of a dangerous level, there is no visible warning, increasing the danger. You should always be careful with your eyes, especially when using a fiber optic microscope which can concentrate all the light from a fiber into your eye. NEVER look into a fiber unless you know no light is present - use a power meter to check it - and anyway, the light is in the infrared and you can't see anything anyway!

Safety in fiber optic installation is not much different from installing any other cable. You may be working with heavy equipment, digging, climbing poles or working in buckets, etc. While fiber itself is not conducting electricity, some cables are conductive and installation may involve working near power cables, so all the usual electrical safety rules need to be understood and followed. You should be aware of all safety standards like OSHA in the US that cover workplace safety.

The real safety issue for splicing and termination is always about small scraps of glass cleaved off the ends of the fibers being terminated or spliced. These scraps are very dangerous! The cleaved ends are extremely sharp and can easily penetrate your skin. If they get into your eyes, they are very hard to flush out. Don't even think about what happens if you eat one. Always wear safety glasses whenever working with fiber and always carefully dispose of fiber scraps.

Always follow these rules when working with fiber.
1. Always wear safety glasses to protect your eyes from fiber scraps.

2. Dispose of all scraps properly. Always use a properly marked container to dispose of later and work on a black pad which makes the slivers of glass easier to spot.

3. Do not drop them on the floor where they will stick in carpets or shoes and be carried elsewhere.

4. Do not eat or drink anywhere near the work area.

Fiber optic splicing and termination use various chemical adhesives and cleaners as part of the processes. Follow the instructions for use (detailed on the chemical's MSDS - material safety data sheet) carefully. Remember, even simple isopropyl alcohol, used as a cleaner, is flammable.

Zero Tolerance for Dirt

With fiber optics, our tolerance to dirt is near zero. Airborne particles are about the size of the core of SM fiber- they absorb lots of light and may scratch connectors if not removed! Dirt on connectors is the biggest cause of scratches on polished connectors and high loss measurements!

1. Try to work in a clean area. Avoid working around heating outlets, as they blow dust all over you

2. Always keep dust caps on connectors, bulkhead splices, patch panels or anything else that is going to have a connection made with it.

3. Use special fiber optic cleaners or lint free pads and isopropyl alcohol to clean the connectors.

4. Ferrules on the connectors/cables used for testing will get dirty by scraping off the material of the alignment sleeve in the splice bushing - creating an attenuator. You can see the front edge of the connector ferrule getting black! Use the metal or ceramic alignment sleeve bulkheads only for testing.

Review Questions

True/False
Indicate whether the statement is true or false.

_____1.   Most outside plant installations are singlemode fiber.

_____2.   Splicing is rare in premises networks.

_____3.   Fiber is used in long distance phone networks because it is much cheaper than copper wire.

_____4.   Light from fiber optic cables is bright and easily visible.

_____5.   Besides causing attenuation, dirt particles can cause scratches on the polished fiber ends.

Multiple Choice
Identify the choice that best completes the statement or answers the question.

_____6.   Outside plant cabling can be installed by _____.
A. Pulling in underground in conduit
B. Direct burial
C. Aerial suspension
D. All of the above

_____7.   Underground cable generally includes a gel, powder or tape for
protection from _____.
A. Pulling friction
B. Lightning strikes
C. Moisture
D. Fiber abrasion

_____8.   Armored cable is used in outside plant installations to

_____.
A. Prevent crushing and rodent damage
B. Protect from dig-up damage
C. Increase pulling tension
D. Conduct lightning strikes

_____9.   Concatenation or the joining of two cables in a long outside plant
run is almost always done by _____.
A. Mechanical splicing
B. Fusion splicing
C. Field installation of connectors
D. Splicing on pigtailled connectors

_____10.   Premise cables in LAN backbones may contain _____.
A. Only multimode fiber
B. Only singlemode fiber
C. Both multimode and singlemode fiber
D. Plastic optical fiber

_____11.   Premises cables must be rated for _____ to meet codes.
A. Pull strength
B. Bend radius
C. Weight in cable trays
D. Fire retardance

_____12.   The protective gear every VDV installer must always wear is

_____.
A. Eye protection
B. Plastic apron
C. Gloves
D. Shoe covers

_____13.   Information on the safety of chemicals used in fiber optics are

_____.
A. Available from National Institutes of Health
B. In MSDS sheets supplied by manufacturers
C. Required to be in every installer's tool kit
D. Rarely useful

_____14.   Always keep _____ on connectors when not connected to
equipment or being tested.
A. Mating adapters
B. Strain relief boots
C. Sticky tape
D. Dust caps

Additional Study And Projects

From the FOA Online Reference Guide, read the reference topics Fiber Optic
Technology and Standards and Safety

Chapter 2
Fiber Optic Jargon

Objectives: From this chapter you should learn:
The language of fiber optics
Systems of measurements used in fiber optics
Specialized fiber optic terms

The key to understanding any technology is understanding the language of the technology – the jargon. We've started this book with an overview of fiber jargon to introduce you to the language of fiber optics and help you understand what you will be reading in the book. While we try to use the most common terminology, some particular applications for optical fiber have their own specialized terms, and when possible, we will try to include those terms also. We suggest you read this section first to help your understanding of the rest of the book and refer back to it when you encounter a term that you do not recognize. You can also use the Definitions in the Appendix of this book or the FOA Online Reference Guide for more explanations.

What Is Fiber Optics?

Fiber optic communications means sending signals from one location to another in the form of modulated light guided through hair-thin fibers of glass or plastic. These signals can be either analog or digital and transmit voice, data or video. Fiber can transport more information longer distances in less time than any copper wire or wireless method. It's powerful and very fast - offering more bandwidth and distance capability than any other form of communication!

The Metric System

Fiber optics, as an international technology, utilizes the metric system as the standard form of measurement. Several of the more common terms used are:

Meter: 3.28 feet, 39.37 inches. Fiber optic cable lengths are generally expressed in meters or kilometers.

Kilometer: 1000 meters / 3,281 feet / 0.62 miles.

Micron: 1 millionth (1/1,000,000th) of a meter. 25 microns equal 0.001 inch. This is the common term of measurement for fiber diameters, most of which are 125 microns in outside diameter.

Nanometer: One billionth of one meter. This term is commonly used in the fiber optics industry to express wavelength of transmitted light, e.g. 850 or 1300 nm.

Fiber

Optical Fiber: Thin strands of highly transparent glass or plastic that guide light, used to transmit communications signals.

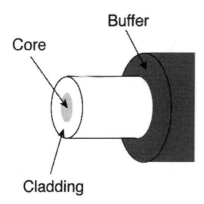

Core: The center of the fiber where the light is transmitted.

Cladding: The outside optical layer of the fiber that traps the light in the core and guides it along - even through curves.

Buffer coating or primary buffer coating: A hard plastic coating on the outside of the fiber that protects the glass from moisture or physical damage. The buffer is what one strips off the fiber for termination or splicing.

Mode: A single "electromagnetic field pattern" or ray of light that travels in fiber.

Multimode fiber: has a larger core (almost always 50 or 62.5 microns - a micron is one millionth of a meter) that transmits many modes or rays of light. Multimode fiber is used with laser or LED sources at wavelengths of 850 and 1300 nm for short distance applications like LANs or security cameras.

Singlemode fiber: has a much smaller core than multimode fiber, only about 8-9 microns, so it only transmits one mode. It can go very long distances at very high speeds. Singlemode is used for telephony (long distance, metropolitan and fiber to the home) and CATV usually with laser sources at 1310 to 1550 nm or over a broader range for wavelength division multiplexing.

Fiber identification: Fibers are identified by their core and cladding diameters expressed in microns (one millionth of a meter), e.g. 50/125 micron multimode fiber or 9/125 micron singlemode fiber. Most multimode and singlemode fibers have an outside diameter of 125 microns - about 0.005 - 5 thousandths of an inch - just slightly larger than a human hair. International standards for fibers call out detailed specifications that also include bandwidth capability or other special characteristics.

Plastic optical fiber (POF): is a large core (usually 1mm) multimode fiber that can be used for short, low speed networks. POF is used in consumer HiFi and as part of a standard for vehicle communication systems called MOST.

Fiber Optic Cable

Cable: Cable provides protection to the fibers from stress during installation and from the environment once it is installed. Cables may contain from only one to hundreds of fibers inside. Cables come in three varieties: tight buffer with a thick plastic coating on the fibers for protection, used mainly indoors, loose-tube, where fibers with only a primary buffer coating are inside plastic tubes, and ribbon, where fibers are made into ribbons to allow small cables with the largest numbers of fibers.

Stiffener / strength member

Binder tape

Aramid fibers

Fibers

Jacket: The tough outer covering on the cable. Cables installed inside buildings must meet fire codes by using special jacketing materials.

Strength members: Aramid fibers (Kevlar is the Dupont trade name) used as strength members in the cable to allow pulling the cable or suspending it for aerial installation. The term is also used for the steel or fiberglass rod in the center of some cables used to stiffen it to prevent kinking as well as provide pulling strength.

Armor: Prevents crushing and discourages rodents from damaging cable by chewing through it. Some cable called armored also includes layers of strengthening wires for use in extreme environments such as encountered by submarine cables.

Sheath: A term used for the combination of the jacket, armor and any other elements used to protect the fibers in a cable .

Outside Plant Installations

Outside plant installations fall into four general categories, depending on the placement of the cable. Each requires cable types chosen for the installation and specialized equipment for placement.

Underground: Cables placed underground in conduit, often inside innerduct pulled in the conduit. Cables can also be blown into duct lines installed by trenching or plowing.

Direct Buried: Cable placed underground without conduit, placed in trenches, plowed into the ground or installed by directional boring.

Aerial: Cable placed above ground on utility poles.

Submarine: Cables placed underwater, including those in shallow water such as lakes or rivers as well as those used for ocean crossings.

Termination and Splicing

Connector: A non-permanent device for connecting two fibers in a non-permanent joint or connect fibers to equipment. Connectors are expected to be disconnected occasionally for testing or rerouting fibers.

Splice: a permanent joint between two fibers primarily used to *concatenate* (join) long fibers in outside plant installations and attach pigtails to terminate them.

Mechanical Splice: A splice where the fibers are aligned created by mechanical means.

Fusion Splice: A splice created by welding or fusing two fibers together.

Fusion Splicer: An instrument that splices fibers by fusing or welding them, typically by electrical arc.

Hardware: Terminations and Splices require hardware for protection and management: patch panels, splice closures, etc.

Fiber Performance Specifications

Attenuation: The reduction in optical power as it passes along a fiber, usually expressed in decibels (dB). For fibers, we talk about attenuation coefficient or attenuation per unit length (dB/km).

Bandwidth: The range of signal frequencies or bit rate within which a fiber optic component, link or network will operate.

Decibels (dB): A unit of measurement of optical power that indicates relative power. dB is a logarithmic scale where 10 dB equals a factor of 10 times. For example, 3 dB is a factor or two, 10 dB a factor of ten. Negative dB indicates loss, so -10 dB means a reduction in power by 10 times, -20 dB means another 10 times or 100 times overall, -30 means another 10 times or 1000 times overall and so on.

dB: Optical power referenced an arbitrary zero level, used to measure loss.

dBm: Optical power referenced to 1 milliwatt, used to measure absolute optical power from transmitters or at receivers. See optical power.

Loss, optical Loss: The amount of optical power lost as light is transmitted through fiber, splices, couplers, etc, expressed in "dB."

Optical Power: is measured in "dBm", or decibels referenced to one milliwatt of power. While loss is a relative reading, optical power is an absolute measurement, referenced to standards. You measure absolute power to test transmitters or receivers and relative power in "dB" to test loss.

Dispersion: Pulse spreading caused by modes in multimode fiber (modal dispersion), the difference in speed of light of different wavelengths (CD or chromatic dispersion in multimode or singlemode fiber) or polarization (PMD or polarization mode dispersion in singlemode)

Scattering: The change of direction of light after striking small particles that causes the majority of loss in optical fibers and is used to make measurements by an OTDR

Wavelength: A term for the color of light, usually expressed in nanometers (nm) or microns (m). Fiber is used mostly in the infrared region where attenuation is lowest but infrared light is invisible to the human eye. Most fiber specifications (attenuation, dispersion) are dependent on wavelength.

Tools

Jacket Slitter or Stripper: A cutter for removing the heavy outside jacket of cables

Fiber Stripper: A precise stripper used to remove the buffer coating of the fiber itself for termination. There at three types in common use, called by their trade names (from left): "Miller Stripper", "No-Nik" and "Micro Strip."

Cleaver: A tool that precisely "breaks" the fiber to produce a flat end for polishing or splicing.

Scribe: A hard, sharp tool that scratches the fiber to allow cleaving.

Polishing Puck: for connectors that require polishing, the puck holds the connector in proper alignment to the polishing film.

Polishing Film: Fine grit film used to polish the end of the connector ferrule.

Crimper: A tool that crimps the connector to the aramid fibers in the cable to add mechanical strength.

Fusion Splicer: An instrument that welds two fibers together into a permanent joint.

Fiber Optic Test Equipment

Optical Power Meter: An instrument that measures optical power from the end of a fiber.

Light Source: an instrument that uses a laser or LED to send an optical signal into fiber for testing loss of the fiber or cable

Optical Loss Test Set (OLTS): A measurement instrument that includes both a optical power meter and light source used for measuring insertion loss of installed cable plants or individual cables. The combination of meter and source, either separate instruments or combined, is sometimes also called light source and power meter (LSPM.)

Reference Test Cables: short, single fiber cables with connectors on both ends, used to test unknown cables. A launch cable is attached to the source and used to set the reference power for loss measurements and a receive cable is attached to the power meter.

Mating Adapter: also called splice bushing or couplers, allow two cables with connectors to mate.

Fiber Tracer: An visible light source (LED or flashlight) that allows visual checking of continuity and tracing for correct connections such as duplex connector polarity

Visual Fault Locator (VFL): A high-powered visible laser light source that allows continuity testing, fiber tracing and location of faults near the end of the cable.

Inspection Microscope: used to inspect the end surface of a connector for faults such as scratches, polish or dirt.

Optical Time Domain Reflectometer (OTDR): An instrument that uses backscattered light to take a snapshot of an optical fiber which can be used to measure fiber length, splice loss, fiber attenuation and for fault location in optical fiber from only one end of the cable.

Specialized Testers: Long distance networks may need testing for chromatic dispersion (CD) and polarization mode dispersion (PMD). Systems using wavelength-division multiplexing may need testing for spectral attenuation. Each performance factor has a specialized tester for that specification.

Review Questions

True/False
Indicate whether the statement is true or false.

_____1.   Optical fibers can transmit either voice, data or video and either analog or digital signals.

_____2.   Singlemode fiber has a smaller core than multimode fiber.

Multiple Choice
Identify the choice that best completes the statement or answers the question.

_____3.   In an optical fiber, the light is transmitted through the _____.
         A. Core
         B. Cladding
         C. Buffer
         D. Jacket

_____4.   The diameter of an optical fiber is traditionally measured in _____.
         A. Meters
         B. Millimeters
         C. Microns (micrometers)
         D. Nanometers

_____5.   Rays of light transmitted in multimode fiber are called _____.
         A. Reflections
         B. Refractions
         C. Waves
         D. Modes

_____6.   Loss of a fiber or any fiber in a cable is measured in _____.
         A. dB
         B. dBm
         C. milliwatts

_____7.   10 dB corresponds to a factor of _____ in power.
         A. 2
         B. 10
         C. 20
         D. 100

_____8.   A fiber stripper removes the _____ of the fiber.
    A. Core
    B. Cladding
    C. Buffer coating

_____9.   The _____ protects the fiber from harm.
    A. Primary buffer coating
    B. Aramid fiber strength members
    C. Jacket
    D. All of the above

_____10.   Which fiber optic test instrument uses backscattered light for measurements?
    A. OLTS
    B. OTDR
    C. VFL
    D. Tracer

_____11.   The wavelength of light used for most fiber optic systems is in the _____ region and _____ to the human eye.
    A. ultraviolet, invisible
    B. solar, visible
    C. infrared, invisible

Additional Study And Projects

Review manufacturer's websites, catalogs or datasheets to see what fiber optic products are available. See if they use different terminology and if it is based on trade names.

Chapter 3
Fiber Optic Communications

Objectives: From this chapter you should learn:
The advantages of optical fiber as a communications medium
How optical fiber is used in communications systems
Other uses for fiber optics

Why use fiber?

Fiber has become the communications medium of choice for telephones, cell phones, CATV, LAN backbones, security cameras, industrial networks, just about every kind of communications.

The biggest advantage of optical fiber is the fact it is the most cost effective means of transporting information. Fiber can transport more information longer distances in less time than any other communications medium, as the photo above from the late 1970s showing cables of equal capacity illustrates so well. The bandwidth and distance capability of fiber means that fewer cables, fewer repeaters, less power and less maintenance are needed. In addition, fiber is unaffected by the interference of electromagnetic radiation which makes it possible to transmit information and data with less noise and less error. Fiber is lighter than copper wires which makes it popular for aircraft and automotive applications. These advantages open up the doors for many other advantages that make the use of optical fiber the most logical choice in data transmission.

These advantages have led to fiber becoming the transport medium of choice for practically all data, voice and video communications.

Both telcos and CATV operators use fiber for economic reasons, but their cost justification requires adopting new network architectures to take advantage of fiber's strengths. LAN and premises network designers and installers now realize that they must also adopt new network architectures too. A properly designed premises cabling network can also be less expensive when done in fiber instead of copper. Conversion from copper networks is easy with media converters, gadgets that convert most types of systems to fiber optics. Even adding the cost of the media converters, the fiber optic network will usually be less than copper when the proper architecture is used.

Fiber Optic Communication Networks

Outside Plant Networks

Telephone Networks
Telephone networks were the first major users of fiber optics. Fiber optic links were used to replace copper or digital radio links between telephone switches, beginning with long distance links, called long lines, where fiber's distance and bandwidth capabilities made fiber significantly more cost effective. Telcos use fiber to connect all their central offices and long distance switches because it has thousands of times the bandwidth of copper wire and can carry signals hundreds of times further before needing a repeater - making the cost of a phone connection over fiber only a few percent of the cost of the same connection on copper.

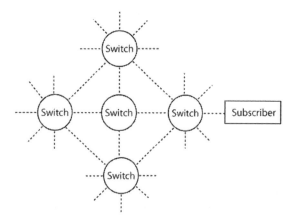

Today, with the exception of some rugged or remote locations, the entire telephone backbone is fiber optics. Cables on the land are run underground, direct buried or aerially, depending on the geography and local regulations. Connections around the world are run primarily on undersea cables which now link every continent and most island nations with the exception of Antarctica.

After long distance links were converted to fiber, telcos began replacing shorter links between switches with fiber, for example between switches in the same metropolitan area. Today, practically all the telephone networks have been converted to fiber. Telcos and other groups are now running fiber right to the home, (FTTH) using low cost passive optical network (PON) systems that use splitters to share the cost of some fiber optic components among as many as 32 subscribers. See Appendix C for more details on FTTH.

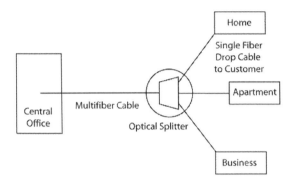

Even cell phone networks are connected to fiber backbones. It is more efficient and less expensive than using scarce wireless bandwidth for backbone connections. Cell phone towers with many antennas will have large cable trays or pedestals where fiber cables connect to the antenna electronics.

The Internet
The Internet has always been based on a fiber optic backbone. It started as part of the telephone network when it was primarily voice but has become the largest communications network as data traffic has outgrown voice traffic. Now the telcos are moving their voice communications to Internet protocol (IP) for lower costs.

CATV
Most CATV systems are using fiber backbones too. CATV companies use fiber because it gives them greater reliability and the opportunity to offer new services, like phone service and Internet connections.

CATV used to have a terrible reputation for reliability, not really a problem with the service itself but with network topology. CATV uses very high frequency analog signals, up to 1 GHz, which has high attenuation over coax cable. For a city-wide system, CATV needed many amplifiers (repeaters) to reach the users at the end of the system; 15 or more we common. Amplifiers failed often, meaning that subscriber downstream of the failed amp lost signal. Finding and fixing failed amps was difficult and time consuming, causing subscriber complaints.

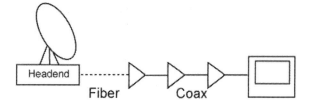

The development of highly linear distributed feedback (DFB) lasers allowed CATV systems to be converted to analog optical systems. CATV companies "overbuild" with fiber, often lashing fiber optic cables to installed aerial coax cable. They connect their headends with fiber and then take fiber into the neighborhood. They often lash the fiber cable onto the aerial "hardline" coax used for the rest of the network or pull it in the same conduit underground. Using this hybrid fiber-coax (HFC) architecture fiber allows them to break their network into smaller service areas connected with coax cable, typically fewer than 4 amplifiers deep, that prevent large numbers of customers from being affected in an outage, making their network more reliable and easier to troubleshoot, providing better service and customer relations.

The fiber also gives CATV operators a return path which they use for Internet and telephone connections, increasing their revenue potential. Most current CATV systems still use AM (analog) systems which simply convert the electrical TV signals into optical signals. CATV companies will probably convert to more digital transmission in the future.

CATV is even developing its own version of fiber to the home called RF over glass (RFOG.) This uses a interface at the home that is like a cable modem but with an optical input that accepts the same analog radio frequency (RF) signals that are used throughout the HFC network.

Security Systems
Security systems are more secure on fiber. Practically any system today has a fiber optic option. CCTV cameras used for surveillance often use fiber for it's distance capability and security, especially in large buildings like airports and metropolitan networks. Fiber also has much more bandwidth than coax so several cameras can be multiplexed onto one fiber. Bidirectional links allow controlling pan, zoom and tilt (PZT) cameras. Other security devices like intrusion alarms or perimeter alarms can utilize fiber and some even use fiber optic sensors.

Metropolitan Networks
Many cities have incorporated fiber optics into their communications networks. Metropolitan networks use fiber for many other applications besides CCTV surveillance cameras, including connecting public service agencies such as fire, police and other emergency services, hospitals, schools and traffic management systems. Cities can install cables to strategic locations so various services can share the fibers in the cables, saving installation costs.

Cities are also learning to bury extra conduits every time a roadway is dug up so when cables need installing, no further construction is needed.

Utility Networks
Utilities use fiber for communications, CCTV surveillance and network management. Electrical utilities have used fiber optics for decades for communications and managing their distribution systems. They realized quickly that fiber's immunity to electromagnetic interference would allow them to operate communications and control networks in close proximity to electrical circuits without problems. Electrical utilities take full advantage of fiber's immunity to noise also, even running fiber inside high voltage power distribution cables. Some utilities install fibers inside their high voltage distribution networks and lease fibers to other telecommunications companies. Utilities use fiber in one non-communications application; fiber optic sensors allow monitoring high voltage and current in their distribution systems. The interest in "smart grid" management of power distribution to enhance efficiency is based on using fiber optics for network management.

Premises Networks

Premises networks, mostly computer LANs (local area networks) use fiber optics primarily in the backbone but increasingly to the desk and to connect wireless access points. The LAN backbone often needs longer distances than copper cable (Cat 5/5e/6/6A) can provide and of course, the fiber offers higher bandwidth for future expansion. Fiber's ability to handle network upgrades meant that one fiber type outlived 9 generations of copper cables in LANs. New fiber types (OM3 and OM4) offer future potential for upgrades while copper continues to struggle with network speed increases.
Until recently large corporate LANs use fiber backbones with copper wire to the desktop. LAN switches and hubs are usually available with fiber optic ports but PCs have interfaces to Ethernet on copper. Inexpensive media converters allow connecting PCs to fiber. Fiber to the desk can be cost effective if properly designed using centralized fiber architecture without local switching in the telecom closet, but many users no longer want to be "tethered" to a network cable. Desktop computer sales are declining and laptops are the PC of choice for most users, with wireless connections to the network. Generally only high data users like engineers and graphics designers use desktop workstations; everybody else gets a wireless-connected laptop.

Optical LANs

Since the late 1990s, international standards have recognized LANs using fiber to the desktop (FTTD) using centralized fiber architectures. Here the typical backbone cabling, Ethernet switches in a telecom closet and horizontal cabling are replaced by a direct fiber network, with either medial converters or fiber switches providing the conversion between the copper and fiber systems. The advantage of centralized fiber is there is on need for placing switches in a telecom closet with their requirements for power, grounds and air conditioning. In fact, you don't need a telecom closet at all.

More recently, optical LANs have been built using the same electronics and cabling as fiber to the home (FTTH). A typical enterprise LAN is similar to the FTTH network in a multi-dwelling unit (apartments, flats, condominiums) and the economies of scale for FTTH with over 100 million subscriber connections makes the electronics much less expensive than even commodity copper switches.

These optical LANs (OLANs) use passive optical network architecture of FTTH, generally gigabit GPON or EPON versions that operate bi-directionally over a single fiber, using all singlemode like the telephone systems from which FTTH was derived. Devices connect to the OLAN with regular copper UTP patchcords. These OLANs are typically much less expensive to install than regular structured cabling LANs and use much less power.

Industrial Networks

Industrial plants use fiber for it's ruggedness, distance and noise immunity. In an industrial environment, electromagnetic interference (EMI) is often a big problem. Motors, relays, welders and other industrial equipment generate a tremendous amount of electrical noise that can cause major problems with copper cabling, especially unshielded cable like UTP. In order to run copper cable in an industrial environment, it is often necessary to pull it through conduit to provide adequate shielding. Fiber is also very flexible, so many industrial robots use fiber for controls, often plastic fiber.

Fiber optics has complete immunity to EMI. You only need to choose a cable type that is rugged enough for the installation, with breakout cable being a good choice for it's heavy-duty construction. The fiber optic cable can be installed easily from point to point, passing right next to major sources of EMI with no effect. Conversion from copper networks is easy with media converters, adapters that convert most types of systems to fiber optics. Even with the cost of the media converters, the fiber optic network will usually be less than copper cable run in conduit.

Military and Platforms

The military uses fiber everywhere, on bases, platforms (ships and planes), and on the battlefield because it's hard to damage, tap or jam. Airplanes use fiber for its reliability and noise immunity, but also like the lighter weight of fiber. Even millions of cars have fiber networks connecting all the electronics because fiber is immune to noise and saves weight.

Designing Fiber Optic Networks

This is a big topic so there is a complete chapter on the subject later in the book. Fiber's extra bandwidth and distance capability makes it possible to do things not possible with copper wire or wireless. First and foremost, it's necessary to understand thoroughly what signals are to be transmitted over the fiber and the specifications of the transmission equipment. Then map and visit the work site to understand where the fiber optic cable plant needs to be installed. Know the standards but use common sense in designing the installation. Consider what are the possible problems and work around or prevent them. Don't cut corners which may affect performance or reliability. Document everything completely. Plan for future expansion and restoration in case of problems. There is no substitute for experience and common sense here!

Review Questions

True/False
Indicate whether the statement is true or false.

_____1.   The biggest advantage of optical fiber is the fact it is the most cost effective means of transporting information.

_____2.   Telephone networks have been converted to fiber, including long distance and metropolitan networks, but fiber to the home (FTTH) is not yet feasible.

Multiple Choice
Identify the choice that best completes the statement or answers the question.

_____3.   Today, with the exception of some _____, the entire
          telephone backbone is fiber optics..
          A. Rugged or remote locations
          B. Ultra-high speed connections
          C. Large cities
          D. Triple play systems

_____4.   _____ companies "overbuild with fiber, often lashing fiber optic
          cables to installed aerial coax cable.
          A. Independent telephone
          B. CATV
          C. Utilities
          D. Private network

_____5.   Copper networks can be converted to fiber optics using
          _____.
          A. Fiber hubs
          B. Media converters
          C. Patch panels
          D. Rewiring

Multiple Response
*Identify one or more choices that best complete the statement or answer the
question.*

_____6.   The bandwidth and distance capability of optical fiber means that
          _____. (choose all that apply)
          A. Fewer cables are needed
          B. Fewer repeaters are needed
          C. Less power is consumed by the network
          D. Less maintenance is required

_____7.   Which of the following communications systems typically use fiber
          optic backbones? (choose all that apply)
          A. Telephones
          B. CATV
          C. Internet
          D. Cell Phones

Additional Study And Projects

Read the FOA Online Reference Guide sections on Premises Networks and FTTH.

See what kinds of communications equipment are available by looking at websites of companies offering systems, media converters, etc.

Chapter 4
Fiber Optic Transmission Systems And Components

Objectives: From this chapter you should learn:
How fiber optic data links and transmission systems work
What components are used in transceivers
Types of sources and detectors used in transceivers
Performance parameters of fiber optic transmission systems

Fiber Optic Data Links

Fiber optic transmission systems use data links that work similar to the diagram shown above. Each fiber link consists of a transmitter on one end of a fiber and a receiver on the other end. Most systems operate by transmitting in one direction on one fiber and in the reverse direction on another fiber for full duplex operation. It's possible to transmit both directions on one fiber but it requires couplers to do so and fiber is less expensive than couplers. A FTTH passive optical network (PON) is one of the few systems using bidirectional transmission over a single fiber because its network architecture is based around couplers already. See Appendix B for more information on FTTH.

Most systems use a "transceiver" which includes both transmitter and receiver in a single module. The transmitter takes an electrical input and converts it to an optical output from a laser diode or LED. The light from the transmitter is coupled into the fiber with a connector and is transmitted through the fiber optic cable plant. The light from the end of the fiber is coupled to a receiver where a detector converts the light into an electrical signal which is then conditioned properly for use by the receiving equipment.

Analog or Digital

Analog signals are continuously variable signals where the information in the signal is contained in the amplitude of the signal over time. Digital signals are sampled at regular time intervals and the amplitude converted to digital bytes so the information is a digital number. Analog signals are the natural form of most data, but are subject to degradation by noise in the transmission system. As an analog signal is attenuated in a cable, the signal to noise ratio becomes worse so the quality of the signal degrades. Digital signals can be transmitted long distances without degradation as the signal is less sensitive to noise.

Analog

Digital

Fiber optic datalinks can be either analog or digital in nature, although most are digital. Telephone and computer networks are digital, CATV is currently using analog transmission but will be converting to digital and CCTV may be either.

Both analog and digital links have some common critical parameters and some major differences. For both, the optical loss margin or power budget is most important. Analog datalinks will be tested for signal to noise ratio to determine link margin, while digital links use bit error rate as a measure of performance. Both links require testing over the full bandwidth specified for operation, but most data links are now specified for a specific network application, like AM CATV or RGB color monitors for analog links and SONET, Ethernet or Fibre Channel for digital links.

Packaging

Transceivers are usually packaged in industry standard packages to allow multiple sources to be accommodated in transmission equipment. Modules connect to a duplex connector on the optical end and a standard electrical interface on the other end. Transceivers are powered from the equipment they are built into.

Sources for Fiber Optic Transmitters

The sources used for fiber optic transmitters need to meet several criteria: it has to be at the correct wavelength, be able to be modulated fast enough to transmit data and be efficiently coupled into fiber.

Four types of sources are commonly used, LEDs, fabry-perot (FP) lasers, distributed feedback (DFB) lasers and vertical cavity surface-emitting lasers (VCSELs). All convert electrical signals into optical signals, but are otherwise quite different devices. All four are tiny semiconductor devices (chips). LEDs and VCSELs are fabricated on semiconductor wafers such that they emit light from the surface of the chip, while F-P and DFB lasers emit from the side of the chip from a laser cavity created in the middle of the chip.

Because of their fabrication methods, LEDs and VCSELs are cheap to make. Lasers are more expensive because creating the laser cavity inside the device is more difficult and the chip must be separated from the semiconductor wafer and each end coated before the laser can even be tested to see if its good.

LED   F-P laser   VCSEL

LEDs have much lower power outputs than lasers and their larger, diverging light output pattern makes them harder to couple the light output into fibers, limiting them to use with multimode fibers. LED devices have much less bandwidth than lasers and are limited to systems operating up to about 250 MHz or around 200 Mb/s.

Lasers have less diverging light outputs and are easily coupled to singlemode fibers, making them ideal for long distance high speed links. Lasers have very high bandwidth capability, most being useful to well over 10 GHz or 10 Gb/s.

Typical Fiber Optic Source Specifications

Device Type	Wavelengths (nm)	Power into Fiber (dBm)	Bandwidth	Fiber Types
LED	850, 1300	-30 to -10	<250 MHz	MM
Fabry-Perot Laser	850,1310 (1280-1330), 1550 (1480-1650)	0 to +10	>10 GHz	MM, SM
DFB Laser	1550 (1480-1650)	0 to + 13 (+25 with fiber amplifier)	>10 GHz	SM
VCSEL	850	-10 to 0	>10 GHz	MM

Another big difference between LEDs and lasers is the spectral output. LEDs have a very broad spectral output which causes them to suffer chromatic dispersion in fiber (see Chapter 5 on optical fiber), while lasers have a narrow spectral output that suffers very little chromatic dispersion. DFB lasers, which are used in long distance and DWDM systems, have the narrowest spectral width which minimizes chromatic dispersion on the longest links. DFB lasers are also highly linear (that is the light output directly follows the electrical input with little distortion) so they can be used as sources in analog (AM) CATV systems.

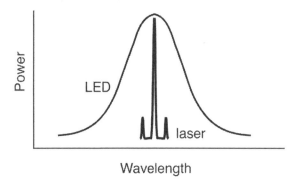

The choice of these devices is determined mainly by speed and fiber compatibility issues. Short, low speed multimode systems can use LEDs. As many premises systems using multimode fiber have exceeded bit rates of 1 Gb/s, lasers (mostly VCSELs) have replaced LEDs. The output of the LED is very broad but lasers are very focused, and the sources will have very different modal fill in the fibers. The restricted launch of the VCSEL or any laser makes the effective bandwidth of the fiber higher, but laser-optimized fiber, usually OM3 or OM4, is the choice for lasers.

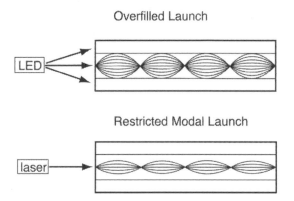

Singlemode systems use lasers, typically the fabry-perot type for shorter digital links, while DFB lasers are preferred for longer, faster links, especially when wavelength division multiplexing is used.

The electronics for a transmitter are simple. They convert an incoming pulse (voltage) into a precise current pulse to drive the source. Lasers generally are biased with a low DC current and modulated above that bias current to maximize speed.

Detectors for Fiber Optic Receivers

Receivers use semiconductor detectors (photodiodes or photodetectors) to convert optical signals to electrical signals. Silicon photodiodes are used for short wavelength links (650 for POF and 850 for glass MM fiber). Long wavelength systems usually use InGaAs (indium gallium arsenide) detectors as they have lower noise than germanium which allows for more sensitive receivers.

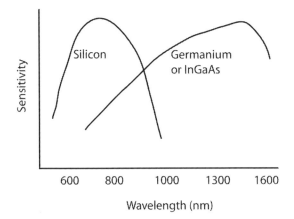

Very high speed systems sometimes use avalanche photodiodes (APDs) that have higher bandwidth capability than other photodiodes. APDs are biased at high voltage to create gain in the photodiode, increasing sensitivity and frequency capability. These devices are more expensive and more complicated to use but offer significant gains in performance.

Specialty Fiber Optic Transmission Components

Wavelength Division Multiplexing
Since light of different wavelengths does not mix within the fiber, it is possible to transmit signals at several different wavelengths on a single fiber simultaneously.   While fiber is inexpensive, installing new cables can be expensive, so utilizing installed fibers for carrying additional signals can be very cost effective.
Wavelength division multiplexing (WDM) was first used with multimode fiber in the earliest days of fiber optics, using both 850 and 1310 nm on multimode

fiber, sometimes carrying two signals in the same direction and sometimes allowing bidirectional transmission on one fiber. When used in bidirectional transmission on a single fiber, the two different wavelengths prevent crosstalk. When used in the same direction, filters remove one wavelength to prevent crosstalk. Both of these techniques are used in FTTH.

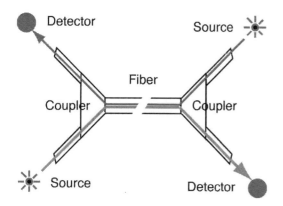

Bidirectional WDM on one fiber

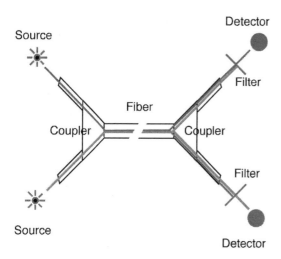

WDM with two wavelengths on one fiber in the same direction.

Singlemode transmission networks can carry signals at 10 Gb/s on 64 or more wavelengths, which is called dense wavelength division multiplexing (DWDM). Coarse wavelength division multiplexing (CWDM) uses new low water peak fibers to transmit signals on lasers in the range of 1260 to 1670 nm. Both systems work by coupling many wavelengths into one fiber using an optical coupler, then separating them at the receiving end with a WDM coupler that aims each wavelength at a separate fiber. Multimode systems using WDM have been less popular, but some standards use coarse WDM to carry multiple signals at greater than 1 Gb/s over laser-optimized multimode fibers to create higher bit rate links.

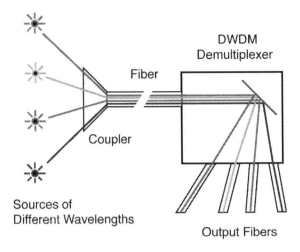

DWDM Demultiplexer

Fiber

Coupler

Sources of
Different Wavelengths

Output Fibers

Repeaters And Fiber Amplifiers

While the low loss of optical fiber allows signals to travel hundreds of kilometers, extremely long haul lines and submarine cables require regenerators or repeaters to amplify the signal periodically. In the beginning, repeaters basically consisted of a receiver followed by a transmitter. The incoming signal was converted from a light signal to an electrical signal by a receiver, cleaned up to remove as much noise as possible, then was retransmitted by another laser transmitter. These repeaters added noise to the signal, consumed much power and were complicated, which means they were a source of failure. They also had to be made for the specific bit rate of transmission and upgrading required replacing all the repeaters, a really difficult task in an undersea cable!

The solution to fiber optic repeaters was the fiber amplifier. The typical fiber amplifier works in the 1480-1650 nm band. It consists of a length of fiber doped with Erbium pumped with a laser at 980 or 1480 nm. The pump laser supplies the energy for the amplifier, while the incoming signal stimulates emission as the pulse passes through the doped fiber. The stimulated emission stimulates more emission, so there is a rapid, exponential growth of optical power in the doped fiber. Gains of >40 dB (10,000X) are possible with power outputs >+26 dBm (400 mW).

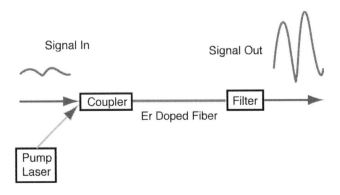

Signal In

Signal Out

Coupler

Er Doped Fiber

Filter

Pump Laser

Besides being used as repeaters, fiber amplifiers are used to increase signal level for CATV systems, which require high power levels at the receiver to maintain adequate signal to noise performance, allowing longer cable runs or using splitters to "broadcast" a single signal through a coupler to many fibers, saving the cost of additional transmitters. In telephony, fiber amplifiers combine with DWDM (dense wavelength division multiplexers) to overcome the inefficiencies of DWDM couplers for long haul transmission.

Fiber Optic Network Optical Wavelength Transmission Bands
As fiber optic networks have developed for longer distances, higher speeds and wavelength-division multiplexing (WDM), fibers have been used in new wavelength ranges, now called "bands," where fiber and transmission equipment can operate more efficiently.
Singlemode fiber transmission began in the "O-band" just above the cutoff wavelength of the SM fiber developed to take advantage of the lower loss of the glass fiber at longer wavelengths and availablility of 1310 nm diode lasers. (Originally SM fibers were developed for 850 nm lasers where the fiber core was about half what it is for today's conventional SM fiber (5 microns as opposed to 8-9 microns at 1310 nm.)
To take advantage of the lower loss at 1550 nm, fiber was developed for the C-band. As links became longer and fiber amplifiers began being used instead of optical-to-electronic-to-optical repeaters, the C-band became more important. With the advent of DWDM (dense wavelength-division multiplexing) which allowed multiple signals to share a single fiber, use of this band was expanded. Development of new fiber amplifiers (Raman and thullium-doped) promise to expand DWDM upward to the L-band.
Several low-cost versions of WDM are in use, generally referred to as Coarse WDM or CWDM which uses broadly separated laser wavelengths. Most do not work over long distances so do not require amplification, broadening the wavelength choice. The most popular is FTTH PON systems, sending signals downstream to users at 1490 nm and using low cost 1310 nm transmission upstream. Early PON systems also use 1550 downstream for TV, but that is being replaced by IPTV on the downstream digital signal at 1490 nm. Other systems use a combination of S, C and L bands to carry signals because of the lower attenuation of the fiber. Some systems even use lasers at 20 nm spacing over the complete range of 1260 to 1660 nm but only with low water peak fibers.
Manufacturers have been able to make singlemode fiber with low-water peaks, opening up a new transmission band (E-band), which has proven useful for CWDM. It is probably mostly useful as an extension of the O-band but few applications have been proposed and it is very energy-intensive for manufacture.

DWDM Band Wavelength Range

Band Name	Wavelengths	Description
O-band	1260 – 1360 nm	Original band, PON upstream
E-band	1360 – 1460 nm	Water peak band
S-band	1460 – 1530 nm	PON downstream
C-band	1530 – 1565 nm	Lowest attenuation, original DWDM band, compatible with fiber amplifiers, CATV
L-band	1565 – 1625 nm	Low attenuation, expanded DWDM band
U-band	1625 – 1675 nm	

Data Link Performance And Link Power Budget

Measuring Data Transmission Quality

Just as with copper wire or radio transmission, the performance of the fiber optic data link can be determined by how well it transmits data; how well the reconverted electrical signal out of the receiver matches the input to the transmitter.

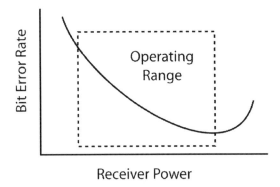

The ability of any fiber optic system to transmit data ultimately depends on the optical power at the receiver as shown above, which shows the data link bit error rate as a function of optical power at the receiver. (BER is the inverse of signal-to-noise ratio, e.g. high BER means poor signal to noise ratio.) Either too little or too much power will cause high bit error rates. Too much power, and the receiver amplifier saturates, too little and noise becomes a problem as it interferes with the signal. This receiver power depends on two basic factors: how much power is launched into the fiber by the transmitter and how much is lost by attenuation in the optical fiber cable plant that connects the transmitter and receiver.

Link Power Budget
The optical power budget of the link is determined by two factors, the sensitivity of the receiver, which is determined in the bit error rate curve above and the output power of the transmitter into the fiber. The minimum power level that produces an acceptable bit error rate determines the sensitivity of the receiver. The power from the transmitter coupled into the optical fiber determines the transmitted power. The difference between these two power levels determines the loss margin (power budget) of the link.

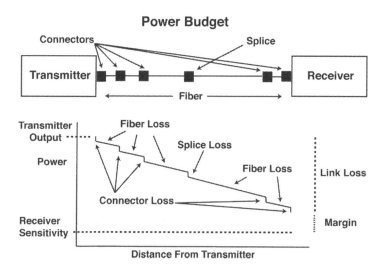

High speed links like gigabit or 10gigabit Ethernet LANs on multimode fiber or extremely long distance OSP links have derating factors for the bandwidth of fiber caused by the dispersion or spreading out the digital data pulses. Older 62.5/125 OM1 fiber will generally operate only on shorter links while links on 50/125 OM3 or OM4 laser-optimized fiber will go the longest distance. Even long distance singlemode fiber links may have limitations caused by chromatic or polarization-mode dispersion.

If the link is designed to operate at several different bit rates, it is necessary to generate the performance curve for each bit-rate. Since the total power in the signal is a function of pulse width and pulse width will vary with bit-rate (higher bit-rates means shorter pulses), the receiver sensitivity will degrade at higher bit-rates.

Every manufacturer of datalinks components and systems specifies their link for receiver sensitivity (perhaps a minimum power required) and minimum power coupled into the fiber from the source. Typical values for these parameters are shown in the table below. In order for a manufacturer or system designer to test them properly, it is necessary to know the test conditions. For data link components, that includes input data frequency or bitrate and duty cycle, power supply voltages and the type of fiber coupled to the source. For systems, it will be the diagnostic software needed by the system.

Typical Fiber optic link/system performance parameters

Link type	Fiber	Source/ Fiber Type	Wave- length (nm)	Transmit Power (dBm)	Receiver Sensitivity (dBm)	Link Margin (dB)
Telecom	SM	Laser	1310/ 1550	+3 to -6	-30 to -45	30 to 40
	SM	DWDM	1550	+20 to 0	-30 to -45	40 to 50
Datacom	MM	LED/ VCSEL	850	-3 to -15	-15 to -30	3 to 25
	MM or SM	Laser	1310	-0 to -20	-15 to -30	10 to 25
CATV(AM)	SM	Laser	1310/ 1550	+10 to 0	0 to -10	10 to 20

Of all the datacommunications links and networks, there are many vendor-specific fiber optic systems, but there are also a number of industry standard networks such as Ethernet that have fiber specific versions. These networks have agreed upon specifications common to all manufacturers' products to insure interoperability. FOA Tech Topics includes a summary of specifications for many of these systems.

Long Distance Considerations
Fiber optic links can now be hundreds or even thousands of kilometers long and operate at 10 gigabits per second or more – certainly lots more in the future – and at many wavelengths over a single fiber. Problems that are ignorable on short or metropolitan links may become extremely important on long links. The next chapter on optical fiber will cover topics like chromatic dispersion, polarization mode dispersion and spectral attenuation that can be important in these long links.

Review Questions

True/False
Indicate whether the statement is true or false.

_____1.   Fiber optic links generally use two fibers for full duplex (bidirectional) links.

_____2.   LEDs have higher output power and bandwidth than lasers.

Multiple Choice
Identify the choice that best completes the statement or answers the question.

_____3.   Singlemode fiber systems covering long distances and using DWDM use _____ sources.
A. F-P laser
B. DFB laser
C. VCSEL
D. LED

_____4.   Wavelength division multiplexing uses _____ to transmit multiple signals on a single fiber.
A. The ability of fiber to transmit multiple wavelengths without mixing
B. F-P Lasers
C. The wide spectral width of lasers
D. The high fiber bandwidth

_____5.   CWDM systems require _____ to allow transmitting in the E-Band (1260-1360 nm).
A. Low water peak fiber
B. DFB lasers
C. 1490 nm pump lasers

_____6.   Long wavelength singlemode links at wavelengths in the range of 1300-1650 nm links must use _____ detectors in the receiver for the best sensitivity performance.
A. Silicon
B. Germanium
C. InGaAs

_____7.   Fiber amplifiers used in DWDM systems work in the _____
           wavelength range.
           A. 650-850
           B. 850-1300
           C. 1300-1550
           D. 1480-1650

Multiple Response
Identify one or more choices that best complete the statement or answer the question.

_____8.   Singlemode transceivers use _____ sources for their higher
           coupled power and bandwidth.
           A. LED
           B. VCSEL
           C. F-P lasers
           D. DFB lasers

_____9.   Multimode transceivers use _____ sources depending on
           their requirements for coupled power and bandwidth.
           A. LED
           B. VCSEL
           C. F-P lasers
           D. DFB lasers

Additional Study And Projects
Review websites of manufacturers of fiber optic sources, detectors and transceivers to see what performance specifications are quoted and what applications supported.
In class or lab, set up a fiber optic link and see how it works. The link can be built from components or from commercially available media converters.

Chapter 5
Optical Fiber

Objectives: From this chapter you should learn:
How optical fiber transmits light
Types of fiber
Physical characteristics of various types of fibers
Fiber performance specifications
Applications for various fibers

What is Optical Fiber?

Optical fiber is the communications medium that works by transmitting optical (light) signals down extremely pure hair-thin strands of glass or plastic fiber. The light is "guided" down the center of the fiber which is called the "core". The core is surrounded by a optical material called the "cladding" that traps the light in the core using an optical technique called "total internal reflection." The fiber itself is coated by a "buffer" to protect the fiber from moisture and physical damage. The buffer is what one strips off the fiber for termination or splicing.

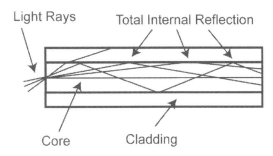

The core and cladding are usually made of ultra-pure glass, although some fibers are all plastic or a glass core and plastic cladding. The core is designed to have a higher index of refraction (an optical parameter that is a measure of the speed of light in the material) than the cladding. The lower index of refraction of the cladding makes the light rays bend as they pass from the core to cladding and causes "total internal reflection" to trap light in the core up to a certain angle, which defines the "numerical aperture" of the fiber. Glass fiber is coated with a protective plastic covering called the "primary buffer coating" that protects it from moisture and other damage. Additional protection is provided by the "cable" which has the fibers and strength members inside an outer protective covering called a "jacket" or "sheath."

Manufacturing Optical Fiber
The manufacturing of optical fiber to sub-micron precision is an interesting process involving making ultra-pure glass and pulling it into strands the size of a human hair. The process begins with the manufacture of a perform, a large diameter glass rod which has the exact same optical cross section as a fiber but is hundreds of times larger. The end of the rod is heated and a thin strand of fiber is pulled from the perform and wound on large reels. After manufacture, the fiber is tested and them made into cable.

Fiber Types

Multimode and Singlemode Types
The two basic types of fiber are multimode and singlemode. Within these categories, fibers are identified by their core and cladding diameters expressed in microns (one millionth of a meter), e.g. 50/125 micron multimode fiber which has a 50 micron core diameter and a 125 micron cladding diameter.
Most fibers are 125 microns in outside diameter - a micron is one one-millionth of a meter and 125 microns is 0.005 inches- a bit larger than the typical human hair.
Multimode fiber has light traveling in the core in many rays, called modes. It has a larger core (almost always 50 or 62.5 microns) which supports the transmission of multiple modes (rays) of light. Multimode is generally used with LED sources at wavelengths of 850 and 1300 nm (see below!) for slower local area networks (LANs) and lasers at 850 (VCSELs) and 1310 nm (Fabry-Perot lasers) for networks running at gigabits per second or more.
Singlemode fiber has a much smaller core, only about 8-10 microns, so that the light travels in only one ray (mode.) It is used for telephony and CATV with laser sources at 1300 and 1550 nm because it has lower loss and virtually infinite bandwidth.
There are two other types of multimode fibers that have limited applications

for communications. Plastic Optical Fiber (POF) is a large core (about 1mm) fiber, usually step index, with high attenuation that is used for short, low speed networks. PCS/HCS (plastic or hard clad silica, plastic cladding on a glass core) is a step index fiber with a glass core (around 200 microns) and a thin plastic cladding. Like all step index fibers, they are limited to slow or short links due to their limited bandwidth.

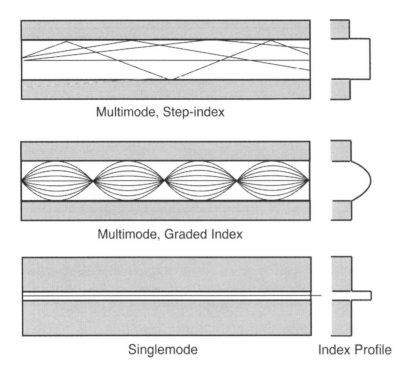

Multimode, Step-index

Multimode, Graded Index

Singlemode   Index Profile

Step Index Multimode
Step index multimode fiber was the first fiber design. The core of step index multimode fiber is made completely of one type of optical material and the cladding is another type with different optical characteristics. It has higher attenuation and is too slow for many uses, due to the dispersion caused by the different path lengths of the various modes traveling in the core. Step index fiber is not widely used - only POF and PCS/HCS (plastic or hard clad silica, plastic cladding on a glass core) use a step index design today. POF is mainly used for consumer audio and TV links.

Graded Index Multimode
Graded index multimode fiber uses variations in the composition of the glass in the core to compensate for the different path lengths of the modes. It offers hundreds of times more bandwidth than step index fiber - up to about 4 gigahertz per km of fiber. Two sizes of multimode fiber are in use, 50/125 and 62.5/125, where the numbers represent the core/cladding diameter in microns. Graded index multimode fiber is primarily used for premises networks, LANs, fiber to the desk, CCTV and other security systems.

Singlemode

Singlemode fiber shrinks the core down so small that the light can only travel in one ray or mode, hence the name singlemode. This increases the bandwidth to almost infinity - but it's practically limited to about 100,000 gigahertz - that's still a lot! Singlemode fiber is often described as having a core diameter of 8-10 microns and a cladding diameter of 125 microns, which can be confusing. What is generally called the core size of singlemode fiber is not the diameter of the glass core itself, but is the "mode field diameter," the effective size of the core which depends on the wavelength of the light being transmitted down the fiber.

Singlemode fiber is used for most outside plant networks such as telco, FTTH, CATV, municipal networks and long data links such as utility grid management. Some high speed LAN backbones, usually on campuses, also use singlemode fibers.

Specialty Fibers

Specialty fibers have been developed for applications that require unique fiber performance specifications. Bend-insensitive fibers, both multimode and singlemode, are used for patchcords and fibers in tight enclosures. Erbium-doped singlemode fibers are used in fiber amplifiers, devices used in extremely long distance networks to regenerate signals. Fibers are optimized for bandwidth at wavelengths appropriate for DWDM systems or to reverse chromatic dispersion. Some specialty fibers are designed to be sensitive to physical parameters so they can be used as sensors to measure that parameter. This is an active area of fiber development.

Fiber Sizes and Types

Fiber comes in two basic types, singlemode and multimode. Except for fibers used in specialty applications, singlemode fiber can be considered as one size and type. If you deal with long haul telecom or submarine cables, you may have to work with specialty singlemode fibers.

POF   PCS & HCS   Singlemode   50/125   62.5/125

Fiber Types and Typical Specifications

Core/Cladding	Attenuation	Bandwidth	Applications/Notes
Multimode Graded-Index	**@850/1300 nm**	**@850/1300 nm**	
50/125 microns (OM2)	3/1 dB/km	500/500 MHz-km	Laser-rated for GbE LANs
50/125 microns (OM3)	3/1 dB/km	2000/500 MHz-km	Optimized for 850 nm VCSELs
50/125 microns (OM4)	3/1 dB/km	3600/500 MHz-km	Optimized for 850 nm VCSELs >10Gb/s
62.5/125 microns (OM1)	3/1 dB/km	160-200/500 MHz-km	LAN fiber (FDDI grade)
100/140 microns	3/1 dB/km	150/300 MHz-km	Obsolete
Singlemode	**@1310/1550 nm**	**@1310/1550 nm**	
9/125 microns (OS1, B1.1, or G.652)	0.4/0.25 dB/km	~100 Terahertz	Standard SM fiber, Telco/CATV, long high speed LANs
9/125 microns (OS2, B1.3, or G.652)	0.4/0.25 dB/km	~100 Terahertz	Low water peak fiber
9/125 microns (B2, or G.653)	0.4/0.25 dB/km	~100 Terahertz	Dispersion shifted fiber
9/125 microns (B1.2, or G.654)	0.4/0.25 dB/km	~100 Terahertz	Cutoff shifted fiber
9/125 microns (B4, or G.654)	0.4/0.25 dB/km	~100 Terahertz	Non-Zero Dispersion Shifted Fiber
9/125 microns (G.657)	0.4/0.25 dB/km	~100 Terahertz	Bend-insensitive versions of all types above
Multimode Step-Index	**@850 nm**	**@850 nm**	
200/240 microns	4-6 dB/km	50 MHz-km	Glass core with plastic cladding, slow LANs & links
POF (plastic optical fiber)	**@ 650 nm**	**@ 650 nm**	
1 mm	~ 1 dB/m	~5 MHz-km	Slow, short links & vehicles

OM* refers to TIA types, B* refers to IEC types, G.* refers to ITU types

Multimode fibers originally came in several sizes, optimized for various networks and sources, but the data industry standardized on 62.5 core fiber in the mid-80s (62.5/125 fiber has a 62.5 micron core and a 125 micron cladding. It's now called OM1 standard fiber. Recently, as gigabit and 10 gigabit networks have become widely used, an old fiber design has been revived. 50/125 fiber was used from the late 70s with lasers for telecom applications before singlemode fiber became available. 50/125 fiber (OM2 standard) offers higher bandwidth with the laser sources used in the gigabit LANs and can allow gigabit links to go longer distances. Newer OM3 and OM4 laser-optimized 50/125 fiber today is considered by most to be the best choice for multimode applications.

The most common step index fibers are plastic optical fiber which generally has a 1mm diameter. Plastic-clad silica or hard-clad silica has a plastic cladding on a glass core and is generally 250 microns diameter with a 200 micron core.

Mixing Fiber Types

Generally, you cannot mix and match fibers. The difference in the cores of the fibers can lead to high losses when transmitting from a larger fiber to a smaller fiber. Transmitting from a smaller fiber to a larger fiber will not suffer losses due to mismatches since the transmitting fiber is smaller than the receiving fiber.   Trying to connect singlemode to multimode fiber can cause 20 dB loss - that's 99% of the power. Even connections between 62.5/125 and 50/125 can cause a significant loss of 3 dB – half the power. Some different singlemode fibers may also have high losses when spliced, a result of different mode field diameters or index profiles.

Fiber Specifications

The usual fiber specifications are size (core/cladding diameter in microns), attenuation coefficient (dB/km at appropriate wavelengths) and bandwidth. Bandwidth for multimode fiber will include modal bandwidth and chromatic dispersion. Singlemode fibers will have specifications for chromatic and polarization-mode dispersion. While manufacturers have other specs for designing and manufacturing the fiber to industry standards, like numerical aperture (the acceptance angle of light into the fiber), ovality (how round the fiber is), concentricity of the core and cladding, etc., these specs do not generally affect users who specify fibers for purchase or installation.

Attenuation

The primary specification of optical fiber is the attenuation. Attenuation means a loss of optical power. The attenuation of an optical fiber is expressed by the attenuation coefficient which is defined as the loss of the fiber per unit length, in dB/km. Fiber attenuation varies significantly with the wavelength of light.

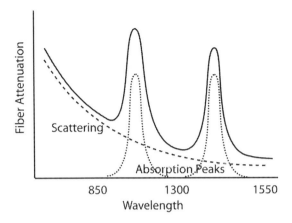

The attenuation of the optical fiber is a result of two factors, absorption and scattering. The absorption is caused by the absorption of the light and conversion to heat by molecules in the glass. Primary absorbers are residual OH+ and dopants used to modify the refractive index of the glass. This absorption occurs at discrete wavelengths, determined by the elements absorbing the light. The OH+ absorption is predominant, and occurs most strongly around 1000 nm, 1400 nm and above1600 nm.

The largest cause of attenuation is scattering. Scattering occurs when light collides with individual atoms in the glass. Light that is scattered at angles outside the numerical aperture of the fiber will be absorbed into the cladding or transmitted back toward the source Scattering is also a function of wavelength, proportional to the inverse fourth power of the wavelength of the light. Thus if you double the wavelength of the light, you reduce the scattering losses by 2 to the 4th power or 16 times.

For example, the loss of multimode fiber is much higher at 850 nm (called short wavelength) at 3 dB/km, while at 1300 nm (called long wavelength) it is only 1 dB/km. That means at 850 nm, half the light is lost in 1 km, while only 20% is lost at 1300 nm.

Therefore , for long distance transmission, it is advantageous to use the longest practical wavelength for minimal attenuation and maximum distance between repeaters. Together, absorption and scattering produce the attenuation curve for a typical glass optical fiber shown above.

Fiber optic systems transmit in the "windows" created between the absorption bands at 850 nm, 1300 nm and 1550 nm, where physics also allows one to fabricate lasers and detectors easily. Plastic fiber has a more limited wavelength band, that limits practical use to 660 nm LED sources.

The attenuation of multimode graded-index fiber is also dependent on how light is transmitted in the fiber, which is called mode power distribution. Bandwidth is affected by mode power distribution also, so modal effects in multimode fiber are discussed below.

Bend-Insensitive Fibers

When installing small fiber count cables indoors and routing patchcords around patch panels, fiber optic cables may be subjected to tight bends. This stress can cause bending losses in the fibers and even long term failure. Fiber manufacturers now offer bend-insensitive fibers, both singlemode and multimode, that are more tolerant of tight bending. One manufacturer even demonstrates the fiber by attaching it to wooden studs with a staple gun, a practice we strongly suggest you do not try – it's just for demonstrations! Bend insensitive fibers are a big advantage for patchcords or whenever fibers are subjected to stress, but manufacturers should be consulted to see if these fibers require special techniques for splicing, termination or testing.

Low Water Peak Fibers

Low water peak fiber results from careful manufacturing of singlemode fiber to reduce the water in the fiber (in the form of OH- ions) that causes higher spectral attenuation at around 1244 and 1383 nm. At the water peaks, legacy fibers may have attenuation coefficients around 2 dB/km while low water peak fibers may be as low as 0.4 dB/km. With the development of low water peak fibers, the possibility of transmission in the complete spectral range from 1260 to 1675 nm has been made possible. Coarse wavelength division multiplexing (CWDM) uses lasers over this entire wavelength range while dense wavelength division multiplexing uses more closely spaced lasers at wavelengths above 1500 nm.

Modal Effects on Multimode Fiber Attenuation

In multimode fibers, some light rays travel straight down the axis of the fiber while all the others wiggle or bounce back and forth inside the core. In step index fiber, the off axis rays, called "higher order modes" bounce back and forth from core/cladding boundaries as they are transmitted down the fiber. Since these high order modes travel a longer distance than the axial ray, they are responsible for the modal dispersion that limits the fiber's bandwidth. In graded index fiber, the reduction of the index of refraction of the core as one approaches the cladding causes the higher order modes to follow a curved path that is longer than the axial ray (the "zero order mode"), but by virtue of the lower index of refraction away from the axis, light speeds up as it approaches the cladding and it takes approximately the same time to travel through the fiber. Thus the "dispersion" or variations in transit time for various modes is minimized and bandwidth of the fiber is maximized.

However, the fact that the higher order modes travel farther in the glass core means that they have a greater likelihood of being scattered or absorbed, the two primary causes of attenuation in optical fibers. Therefore, the higher order modes will have greater attenuation than lower order modes, and a long length of fiber that was fully filled (all modes had the same power level launched into them) will have a lower amount of power in the higher order modes than will a short length of the same fiber.

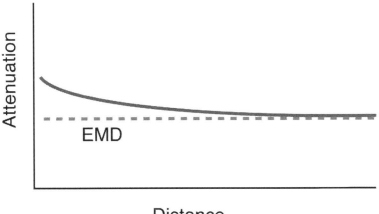

Distance

This change in "modal distribution" between long and short graded-index fibers is described as a "transient loss", and can make significant differences in the attenuation measurements one makes with the fiber, depending on the characteristics of the source. Transient loss not only changes the modal distribution, it changes the effective core diameter and numerical aperture also which can affect the losses of terminations or splices. The term "equilibrium modal distribution" (EMD) is used to describe the modal distribution in a long fiber which has lost most of the higher order modes. A "long" fiber is one in EMD, while a "short" fiber has all its initially launched higher order modes.

Modal conditions in the fiber can greatly affect measurements of the loss of the fiber and any terminations or splices associated with it. Various methods have been used to control modal conditions to make measurements more repeatable. These are discussed in the chapter on testing.

Modal Effects on Singlemode Fiber Attenuation

While the heading may sound contradictory, singlemode fiber can transmit multiple modes for short distances, perhaps as long as 100 meters. This generally occurs with coupled power from lasers or after a connector or splice. To prevent multimode effects, one uses a mode filter made by a small loop of the fiber whenever making measurements with singlemode fibers.

Dispersion in Multimode and Singlemode Fiber

Modal Effects on Multimode Fiber Bandwidth

Multimode fiber's information transmission capacity is limited by two separate components of dispersion: modal and chromatic. Modal dispersion comes from the fact that the index profile of the multimode fiber isn't perfect. The graded index profile was chosen to theoretically allow all modes to have the same group velocity or transit speed along the length of the fiber. By making the outer parts of the core a lower index of refraction than the inner parts of the core, the higher order modes speed up as they go away from the center of the core, compensating for their longer path lengths.

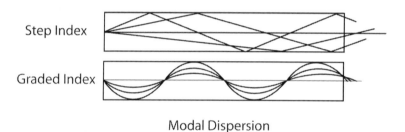

Modal Dispersion

In an idealized fiber, all modes have the same group velocity (speed) and no modal dispersion occurs. But in real fibers, the index profile is a approximation and all modes are not perfectly transmitted, allowing some modal dispersion. Since the higher order modes have greater deviations from an ideal fiber, the modal dispersion of a fiber (and therefore its laser bandwidth) tends to be very sensitive to modal conditions in the fiber. The bandwidth of a particular fiber is proportional to the length of the fiber, since dispersion occurs all along the fiber. However, the bandwidth of longer fibers degrades nonlinearly as the higher order modes are attenuated more strongly. The concern for dispersion in multimode fibers today focuses on 850 nm systems using VCSELs, vertical-cavity surface-emitting lasers, the most practical source for high speed links. As Ethernet LAN and Fibre Channel and other data center links have gotten faster, multimode fiber has been optimized for those applications over a few hundred meters of multimode fiber. Thus multimode fiber bandwidth performance has been increasing from OM1 fiber to OM4 as shown in the table of fiber specifications above.

Most fibers have been tested in the factory for bandwidth where the test source overfills the fiber, that is all modes are carrying light. Recent developments in laser-optimized fibers have caused new test methods to be developed, either limiting the modal fill of the fiber or using dispersion test methods that look at modes separately.

Chromatic Dispersion

The second factor in fiber bandwidth, chromatic dispersion (CD), affects both multimode and singlemode fiber. Chromatic dispersion is caused by the fact that glass fibers transmit light of slightly different wavelengths at different speeds. The ratio of the speed of light in a medium to the speed in a vacuum defines the index of refraction or refractive index of the material. For optical fiber, the effective index of refraction is about 1.45, so the speed of light in glass is about 2/3 the speed of light in a vacuum. But the index of refraction, and thereby the speed of light in the fiber, is a function of the wavelength of light, the principle we all know from seeing a prism break light into a spectrum.

Remember a prism spreads out the spectrum of incident light since the light travels at different speeds according to its color and is therefore refracted at different angles. The usual way of stating this is the index of refraction of the glass is wavelength dependent. Thus a carefully manufactured multimode graded index profile can only be optimized for a single wavelength, usually near 850 or 1300 nm, and light of other colors will suffer from chromatic dispersion. Even light in the same mode will be dispersed if it is of different wavelengths.

Chromatic dispersion is a big problem in multimode fiber with LED sources, which have broad spectral outputs, unlike lasers which concentrate most of their light in a narrow spectral range. Early high speed systems like FDDI at only 100 Mb/s but based on LEDs at 1300 nm, suffered such intense chromatic dispersion that chromatic dispersion was as large a factor as modal dispersion and transmission was limited to only two km of 62.5/125 fiber. Newer high speed multimode systems use fiber optimized for 850 nm VCSEL sources where modal dispersion is the main consideration.

Dispersion in Singlemode Fiber
Singlemode fiber only transmits one mode of light, so modal dispersion is not an issue. Chromatic dispersion however also affects long links in singlemode systems, even with lasers, so fiber and sources are optimized to minimize chromatic dispersion in the long distance links. As singlemode systems have

become longer and faster, another dispersion factor has become important, polarization mode dispersion (PMD). PMD occurs because of the speed differences in polarized light propagating in the fiber.

What Causes Chromatic Dispersion

There are two factors that cause chromatic dispersion in singlemode fibers: material dispersion and waveguide dispersion.

Material dispersion is caused by the variation of the index of refraction in a given material, glass in this case, over wavelength. Looking at the graph below, the variation of the index of refraction over the entire spectrum covered by fiber optics may seem small, only a few percent, but when you are dealing with very high speed pulses over very long distances it can add up.

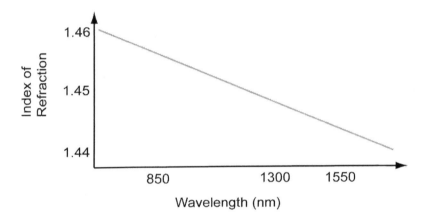

Waveguide Dispersion

Waveguide dispersion is a bit more complex. In singlemode fiber, the wavelength of the light is not that much bigger than the core of the fiber and (we'll leave out the complex physics) as a result the light traveling down the fiber actually travels in an area that exceeds the diameter of the core, which we call the "mode field diameter" of the fiber. The mode field diameter is a function of the wavelength of the light, with longer wavelengths traveling in a larger mode field diameter. Thus part of the light is traveling in the geometric core of the fiber and part is traveling in the cladding. Since the core is made of a higher index of refraction glass than the cladding, the light in the cladding travels faster than the light in the core. Longer wavelengths have larger mode field diameters so they suffer more material dispersion.

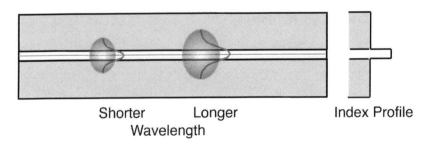

Shorter   Longer   Index Profile
Wavelength

Engineered Dispersion in Fibers

Material and waveguide dispersion have opposite variations with wavelength, so careful design of the fiber materials and index profiles allows the fiber to have a "zero dispersion wavelength." On either side of that wavelength, dispersion increases. The importance of chromatic dispersion is a function of the application for the fiber. As a result, different SM fibers have been developed for the requirements of specific applications. The table of fiber types earlier in the chapter shows the types of singlemode fibers currently in use and how they are optimized.

Dispersion Compensation

As mentioned earlier, the dispersion characteristics of a fiber can be manipulated by the materials and design of the fiber. In fact, fibers can be made that have CD inverse to the typical fibers and of a greater magnitude. So a length of dispersion compensation fiber can be added to a link, usually at a repeater (optical amplifier) that reverses the CD of the fiber span before it. Such fibers tend to have high loss and bend sensitivity, so alternatively a dispersion compensator made from a specialized component called a bragg grating can be used, but it has a more limited use and higher cost.

Chromatic Dispersion in the Cable Plant

As with any other component, optical fiber performance parameters can vary from batch to batch, so a long concatenated cable plant with many different fibers will have a end-to-end chromatic dispersion which is an integration of the CD of all the individual fibers. Therefore fiber in long distance links will probably be tested for CD after installation or before upgrading a link to higher bit rate electronics.

Polarization Mode Dispersion

Polarization mode dispersion (PMD)in singlemode fiber is a bit more complex. Polarization is a phenomenon of light traveling in a medium as a wave with components at right angles. Some materials, like a glass optical fiber, have a different index of refraction for each of those components of the light wave, which is called birefringence. And a different index of refraction means light travels at a different speed, so in the simplest visualization, PMD in fiber looks like the drawing below, where each component of the polarized light travels at a different speed, causing dispersion. The magnitude of PMD in a fiber is expressed as this difference, which is known as the differential group delay (DGD) and called $\Delta\tau$ ("delta Tau").

PMD is caused by the birefringence of the fiber which can be influenced by two factors, material birefringence and waveguide birefringence, similar to CD, but more complex. Waveguide birefringence is caused by geometrical variations in the fiber such as concentricity or ellipticity. Material birefringence is mainly caused by stress on the fiber.

Waveguide Birefringence

Material Birefringence

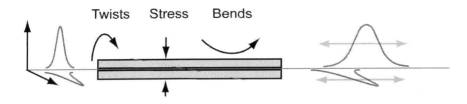

PMD is a complex issue in installed optical fiber. In a long concatenated fiber, each fiber can have different waveguide and material birefringence characteristics caused by the random characteristics of each fiber in the link and variations of the stress on the fiber. Variations are particularly noticeable in aerial fiber, where the PMD may vary considerably according to temperature and wind speed buffeting the fiber!
PMD causes pulse broadening and/or jitter in the received electrical signal, potentially causing errors in the reception of the signals. Since the PMD

can vary over time, an extra margin of 1 to 3 dB is often added to the power budget to accommodate variation in PMD.

PMD is an important issue as data rates on long distance links increases to 40 Gb/s and 100 Gb/s. Unfortunately, there are no reliable compensation schemes for PMD, so the only solution is to test links to be upgraded for PMD using one or more of the standardized test methods.

Review Questions

Multiple Choice
Identify the choice that best completes the statement or answers the question.

_____1.   Singlemode fiber has a _____ light-carrying core than multimode fiber.
A. Smaller
B. Larger
C. Same size

_____2.   What is the core size of singlemode fiber?
A. 5 mm
B. 9 microns
C. 50 microns
D. 63.5 microns

_____3.   Singlemode fiber has _____ bandwidth than multimode fiber.
A. More
B. Less
C. The same

_____4.   What wavelengths are appropriate for use with singlemode fiber?
A. 650 & 850 nm
B. 850 & 1300 nm
C. 1310 & 1550 nm
D. 850 & 1490 nm

_____5.   The diameter of the core in OM2 and OM3 multimode fiber is how large?
A. 50 microns
B. 62.5 microns
C. 62.5 mm
D. 9 mm

_____6.   Which of the following fiber specifications is most important to the
             user and is an important factor in testing?
             A. Attenuation
             B. Bandwidth
             C. Numerical aperture
             D. Core-cladding concentricity

_____7.   The largest contributor to fiber attenuation is _____.
             A. Absorption
             B. Scattering
             C. Bending losses
             D. Microbends

_____8.   Which fiber typically has the largest core?
             A. POF
             B. Multimode Step Index
             C. Multimode Graded Index
             D. Singlemode

_____9.   The loss of a singlemode fiber is lowest at _____.
             A. 850 nm
             B. 1300 nm
             C. 1310 nm
             D. 1550 nm

_____10.   Which type of dispersion affects singlemode fiber as well as
             multimode fiber?
             A. Modal
             B. Differential
             C. Chromatic
             D. Polarization mode

_____11.   Which types of dispersion needs to be tested in long singlemode
             fiber links?
             A. Modal
             B. Differential Modal
             C. Chromatic
             D. Polarization mode

Additional Study And Projects

Examine samples of optical fiber including bare fiber, buffered fiber, tight buffered fiber and POF, following safety procedures. Couple light from a flashlight or laser pointer through POF to see how light is transmitted.

Learn how optical fiber is manufactured by reading the page on the FOA Online Reference Guide or fiber manufacturers web pages.

Learn how mismatched fiber losses occur and how large they can be from the page on the FOA Online Reference Guide.

Chapter 6
Fiber Optic Cable

Objectives: From this chapter you should learn:
The types of fiber optic cables and their applications
Differences between outside plant and premises cables
Specifications for fiber optic cables

Fiber Optic Cable Design

Fiber optic cable provides protection for the optical fiber or fibers within it appropriate for the environment in which it is to be installed. Cable refers to the complete assembly of fibers, strength members and jacket. Fiber optic cables come in many different types, depending on the number of fibers and how and where it will be installed. It is important to choose cable carefully as the choice will affect how easy the cable is to install, splice or terminate, what it will cost and how long it will last in the field.

Cable's job is to protect the fibers from the environment encountered in any installation. Outdoors, it depends on whether the cable is buried directly, pulled in conduit, strung aerially or even placed underwater. Will the cable become wet or moist? Will it have to withstand high pulling tension for installation in conduit or continual tension in an aerial installation? Will the cable be exposed to chemicals or have to withstand a wide temperature range? What about being gnawed on by a squirrel, woodchuck or prairie dog? Indoors, cables don't have to be so strong to protect the fibers, but they have to meet all fire code provisions so the cable jacket has to be flame-retardant.

Outside plant cable designs are optimized for the application type. In OSP installations, cables may be underground, direct buried, aerial or submarine (or simply underwater.)

Underground cables are generally installed in conduit which is usually a 4 inch (10 cm) conduit with several innerducts for pulling cables. Here cables are designed for high pulling tension and lubricants are used to reduce friction on longer pulls. Automated pulling equipment that limits pulling tension protects the cables. Very long runs or those with more bends in the conduit may need intermediate pulls where cable is pulled, figure-8ed and then pulled to the next stage or intermediate pulling equipment is used. An alternative is to install duct lines and blow special lightweight cables into the ducts which can be faster and less stressful on the cable.

Splices on underground cables are generally stored above ground in a pedestal or in a vault underground. Sufficient excess cable is needed to allow splicing in a controlled environment, usually a splicing trailer, and the storage of excess cable must be considered in the planning stage.

Direct buried cable is placed underground without conduit. Here the cable must be designed to withstand the rigors of being buried in dirt, so it is generally a more rugged cable, armored to prevent harm from rodent chewing or the pressures of dirt and rocks in which it is buried. Direct burial is generally limited to areas where the ground is mostly soil with few rocks down to the depth required so trenching or plowing in cable is easily accomplished. Splices on direct buried cables can be stored above ground in a pedestal or buried underground. Sufficient excess cable is needed to allow splicing in a controlled environment, usually a splicing trailer, and the storage of excess cable must be considered.

Aerial installations go from pole to pole, but the method of securing cables can vary depending on the situation. Some cables are lashed to messengers or other cables, such as CATV where light fiber cables are often lashed to the heavy coax already in place. Cables are available in a "8" configuration with an attached steel messenger that provides the strength to withstand tension on the cable. Some cables are made to directly be supported without a messenger, called all-dielectric self-supporting cables that use special hardware on poles to hold the cables. Optical ground wire is used by utilities for high voltage distribution lines. This cable is an electrical cable with fibers in the middle in a hermetically-sealed metal tube. It is installed just like standard electrical conductors. Splices on aerial cables can be supported on the cables or placed on poles or towers, Most splices are done on the ground, although it is sometimes done in a bucket or even on a tent supported on the pole or tower. Hardware is available for coiling and storing excess cable.

Sometime OSP installations involve running cables across rivers or lakes where other routes are not possible. Special cables are available for this that are more rugged and sealed. Even underwater splice hardware is available. Landings on the shore need to be planned to prevent damage, generally by burying the cable close to shore and marking the landing. Transoceanic links are similar but much more complex, requiring special ships designed for cable laying.

Since OSP applications often use significant lengths of cables, the cables can be made to order, allowing optimization for that particular installation. This usually allows saving costs but requires more knowledge on the part of the user and more time to negotiate with several cable manufacturers.

Cable Construction

All fiber optic cables are comprised of multiple layers of protection for the fibers. Most all start with standard fiber with a primary buffer coating (250 microns diameter) and add:

Tight Buffer Coating
(for tight buffer cables like simplex, zipcord, distribution and breakout types)
A soft protective coating 900 microns outside diameter is applied directly
to the 250 micron coated fiber to provide additional protection for the fiber,
allowing easier handling and direct termination by applying a connector on the
fiber.

Loose Tubes (loose tube cables)
Small, thin plastic tubes containing as many as a dozen 250 micron buffered
fibers are used to protect fibers in cables rated for outside plant use. They
allow the fibers to be isolated from high pulling tension and can be filled with
water-blocking materials (gel, dry tape or powder) to prevent moisture entry.

Strength members
Strength members are usually aramid yarn, the same used in bulletproof
vests, often called by the Dupont trade name Kevlar, which absorbs the
tension needed to pull the cable and provides cushioning for the fibers.
Aramid fibers are used not only because they are strong, but they do not
stretch. If pulled hard, they will not stretch but eventually break when tension
exceeds their limits. This ensures that the strength members will not stretch
and then relax, binding the fibers in the cable. The proper method of pulling
fiber optic cables is always to attach the pull rope, wire or tape to the strength
members.
Some cables also include a central fiberglass rod used for additional strength
and to stiffen the cable to prevent kinking and damaging the fibers. When
included, these rods should be attached to swivel pulling eyes for pulling and
clamps in splice closures or patch panels when spliced or terminated. Few
cables today use metallic strength members since it complicates installation
by requiring the cable to be properly grounded and bonded.

Cable Jacket
The outermost layer of protection for the fibers which is chosen to withstand
the environment in which the cable is installed. Outdoor cables will generally
be black polyethylene (PE) which resists moisture and sunlight exposure.
Indoor cables use flame-retardant jackets that can be color-coded to identify
the fibers inside the cable. Some outdoor cables may have double jackets
with a tough layer of armor between them to protect from chewing by rodents
or Kevlar for strength to allow pulling by the jackets.
Indoor cables usually have a flame-retardant PVC (polyvinyl chloride) jacket
for general or riser use and some other special plastic for plenum use in air
handling areas. Indoor-outdoor cables usually have a PE outer jacket that can
be removed to expose a flame-retardant inner jacket for use within buildings.

Protection Against Water and Moisture
Cables installed outdoors require protecting the fibers from water. Either a gel or as is becoming more common, absorbent tape or powder, is used to prevent water from entering the cable and causing harm to the fibers. Generally, this applies to loose tube or ribbon cables, but dry water-blocking is used on some tight buffer cables used in short outdoor runs, such as building to building on a campus or to an outdoor wireless antenna or CCTV camera.

Protection Against Crushing or Rodent Penetration
Some cables have armor, usually metallic but sometimes hard plastic, under the outer jacket resist crushing loads, such as cables installed under floors in data centers or in rocky soil, as well as to prevent rodent penetration. Metallic armor requires that the cable be properly grounded and bonded.

Fiber Optic Cable Types

Tight Buffer Cable Types
There are two basic types of cables, generally defined as tight buffer and loose tube. Tight buffer cables (simplex, zipcord, distribution and breakout) are used in premises applications where cable flexibility and ease of termination are important, more so than ruggedness and pulling strength which characterize loose tube and ribbon types of cable. Generally, tight buffer cables are used indoors and loose tube/ribbon cables outdoors, but some tight buffer cables with moisture protection are used in short runs like on a campus or between buildings.

Simplex And Zip Cord

These types are used mostly for patch cord and backplane applications, but zipcord can also be used for desktop connections. Simplex cables are one fiber, tight-buffered (coated with a 900 micron buffer over the primary buffer coating) with Kevlar (aramid fiber) strength members and jacketed for indoor use. The jacket is usually 3mm (1/8 in.) diameter, but some 2 mm cable is sometimes used with small form factor connectors. Zipcord is simply two of these joined with a thin web.

Distribution Cable

Distribution cable is the most popular indoor cable, as it is small in size and light in weight. They contain several tight-buffered fibers bundled under the same jacket with Kevlar strength members and sometimes fiberglass rod reinforcement to stiffen the cable and prevent kinking. These cables are small in size, and used for short, dry conduit runs, riser and plenum applications. The fibers are double buffered and can be directly terminated, but because their fibers are not individually reinforced, these cables need to be broken out with a "breakout box" or terminated inside a patch panel or junction box to protect individual fibers.

Breakout Cable

Breakout cable is a favorite where rugged cables are desirable or direct termination without junction boxes, patch panels or other hardware is needed. They are made of several simplex cables bundled together inside a common jacket. This is a strong, rugged design, but is larger and more expensive than the distribution cables. It is suitable for conduit runs, riser and plenum applications. It's perfect for industrial applications where ruggedness is needed. Because each fiber is individually reinforced, this design allows for quick termination to connectors and does not require patch panels or boxes. Breakout cable can be more economic where fiber count isn't too large and distances too long, because is requires so much less labor to terminate.

Loose Tube Cable Types

Loose Tube Cable

Loose tube cables are the most widely used cables for outside plant installation because this type of cable offers the best protection for the fibers under high pulling tensions and can be easily protected from moisture with water-blocking gel or tapes. These cables are composed of several fibers together inside a small plastic tube, which are in turn helically wound around a central strength member, surrounded by aramid strength members and jacketed, providing a small, high fiber count cable. This type of cable is ideal for outside plant trunking applications, as it can be made with the loose tubes filled with gel or water absorbent powder to prevent harm to the fibers from water. It can be used in conduits, strung overhead or buried directly into the ground. Some outdoor cables may have double jackets with a metallic armor between them to protect from chewing by rodents or Kevlar for strength to allow pulling by the jackets. Since the fibers have only a thin buffer coating, they must be carefully handled and protected to prevent damage. Loose tube cables with singlemode fibers are generally terminated by spicing pigtails onto the fibers and protecting them in a splice closure. Multimode loose tube cables can be terminated directly by installing a breakout kit, also called a furcation or fan-out kit, which sleeves each fiber for protection.

Ribbon Cable

Ribbon cable is preferred where high fiber counts and small diameter cables are needed. This cable has the most fibers in the smallest cable, since all the fibers are laid out in rows in ribbons, typically of 12 fibers, and the ribbons are laid on top of each other. Not only is this the smallest cable for the most number of fibers, it's usually the lowest cost. Typically 144 fibers in ribbons only has a cross section of about 1/4 inch or 6 mm and the jacket is only 13 mm or 1/2 inch diameter! Some cable designs use a "slotted core" with up to 6 of these 144 fiber ribbon assemblies for 864 fibers in one cable! Since it's outside plant cable, it's gel-filled for water blocking or dry water-blocked. Another advantage of ribbon cable is Mass Fusion Splicers can join a ribbon (12 fibers) at once, making installation fast and easy. Ribbon pigtails are spliced onto the cable for quick termination. Premises cabling also uses some ribbon cables, often in preterminated cabling systems where 12 fibers are terminated in one MTP connector. These cables are common in LAN backbones and data centers.

Armored Cable

Armored cable is used in direct buried outside plant applications where a rugged cable is needed and/or for rodent resistance. Armored cable withstands crush loads well, for example in rocky soil, often necessary for direct burial applications. Cable installed by direct burial in areas where rodents are a problem usually have metal armoring between two jackets to prevent rodent penetration. Another application for armored cable is in data centers, where cables are installed under the floor and one worries about the fiber cable being crushed. Indoor armored cables may have nonmetallic armor. Metallic armored cable is conductive, so it must be grounded properly. As with other fiber optic components, there are different names or meanings used. "Armor" in some companies' jargon denotes a twisted heavy wire rope type cable surrounding the entire poly cable sheath/jacket. Single or double armor (two opposite ply layers of the steel wire) is typically used underwater near shore and shoals. Inner metallic sheath members of aluminum and/or copper are used for strength and for buried cable locating with a tone set.

Aerial Cables
Aerial cables are for outside installation on poles where consideration must be given to continual tension from the cable weight as well as wind and ice loads. Regular outdoor loose tube cables can be helically lashed to a messenger or another cable (common in CATV.) Some cables have heavier jackets and stronger metal or aramid strength members to make them self supporting (called all-dielectric self-supporting or ADSS cable if the strength members are nonconductive.) Self-supporting cables use special hardware to handle the installed tension on the cables caused by the weight of the cables and

environmental factors like wind. Aerial hardware to store slack cable can be mounted on the cable itself or on utility poles.

The cable known as a figure 8 cable has a cable bonded to an insulated steel or all dielectric messenger for support. The messenger is supported at each pole. If the messenger is steel, it must be grounded properly. You can also get figure 8 conduit which can be installed then cable pulled into the aerial conduit.

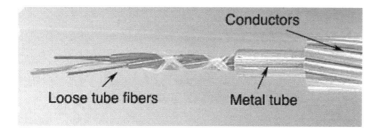

A widely used aerial cable is optical power ground wire (OPGW) which is a high voltage distribution cable with fiber in a metallic tube in the center of the wire surrounded by electrical conductors. The fiber is not affected by the electrical fields and the utility installing it gets fibers for grid management and communications. This cable is usually installed on the top of high voltage towers but brought to ground level for splicing or termination.

Underwater and Submarine Cables
It is often necessary to install fibers under water, such as crossing a river or lake where a bridge other above water location is not possible. For simple applications a rugged direct burial cable may be adequate. For true undersea applications, cables are extremely rugged, with fibers in the middle of the cable inside stainless steel tubes and the outside coated with many layers of steel strength members and conductors for powering repeaters. Submarine cables are completed on shore, then loaded on ships and laid from the ship, often while operational to ensure proper operation.

Other Types of Cable
There are many other types of fiber optic cable available, many unique to one

manufacturer. Every manufacturer has it's own specialties and sometimes uses their own names for common types of cable, so it's a good idea to get literature from as many cable makers as possible. Don't overlook the smaller cable companies; often they can save costs by making special cable just for you, even in relative small quantities.

Air-Blown Cable
Of course the advantages of fiber optic cable includes small size, light weight and flexibility. These advantages have allowed some cables to be installed by blowing into special ducts called duct lines, micro-ducts or sub-ducts which have been installed in larger conduit or even pipes for carrying water, sewage or gas. High pressure compressed air provides an aerodynamic effect, floating the cable on the air stream and carrying it down the duct, allowing installation lengths as long as 2 km (6,500 feet.) Air-blown cable needs to be designed for lightness and flexibility and the jackets are designed to help the air lift and carry the cable down the duct. This method involves less stress on the cable, allowing it to be made lighter and smaller than traditional outside plant cables.

Air-Blown Fiber
Another cable type is not really cable at all. By installing a "cable" which is just a bundle of empty plastic tubes, you can "blow" fibers into the tubes as needed with special equipment using compressed gas. If you need to upgrade, blow out the old fibers and blow in new ones. Both indoor and outdoor versions of air-blown fiber cables are available and it has even been used in FTTH. Special fibers are required that have been coated for easier blowing through the tubes, but any singlemode or multimode fiber is available. It's more expensive to install since the tubes must be installed, special equipment and trained installers are needed but can be cost effective for upgrades.

Hybrid and Composite Cables
These two types of cables are often confused, but almost everybody and the NEC defines them as:

Hybrid cables: Cables that contain two types of fibers, usually multimode and singlemode. These cables are often used in campus and premises backbones where the singlemode fibers may be used in the future.

Composite cables: Cables that contain both fibers and electrical conductors. Underwater tethered vehicles use cables like this, as do some cables used for remote wireless antennas or CCTV cameras. These cables must be properly grounded and bonded for safety.

Choosing a Cable Design

Choosing a cable requires consideration of all the environmental factors involved during installation and during the cable's lifetime. Here are some of the most important factors:

Pulling Strength
Some cable is simply laid into cable trays or ditches, so pull strength is not too important. But other cable may be pulled thorough 2-5 km or more of conduit. Even with special cable lubricant, pulling tension can be high. Most cables get their strength from an aramid fiber (Kevlar□ is the Dupont trade name), a unique polymer thread that is very strong but does not stretch, so pulling on it will not stretch the cable and stress the other components in the cable. The simplest simplex cable has a pull strength of 100-200 pounds, while outside plant cable may have a specification of over 800 pounds.

Bending Radius Limits
The normal recommendation for fiber optic cable bend radius is to ensure the minimum bend radius under tension during pulling is 20 times the diameter of the cable. When not under tension, the minimum recommended long term bend radius is 10 times the cable diameter.

Water Protection
Outdoors, every cable must be protected from water or moisture. Protection starts on the outside with a moisture resistant jacket, usually PE (polyethylene), and a filling of water-blocking material. The usual way has been to flood the cable with a water-blocking gel. It's effective but messy - requiring a gel remover (use the commercial stuff - it's best- -but bottled lemon juice works in a pinch!). A newer alternative is dry water blocking using a water–absorbent tape or powder – similar to the material developed to absorb moisture in disposable diapers. Most cable manufacturers now offer dry water-blocked cables.

Crush Loads or Rodent Penetration
Armored cables are used because their strong jackets withstand crushing and rodent penetration. Direct burial OSP cables are usually armored or installed in conduit. Armored indoor cables are available with NEC rated jackets for placement with other cables under false floors, as in data centers.

Fire Code Ratings For Premises Cables
Every cable installed indoors must meet fire codes. OSP cables can only be run 50 feet (about 15 meters) inside a building without conduit or connecting to a rated premises cable. That means the jacket must be rated for fire resistance, with ratings for general use, riser (a vertical cable feeds flames

more than horizontal) and plenum (for installation in air-handling areas. Most indoor cables use PVC (polyvinyl chloride) jacketing for fire retardance. In the United States, all premises cables must carry identification and flammability ratings per the NEC (National Electrical Code) paragraph 770. In Canada, it's CEC and other countries have similar cable ratings.

These ratings are:

NEC Rating	Description
OFN	Optical fiber non-conductive
OFC	Optical fiber conductive
OFNG or OFCG	General purpose
OFNR or OFCR	Riser rated cable for vertical runs
OFNP or OFCP	Plenum rated cables for use in indoor air-handling spaces or plenums
OFN-LS	Low smoke density

2 FIBER 62.5/125 FDDI (UL) c(UL) TYPE OFNR

Cables without markings should never be installed indoors as they will not pass building inspections. Outdoor cables are not fire-rated and can only be used up to 50 feet indoors. If you need to bring an outdoor cable indoors, consider a double-jacketed cable with PE jacket over a PVC UL-rated indoor jacket. Simply remove the outdoor jacket when you come indoors and you will not have to terminate at the entry point.

Grounding and Bonding
Any cable that includes any conductive metal must be properly grounded and bonded per the NEC for safety. Indoor cables rated OFC, OFCG, OFCR or OFCP and outdoor cables with metallic strength members or armor must be grounded and bonded. All composite cables must be properly grounded and bonded also.

Cable Color Codes
Outdoor cables are generally black but premises cable jackets are color-coded. De facto standard color codes for cable jackets have been yellow jackets for singlemode and orange jackets for multimode but new types of fibers have led to more standardized color codes. With two multimode fibers now in common use, 62.5/125 and 50/125, and several versions of 50/125 fiber, it's important to follow the TIA-598 standard to prevent mixing up cables.

Premises Cable Jacket Color Codes

Fiber Type	Non-Military Applications	Military Applications	Suggested Print Nomenclature
Multimode (50/125) (OM2)	Orange	Orange	50/125
Multimode (50/125) (850 nm Laser-optimized) (OM3 or OM4)	Aqua	Undefined	850 LO 50/125
Multimode (62.5/125) (OM1)	Orange	Slate	62.5/125
Multimode (100/140)	Orange	Green	100/140
Single-mode (OS1, OS2)	Yellow	Yellow	SM/NZDS, SM
Polarization Maintaining Single-mode	Blue	Undefined	Undefined

Fiber Color Codes

Number	Color
1	Blue
2	Orange
3	Green
4	Brown
5	Slate
6	White
7	Red
8	Black
9	Yellow
10	Violet
11	Rose
12	Aqua

Inside the cable or inside each tube in a loose tube cable, individual fibers will be color coded for identification. Fibers generally follow the convention created for telephone wires except fibers are identified individually, not in pairs. Since most loose tube cables have 12 fibers per tube, colors are specified for fibers 1-12, then tubes are color coded in the same manner, up to 144 fiber cables. In ribbon cables, each ribbon is color coded in this format then ribbons are stacked.   For splicing long cable runs from similar cables (called concatenation), like color fibers are spliced to ensure continuity of color codes throughout a cable run.

Choosing Cables

Choosing a fiber optic cable for any given application requires considering installation and environmental requirements plus long-term fiber requirements to cover expansion to newer communications networks. Installation requirements include where and how the cable will be installed, such as pulled in conduit outdoors or placed in cable trays in a building. Long term requirements need to consider moisture or water exposure, expected temperature range, tension (aerial cables), or other environmental factors. You should contact several cable manufacturers and give them detailed specifications for the installation. They will want to know where the cable is going to be installed, how many fibers you need and what kind of fibers (singlemode, multimode or both in what we call "hybrid" cables.) You can also have a "composite" cable that includes copper conductors for signals or power. The cable companies will evaluate your requirements and make suggestions. Then you can get competitive bids.
Since the plan will call for a certain number of fibers, consider adding spare fibers to the cable - fibers are cheap compared to the cost of installing additional cables. Then you won't be in trouble if you break a fiber or two when splicing, breaking-out or terminating fibers. And consider future expansion needs. Most users install many more fibers than needed, especially adding singlemode fiber to multimode fiber cables for campus or premises backbone applications.
Additional information on choosing cables is included in the chapter on fiber optic network design.

Review Questions

True/False
Indicate whether the statement is true or false.

_____1.   Any cable that contains metallic conductors must be properly grounded and bonded.

_____2.`   In order to specify a fiber optic cable properly, you need to specify installation specifications as well as environmental specifications.

Multiple Choice
Identify the choice that best completes the statement or answers the question.

_____3. Cables which contain both multimode and singlemode fibers are called _____.
A. Mixed cables
B. Hybrid cables
C. Composite cables
D. XC cables

_____4. Cables with metallic conductors as well as fiber are called
_____.
A. Mixed cables
B. Hybrid cables
C. Composite cables
D. XC cables

_____5. No cable should be installed indoors unless it _____.
A. Is UL listed for flame retardancy for NEC
B. Is colored orange to indicate fiber optics
C. Is enclosed in innerduct or conduit
D. The length is printed on the cable jacket

_____6. ALL outdoor cables are specifically designed to _____.
A. Include large numbers of fibers
B. Be direct buried for ease of installation
C. Prevent rodent damage to the cable
D. Prevent moisture damage to the fiber

_____7. The design of cables of small size with very large fiber counts is usually _____.
A. Loose tube
B. Ribbon
C. Tight buffer

_____8. The design of cables for high pulling tension in outside plant installations is usually _____.
A. Loose tube
B. Ribbon
C. Tight buffer

_____9.   Aerial cables must be designed and installed to withstand
_____.
A. Continual tension from cable weight
B. Wind
C. Ice
D. All of the above

_____10.   Cables should always be pulled with _____ to prevent
damage.
A. Nylon rope
B. Kellums grip on the jacket
C. Tension gage
D. The cable's strength members

_____11.   Loose tube cable requires a _____ to terminate directly
with connectors, so often pigtails are spliced-on instead.
A. Splice closure
B. Breakout kit
C. Strain relief
D. Tube stuffer

_____12.   Armored cable is used in outside plant installations to
_____ and _____.
A. Prevent rodent damage
B. Protect from damage from crushing
C. Increase pulling tension
D. Conduct lightning strikes

_____13.   The minimum long term bend radius of installed fiber optic cable
is usually specified as no less than _____.
A. 12 inches
B. 1 meter
C. 10 times the cable diameter
D. 20 times the cable diameter

_____14.   Black polyethylene jackets are used on outdoor cables for
_____.
A. Abrasion resistance
B. High tensile load
C. Sunlight and moisture resistance
D. Appearance

Additional Study And Projects

Find manufacturer's websites and see how they specify cables for various applications. Note which cables are UL approved for indoor applications and how they are specified.

Review the FOA videos on cable preparation.

Labs: Examine various fiber optic cables to understand their construction and prepare them for splicing or termination.

Try pulling zipcord by the strength members and then by the jacket. What happens when you pull by the jacket?

Chapter 7
Splices and Connectors

Objectives: From this chapter you should learn:
The difference between splices and connectors
Requirements for connectors and splices
Connector styles
Termination types of connectors
Splice types
Splicing procedures

Splices or Connectors?

Fiber optic joints or terminations are made two ways: 1) splices which create a permanent joint between the two fibers or 2) connectors that mate two fibers to create a temporary joint and/or connect the fiber to a piece of network gear. Either joining method must have two primary characteristics: good optical performance indicated by low loss, minimal reflectance and high mechanical strength. Terminations must also be of the right style to be compatible to the equipment involved and be protected against the environment in which they are installed.

Splices are considered permanent joints and are used for joining most outside plant cables. Fusion splicing is most widely used as it provides for the lowest loss and least reflectance, as well as providing the most reliable joint. Virtually all singlemode splices are fusion. Mechanical splicing is used for temporary restoration and for most multimode splicing.

Connectors are used for terminations, that is the ends of the fibers where they connect to equipment or to patch panels where fiber routing can be changed by patching different fibers together. Different connectors and termination procedures are used for multimode and singlemode fibers. Multimode fibers are relatively easy to terminate, so field termination is generally done by installing connectors directly on tight buffered fibers using the procedures outlined below. Most field singlemode terminations are made by splicing a factory-made pigtail onto the installed cable rather than terminating the fiber directly as is commonly done with multimode fiber. Singlemode terminations require extreme care in assembly, especially polishing, to get good performance (low loss and reflectance), so they are usually done in a clean manufacturing facility using heat-cured epoxy and machine polishing.

Performance Specifications

Optical Loss

The primary specification for connectors and splices is loss or the amount of light lost in the connection. When we say connector loss or splice loss, we really mean "connection" loss - the loss of a mated pair of connectors or a fiber joint, expressed in "dB." The loss of a splice is obviously the light lost in the joint between two fibers. Connection loss is the loss of a connector mated to a reference connector.

Testing a connector requires mating it to a reference connector which must be a high quality connector in order to not adversely affect the measured loss. Testing splices is more difficult, since it is a permanent joint, so splice testing is done indirectly using an instrument called an OTDR. Fusion splicers estimate splice loss but their estimate is generally verified during installation by an OTDR. See Chapter 8 on testing.

Connector and splice loss is caused by a number of factors. Loss is minimized when the two fiber cores are identical, perfectly aligned and touching each other, the connectors or splices are properly finished and no dirt is present at the joint. Only the light that is coupled into the receiving fiber's core will propagate, so all the rest of the light becomes the connector or splice loss.

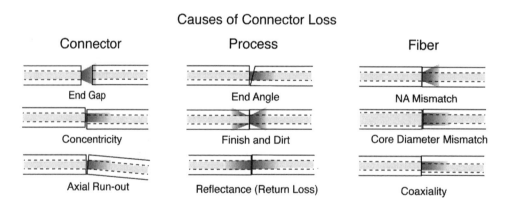

Causes of Connector Loss

Connector	Process	Fiber
End Gap	End Angle	NA Mismatch
Concentricity	Finish and Dirt	Core Diameter Mismatch
Axial Run-out	Reflectance (Return Loss)	Coaxiality

End gaps between the two fibers cause two problems, insertion loss and reflectance. The emerging cone of light from the connector will spill over the core of the receiving fiber and be lost. In addition, the air gap in the joint between the fibers causes a reflection when the light encounters the change n refractive index from the glass fiber to the air in the gap. This reflection (called fresnel reflection) amounts to about 5% in typical flat polished connectors, and means that no connector with an air gap will have less than about 0.3 dB loss. This reflection is called reflectance or optical return loss, and can be a problem in laser-based systems. Connectors use a number of polishing techniques to create a convex end on the fiber to ensure physical contact of the fiber ends to minimize reflectance. On mechanical splices, it is possible to reduce reflections by using non-perpendicular cleaves, which cause back reflections to be absorbed in the cladding of the fiber.

The end the fiber must be properly polished and clean to minimize loss. A rough surface or dirt can scatter and absorb light. Since the optical fiber is so small, typical airborne dirt can be a major source of loss. Whenever connectors are not terminated, they should be covered with dust caps provided by the manufacturer to protect the end of the ferrule from dirt. One should never touch the end of the ferrule, since the oils on one's skin causes the fiber to attract dirt. Before connection and testing, it is advisable to clean connectors with lint-free wipes moistened with isopropyl alcohol or dry fiber cleaners.

Two sources of loss caused by mismatched fibers are directional; numerical aperture (NA) and core diameter differences inherent in the fibers being joined. Differences in these two will create connections that have different losses depending on the direction of light propagation. Light from a fiber with a larger NA will overfill the core of the receiving fiber and be more sensitive to angularity and end gap, so transmission from a fiber of larger NA to one of smaller NA will be higher loss than the reverse direction. Likewise, light from a larger core fiber will have high loss coupled to a fiber of smaller diameter, while one can couple a small diameter fiber to a large diameter fiber with minimal loss, since it is much less sensitive to end gap or lateral offset.

These fiber mismatches occur for two reasons, the occasional need to interconnect two dissimilar fibers and production variances in fibers of the same nominal dimensions. Production variances are only a few microns and contribute only small amounts of loss, but the loss caused by mismatches will be directional, causing larger losses when transmitting from larger to smaller core fibers.

With two multimode fibers in common usage today (50/125 and 62.5/125) and two others which have been used occasionally in the past (100/140 and 85/125) and several types of singlemode fiber in use, it is possible to sometimes have to connect dissimilar fibers or use systems designed for one fiber size on another. If you connect a smaller fiber to a larger one, the coupling losses will be minimal, but connecting larger fibers to smaller ones results in substantial losses at the joint.

Typical connector losses are generally less than 0.3 dB for factory-polished singlemode or multimode connectors using adhesive/polish techniques. Few installers tackle singlemode field termination, generally fusion splicing factory-made pigtails onto the fibers, since SM polishing is not so easy in the field, especially in terms of reflectance. Multimode field terminations are common, since experienced installers can get results comparable to factory-terminations with adhesive/polish techniques. Field termination of prepolished/splice connectors using a precision cleaver (those made for fusion splicing) can produce consistent results around 0.5 dB, while the simple cleaver produces losses more often in the 0.75 dB range. Few industry standards put limits on connector losses, but TIA 568 calls for connection losses of less than 0.75 dB and splice losses at less than 0.3 dB, high losses but limits which will allow use of prepolished/splice connectors and most mechanical splices.

Reflectance

Reflectance or optical return loss (which has also been called "back reflection") of the connector or splice is the amount of light that is reflected back up the fiber toward the source by light reflections off the interface of the polished end surface of the connector and air. It is called fresnel reflection and is caused by the light going through the change in index of refraction at the interface between the fiber (n=1.5) and air (n=1). Reflectance is primarily a problem with connectors but may also affect mechanical splices even though they contain an index matching gel to prevent reflectance. Since fusion splices weld two fibers together, reflectance is generally not a problem, but if a fusion splice shows reflectance, it indicates a problem with the splice, often a bubble from improper fusing.

Reflectance is one component of a connector's loss, representing about 0.3 dB loss for a non-contact or air-gap connector where the two fibers do not make contact. Reflected light may reflect back to the transmitter and interfere with the performance of singlemode lasers or reflect several times from each end of a link to create optical background noise. Minimizing the reflectance is necessary to get maximum performance out of high bit rate singlemode laser-based systems and especially AM modulated CATV signals. In multimode systems, reflections are less of a problem but can add to background noise in the fiber.

Since this is more a problem with singlemode systems, manufacturers have concentrated on solving the problem for their singlemode components but multimode connectors benefit also as any reduction in reflectance also reduces loss. Several schemes have been used to reduce reflectance, mainly using a convex physical contact (PC) polish on the end of the connector ferrule, which reduces the fresnel reflection. The technique involves polishing the end surface of the fiber to a convex surface or even better at a slight angle (APC or angled physical contact) to prevent reflectance.

Splicing Optical Fibers

Splices create a permanent joint between two fibers, so its use is limited to places where cables are not expected to be available for servicing in the future. The most common application for splicing is concatenating (joining) cables in long outside plant cable runs where the length of the run requires more than one cable. Splicing can be used to mix a number of different types of cables such as connecting a 48 fiber cable to six 8 fiber cables going to various locations. Splicing is generally used to terminate singlemode fibers by splicing preterminated pigtails onto each fiber. And of course, splicing is used for OSP restoration.

There are two types of splices, fusion and mechanical. Fusion splicing is most widely used as it provides for the lowest loss and least reflectance, as well as providing the strongest and most reliable joint. Fusion splicing machines are available in two types that splice a single fiber or a ribbon of 12 fibers at one time. Virtually all singlemode splices are fusion. Mechanical splicing is mostly used for temporary restoration and for multimode splicing. In the photo below, a fusion splice is on the left and the rest are various types of mechanical splices.

Splicing in the field is generally done in a trailer or tent to reduce problems from dust and temperature extremes. Fusion splicing in manholes is particularly dangerous because of the possibility of explosive gas in the manhole. Splicing on poles is obviously dangerous too. It's easier to bring extra cable length into a trailer on the ground and work in a clean environment for splicing, placing splices in a closure and testing. The final closure is then placed in location and the extra fiber carefully looped and mounted in an appropriate place.

Color Codes for Splicing
Individual fibers and buffer tubes in loose tube cables are color coded for identification. When splicing similar cables on long runs, fibers should be spliced straight through according to color codes to continue the same color coding for each joined fiber in the concatenated cables. When connecting large fiber count cables to several smaller cables, fibers should be spliced in order and records kept of the connections made.

Fusion Splices
Fusion splices are made by "welding" the two fibers together usually by an electric arc. For safety, fusion splicing should not be done in an enclosed space like a manhole or any potentially explosive atmosphere. The equipment for fusion splicing is usually too bulky for most aerial applications also, so fusion splicing is usually done in a truck or trailer equipped just for that purpose.

Singlemode fusion splicers are highly automated and it's hard to make a bad splice as long as you clean and cleave the fibers properly then follow the directions for using the splicer correctly. Fusion splices are so good today that splice points may not be detectable in OTDR traces. Some splicing machines only do one fiber at a time but mass fusion splicers can do all 12 fibers in a ribbon at once.

The Fusion Splicing Process

Preparing the Fibers
The fusion splicing process is basically the same for all automatic splicing machines. The first step is to strip, clean & cleave the fibers to be spliced. Strip the primary buffer coating to expose the proper length of bare fiber. Clean the fiber with appropriate wipes. Cleave the fiber using the directions appropriate to the cleaver being used. Place each fiber into the guides in the fusion splicing machine and clamp it in place.

Running the splicer program
First choose the proper program for the fiber types being spliced. The splicer will show the fibers being spliced on a video screen. Fiber ends will be inspected for proper cleaves and bad ones will be rejected. That fiber must be cleaved again. The fibers will be moved into position, prefused to remove any dirt on the fiber ends and preheat the fibers for splicing. The fibers will be aligned using the core alignment method used on that splicer. Then the fibers will be fused by an automatic arc cycle that heats them in an electric arc and feeds the fibers together at a controlled rate.
When fusion is completed, the splicing machine will inspect the splice and estimate the optical loss of the splice. It will tell the operator if a splice needs to be remade. The operator removes the fibers from the guides and attach a permanent splice protector by heat-shrinking or clamping clam shell protectors.

Mass (Ribbon) Fusion Splicing

Ribbon cables are fusion spliced one ribbon at a time, rather than one fiber at a time. Thus each ribbon is stripped, cleaved and spliced as a unit. Special tools are needed to strip the fiber ribbon, usually heating it first, then cleave all fibers at once. Many tools place the ribbon in a carrier that supports and aligns it through stripping, cleaving and splicing. Consult both cable and splicer manufacturers to ensure you have the proper directions.

Mechanical Splices
Mechanical splices are alignment fixtures that hold the ends of two fibers together with some index matching gel or glue between them. There are a number of types of mechanical splices, such as small glass tubes or V-shaped metal clamps. The tools to make mechanical splices are inexpensive, but the splices themselves can be more expensive. Many mechanical splices are used for restoration, but with practice they can work well with both singlemode and multimode fiber, and using a quality cleaver such as those used for fusion splicing.

Mechanical Splicing Process

Preparing the Fibers
The splicing process is basically the same for all types of mechanical splices. The first step is to strip, clean & cleave the fibers to be spliced. Strip the primary buffer coating to expose the proper length of bare fiber. Clean the fiber with appropriate wipes. Cleave the fiber using the directions appropriate to the cleaver being used. Using a high quality cleaver such as those provided with fusion splicers will yield more consistent and lower loss splices.

Making The Mechanical Splice
Insert the first fiber into the mechanical splice. Most splices are designed to limit the depth of the fiber insertion by the stripped length of buffer coating on the fiber. Clamp the fiber in place if fibers are held separately. Some splices clamp both fibers at once. Repeat these steps for the second fiber.
You can optimize the loss of a mechanical splice visually using a visual fault locator, a visible laser test source if the fiber ends being spliced are visible. Gently withdraw one of the fibers a slight amount, rotating it slightly and reinserting it until the visible light is minimized, indicating lowest loss.

Making Good Splices, Fusion or Mechanical

Making consistently low loss splices depends on proper techniques and keeping equipment in good shape. Cleanliness is a big issue, of course. Fiber strippers should be kept clean and in good condition and be replaced when nicked or worn. Cleavers are most important, as the secret to good splices - either fusion or mechanical - is having good cleaves on both fibers. Keep cleavers clean and have the scribing blades aligned and replaced regularly. Fusion splicers should be properly maintained and fusing parameters set for the fibers being spliced. For mechanical splices, light pressure on the fiber to keep the ends together while crimping is important. Use a visual fault locator (VFL) to optimize the splice before crimping if possible.

Verifying Splice Loss
Splices are permanent joints that cannot be accessed for individual insertion loss testing with a source and power meter as connectors are tested. Fusion splicers generally provide an estimate of connector loss based on an analysis of data from the alignment system used by the splicer, but it is only an estimate. An insertion loss test of the entire finished cable will be done when installation is finished, but that only allows comparison to the overall loss predicted by the loss budget created during the design phase, not verification of any individual splice.
For concatenations of cables, only an OTDR can see the splice and confirm its loss, but for accurate loss measurements it requires testing from both ends and averaging (see Chapter 8 on Testing.) The OTDR test will also confirm that the splice is not reflective, an important issue in many systems. The limited resolution of the OTDR means that it cannot be used to verify the splices used to terminate fibers with pigtails, but a visual fault locator can be used to check these splices near the ends of the cable.

Choosing a Splice Type
The choice between fusion and mechanical splicing can be made on several parameters including performance, reliability and cost. In addition, installers may choose the type they are most familiar with or already have equipment for.
From a performance standpoint, fusion splices give very low loss and reflectance so they are preferred for singlemode networks. However, fusion may not work well on some multimode fibers, so mechanical splices may be preferred for multimode fiber, unless it is an underwater or aerial application, where the greater reliability of the fusion splice is preferred.
From a reliability standpoint, a fusion splice is the best choice. Properly made and sealed in a splice protector, the splice should last as long as the cable itself. Tests have shown mechanical splices are also long-lasting, but do not have the mechanical strength of a fusion splice.
If cost is the issue, the choice depends on how many splices are going to be made. Fusion splicing requires expensive equipment and but makes

inexpensive splices, while mechanical splices require inexpensive equipment and more expensive splice hardware. If you make a lot of splices (and there may be thousands in an big telco or CATV network,) fusion splices will be less expensive. If you need just a few splices or are preparing for a restoration and do not have a fusion splicer available, mechanical splices may be a logical choice.

Protecting Splices

For protection against the outside plant environment and damage, splices require placement in a protective case. They are generally placed in a splice tray which is then placed inside a splice closure for OSP installations or a patch panel box for premises applications. Indoors, splice trays are often integrated into patch panels to provide for connections to the fibers.
There are probably thousands of different types and options on splice closures. Some are designed for concatenation of long distance cables where two identical cables are spliced together. Some closures are designed for connecting several smaller cables to a larger one for breaking out the larger cable to several destinations. Closures can be used for midspan entry also, where the cable jacket is stripped but most of the buffer tubes are coiled inside without opening, while one or more tubes will be opened and spliced to other cables. Some have cables entering into one end, some have cable entries on both ends.
There are splice closures designed to be buried, mounted on walls, hung from cables or poles. Some are small pedestals themselves. Each type has a particular application and probably every application has a special closure. Even special hardware may be necessary for handling different cable or splice types, so make certain you have the right hardware before using the closure. It is recommended that you work with vendors to find the best closure for your applications then follow their instructions.
Preparing cables for splice closures involves several steps that should be followed in the exact sequence specified by the manufacturer to ensure the cables are properly secured and the closure will seal. For every splice closure, it is important to follow the manufacturer's instructions on stripping the cable to ensure proper lengths of strength members to secure the cable to the closure and proper lengths of buffer tubes to connect to the splice trays. The proper length of fiber is needed to allow splicing and then neatly storing fiber in the splice tray. Inside splice closures and at each end, cables with metallic shielding or strength members must be properly grounded and bonded.

Care should be taken when arranging fibers and splices in splice trays and buffer tubes in the splice closure to prevent stress on the fibers. Arranging fibers inside splice trays may require twisting the fiber but following the closure manufacturer's instructions will minimize the stress on the fiber. Often the fibers are broken as the trays and closure are assembled or re-entered for troubleshooting and repair. Cables must be secured to the splice closure and sealed properly. Generally loose tube cables will have the tubes extending from the entrance of the closure to the tray, where they are secured, then approximately 1 meter of bare fibers are organized in the tray after splicing. Care must be taken to properly bond electrical conductors such as the armor on some cables or center metallic strength members to the closure and at each end.

All closures must be sealed to prevent moisture entry. Closures must be properly secured, with the location being determined by the installation type, and excess cable properly coiled and stored. This may be in a pedestal or vault, on a pole or tower or buried underground.

Connectors

Styles of Fiber Optic Connectors
Since fiber optic technology was introduced in the late 70s, numerous connector styles have been developed - probably over 100 designs. Each new design was meant to offer better performance (less light loss and reflectance) and easier, faster and/or more inexpensive termination.

Of course, the marketplace eventually determines which connectors are successful. However several attempts to standardize connectors have been attempted. Some were unique to networks or systems. FDDI, the first fiber LAN, and ESCON, the IBM mainframe peripheral network, required unique connectors. TIA 568 originally called for SC connectors as a standard, but when users continued to use more STs than SCs and a whole new generation of smaller connectors were introduced, TIA-568B was changed to say that any connector standardized by a FOCIS standard document was acceptable.

The four connectors here show how fiber optic connectors have evolved. The bottom connector is a Deutsch 1000, the first commercially-available fiber optic connector. It was really a mechanical splice, where fibers were held inside the connector with a tiny screw-tightened chuck. The nose piece was spring-loaded, allowing exposing the fiber for cleaving and mating with a small plastic lens in a mating adapter. The mating adapter also had index-matching fluid to reduce loss but it created a dirt problem.

The AT&T Biconic was developed by Bell Labs in the late 1970s. The conical ferrule was molded from glass-filled plastic. The first Biconics had ferrules molded around the fiber, until a die with a tiny 125 micron (0.005 inch) pin in the exact center was developed. When Biconics were adapted to singlemode fiber, the ferrules were ground on a special grinding machine to center the fiber.

LC

SC

Biconic

Deutsch

The SC, which was introduced in the mid-1980s, used a new invention, the molded ceramic ferrule, that revolutionized fiber optic termination. Ceramic was an ideal ferrule material. It could be made cheaply by molding, much cheaper than machining metal for example. It was extremely stable with temperature, having similar expansion characteristics to glass which prevented "pistoning" when the ferrule came unglued, a problem with metal or plastic ferrules. It's hardness was similar to glass which made polishing much easier. And it readily adhered to fibers using epoxies or anaerobic adhesives. Today, virtually all connectors use the ceramic ferrule, usually 2.5 mm diameter (SC, ST, FC) or 1.25 mm diameter (LC, MU.)
The LC connector at the top was introduced in the late 1990s to miniaturize connectors for higher density in patch panels or equipment. It uses a smaller ceramic ferrule, 1.25 mm diameter. The LC is the connector of choice for telecom and high speed data (>1 Gb/s) networks.

SC   ST   LC

While over one hundred connector types have been developed over the history of fiber optics, only the three connectors shown above, the SC, LC and

ST are the most widely used fiber optic connectors today.
The ST (an AT&T Trademark) was one of the first connectors to use ceramic
ferrules and is still one of the most popular connectors for multimode
networks, like most buildings and campuses. It has a bayonet mount and a
long cylindrical ferrule to hold the fiber. Most ferrules are ceramic, but some
are metal or plastic. And because they are spring-loaded, you have to make
sure they are seated properly. If you have high loss, reconnect them to see if
it makes a difference.
SC is a snap-in connector that is widely used in singlemode systems for
it's excellent performance and multimode systems because it was the
first connector chosen as the standard connector for TIA-568 (now any
connector with a FOCIS standard is acceptable.) It's a snap-in connector
that latches with a simple push-pull motion. It is also available in a duplex
configuration.
LC is a relatively new connector that uses a 1.25 mm ferrule, half the size
of the ST. It is often used in duplex form. It is a standard ceramic ferrule
connector, easily terminated with any adhesive. Good performance,
highly favored for singlemode and the connector of choice for multimode
transceivers for gigabit speeds and above, including multimode Ethernet and
Fibre Channel.
You can see more types of fiber optic connectors on the FOA Tech Topics
website.

Connector Popularity
The ST is still one of the most popular multimode connectors because
it is inexpensive and easy to install. The SC connector was specified as
a standard by the old EIA/TIA 568A specification, but its higher cost and
difficulty of installation (until recently) limited its popularity in premises
applications at first. However, newer SCs are much better in both cost and
installation ease, so it has been growing in use, but is now challenged by the
LC, which is the connector of choice for transceivers for systems operating at
gigabit speeds because of its small size and high performance.
Singlemode networks have used FC or SC connectors in about the same
proportion as ST and SC in multimode installations. There are some D4s
out there too. But LCs have become the most popular, again for their
performance and small size.
EIA/TIA 568 now allows any fiber optic connector as long as it has a FOCIS
(Fiber Optic Connector Intermateability Standard) document behind it. This
opened the way to the development of several new connectors, which we call
the "Small Form Factor" (SFF) connectors, including AT&T LC, the MT-RJ, the
Panduit "Opti-Jack," 3M's Volition, the E2000/LX-5 and MU. The LC has been
particularly successful in the US.

Specialty Fiber Optic Connectors

There are a number of specialty fiber optic connectors available such as this multifiber MTP connector used in prefabricated cabling systems, as well as ruggedized industrial connectors, military connectors, underwater or aircraft connectors, plastic optical fiber (POF) connectors, etc. Most have been designed for very specific applications and require extremely rigorous qualification testing. Some like the Mil-C-38999, are copper wiring connectors adapted to hold fiber optic ferrules. Many of these connectors require special cable types, termination procedures, cleaning, handling and test procedures. Refer to manufacturer's instructions whenever dealing with these types of connectors.

Connector Construction

Most connectors available today use ceramic ferrules to hold and align the fibers. Ceramic is used because it adheres well to glass, is easy to polish and has very low thermal expansion like the glass fiber. The back end of the ceramic ferrule is glued or crimped to the connector body. The back of the connector is shaped to accept a crimp sleeve that is used with jacketed simplex cables to crimp the aramid fiber strength members to the connector body, providing mechanical strength to the cable termination.

Cable Boot   Crimp Sleeve   Connector   Dust Cap

Connector Ferrule Shapes & Polishes

Fiber optic connectors can have several different ferrule shapes or finishes, usually referred to as end finish or polish type. Early connectors, which did not have keyed ferrules and could rotate in mating adapters, always had an air gap between the connectors to prevent them rotating and grinding scratches into the ends of the fibers. The ends of the ferrules were polished on hard, flat surfaces.

Connector Ferrule Ends

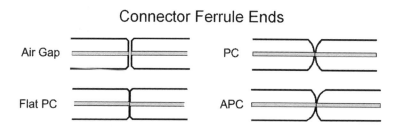

Beginning with the ST and FC which had keyed ferrules, the connectors were designed to contact tightly, what we now call physical contact (PC) connectors. These early connectors were still polished flat on the end. Reducing the air gap reduced the loss and reflectance (very important to laser-based singlemode systems), since light has a loss of about 5% (~0.25 dB) at each air gap and light is reflected back up the fiber. While air gap connectors usually had losses of 0.5 dB or more and a reflectance of -20 dB, PC connectors had lower typical losses of 0.3 dB and a lower reflectance of -30 to -40 dB. PC connectors required polishing on a flat surface with a soft rubber pad to allow the end to be polished convex.

Soon thereafter, it was determined that polishing the connector ferrules to a convex end face would produce an even better connection. The convex ferrule guaranteed the fiber cores were in contact. Losses were under 0.3dB and reflectance -40 dB or better.

The ultimate solution for singlemode systems extremely sensitive to reflections, like CATV or high bit rate telco links, was to angle the end of the ferrule 8 degrees to create what we call an APC or angled physical contact connector. Then any reflected light is at an angle that is absorbed in the cladding of the fiber, resulting in reflectance of >-60 dB.

Connector Color Codes:
Since the earliest days of fiber optics, orange, black or gray was multimode and yellow singlemode. However, the advent of metallic connectors like the FC and ST made color coding difficult, so colored strain-relief boots on the fiber or cable were more often used to identify connectors. Sometimes the connector color is ignored, requiring the user to identify the fiber type from the cable.

The TIA 568 color code for connector bodies and/or boots is Beige for multimode fiber except aqua for laser-optimized fiber, Blue for singlemode fiber, and Green for APC connectors.

Termination Procedures

Multimode connectors are usually installed in the field on the cables after pulling, while singlemode connectors are usually installed by splicing a factory-made "pigtail" onto the fiber. The tolerances on singlemode terminations are much tighter than multimode and the polishing processes are more critical, so singlemode termination is better done in a factory environment using polishing machines. You can install singlemode connectors in the field for low speed data networks, but you may not be able to get losses lower than 1 dB and reflectance may be a problem!
Connectors can be installed directly on most cable types, including jacketed tight buffer types like simplex, zipcord and breakout cables, where the aramid fiber strength members in the cable are crimped or glued to the connector body to create a strong connector. Connectors can be attached to the 900 micron buffered fibers in distribution cables, but the termination is not as rugged as those made to jacketed cables, so they should be placed in patch panels or boxes for protection. The 250 micron buffered fibers in loose tube cables cannot be easily terminated unless they have a reinforcement called a breakout kit or furcation kit installed, where each fiber is covered by a larger plastic tube. Generally loose tube and ribbon cables are terminated by splicing on a terminated pigtail.
Cables can be pulled with connectors already on them if, and a big if, you can deal with two issues: First, the length must be precise. Too short and you have to pull another longer one (its not cost effective to splice), too long and you waste money and have to store the extra cable length. Secondly, the connectors must be protected. Some cable and connector manufacturers offer protective sleeves to cover the connectors, but you must still be much more careful in pulling cables. You might consider terminating one end and pulling the unterminated end to not risk the connectors. There is a growing movement to install preterminated systems with the MTP 12 multifiber connector. It's a very small connector, not much bigger than a ST or SC, but terminates up to 12 fibers. Manufacturers sell multifiber cables with MTPs on them that connect to preterminated patch panels with STs or SCs.

Multimode Terminations
Several different types of terminations are available for multimode fibers. Each version has its advantages and disadvantages, so learning more about how each works helps decide which one to use.

Singlemode Terminations
Singlemode fiber requires different connectors and polishing techniques that are best done in a factory environment. Consequently most SM fiber is generally field terminated by splicing on a factory-terminated pigtail. Singlemode termination requires special connectors with much tighter

tolerances on the ferrule, especially the hole for the fiber. Polishing requires special diamond polishing film on a soft rubber pad and a polishing slurry to get low reflectance. But you can put SM connectors on in the field if you know what you are doing. Expect higher loss and high reflectance.

Adhesive Terminations

Most connectors use epoxies or other adhesives to hold the fiber in the connector ferrule and polish the end of the fiber to a smooth finish. Follow termination procedures carefully, as they have been developed to produce the lowest loss and most reliable terminations. Use only the specified adhesives, as the fiber to ferrule bond is critical for low loss and long term reliability! We've seen people use hardware store epoxies, Crazy Glue, you name it. And they regretted doing it. Only adhesives approved by manufacturers or other distributors of connectors should be used. If the adhesive fails, not unusual when connector ferrules were made of metal, the fiber will "piston" - sticking out or pulling back into the ferrule - causing high loss and potential damage to a mated connector.

The polishing process involves three steps but only takes a minute: "air polishing" to grind down the protruding fiber, polishing on a soft pad with the fiber held perpendicular to the polishing surface with a polishing puck and a quick final fine polish.

Epoxy/Polish

Most connectors, including virtually all factory made terminations, are the simple "epoxy/polish" type where the fiber is glued into the connector with epoxy and the end polished with special polishing film. These provide the most reliable connection, lowest losses (less than 0.5 dB) and lowest costs, especially if you are doing a lot of connectors. The small bead of hardened epoxy that surrounds the fiber on the end of the ferrule even makes the cleaving and polishing processes much easier - practically foolproof. The epoxy can be allowed to set overnight or cured in an inexpensive oven. A "heat gun" should never be used to try to cure the epoxy faster as the uneven heat may not cure all the epoxy or may overheat some of it which will prevent it ever curing. Don't use "Hot Melt" ovens either, as they use a much higher temperature and will ruin the epoxy.

"Hot Melt" Adhesive/Polish

This is a 3M trade name for a connector that already has the epoxy (actually a heat set glue) inside the connector. You insert the connector in a special oven. In a few minutes, the glue is melted, so you remove the connector, insert the stripped fiber, let it cool and it is ready to polish. Fast and easy, low loss, but not as cheap as the epoxy type, it has become the favorite of lots of contractors who install relatively small quantities of connectors. Remember you need a special Hot Melt oven, as it needs a much higher temperature than is used for curing epoxy.

Anaerobic Adhesive/Polish

These connectors use a quick setting "anaerobic" adhesive that cures faster than other types of adhesives. Various techniques of applying adhesive are used, including injecting it into the connector before inserting the fiber or simply wiping adhesive onto the fiber before inserting it in the connector. These adhesives dry in 5 minutes alone or in 30 seconds when used with a chemical accelerator.

Anaerobic connectors work well if your technique is good, but some do not have the wide temperature range of epoxies. A lot of installers are using Loctite 648, with or without the accelerator solution, that is neat and easy to use.

The Termination Process

For all types of adhesive/polish connectors, the termination process is similar. You start by preparing the cable, stripping off the outer jacket and cutting off strength members. Next you strip the fiber with a special tool that removes the plastic buffer coatings without damaging the fiber. The fiber is then cleaned and set aside. Adhesive is applied to the connector or fiber and the fiber is inserted and crimped into the connector body.

After the adhesive is set, the fiber is then cleaved close to the end of the ferrule. Polishing takes three steps. First "air polish" to grind down the cleaved fiber to near the end surface of the ferrule. Then polish on two different grades of abrasive film placed on a rubber pad using a polishing puck to keep the fiber perpendicular to the surface.

Inspect the polished end of the connector ferrule with a fiber optic inspection microscope. See the Testing Chapter for more information on connector inspection.

An experienced installer can terminate multifiber cables in about one minute per fiber, using the time required to cure the adhesive to prepare other connectors and reduce the time per connector.

It's important to follow termination procedures carefully, as they have been developed to produce the lowest loss and most reliable terminations. Use only the specified adhesives, as the fiber to ferrule bond is critical for low loss and long term reliability. And, like everything else, practice makes perfect!

Crimp/Polish

Rather than glue the fiber in the connector, these connectors use a crimp on the fiber to hold it in. Most types available in the past offered marginal loss performance and are thus no longer available. Expect to trade higher losses for the faster termination speed. A good choice if you only install small quantities and your customer will accept them.

Prepolished/splice (also called "cleave & crimp")

Some manufacturers offer connectors that have a short stub fiber already epoxied into the ferrule and polished and a mechanical or fusion splice in the back of the connector, so you just cleave a fiber and splice the connector to the fiber, a process which can be done very quickly. Several connectors use a fusion splice instead of a mechanical splice to attach the connector.

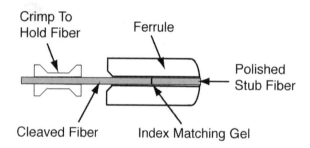

Crimp To Hold Fiber

Ferrule

Polished Stub Fiber

Cleaved Fiber

Index Matching Gel

This method has both good and bad points. The manufacturing process is complex so these connectors are costly, as much as ten times as much as an adhesive/polish type, since they require careful manufacturing. Some of that extra cost can be recovered in lower labor costs for installation. You must have a good cleave on the fiber you are terminating to make them low loss, as the fiber cleave is a major factor in the loss of a mechanical splice. Using a high quality cleaver like those used for fusion splicing, available from some manufacturers as part of their termination kits, is recommended. Even if you do everything correctly, loss will be somewhat higher, because you have a connection loss plus a splice loss in every connector. For prepolished connectors with mechanical splices, typical losses are 0.5-1 dB. For those with fusion splices, the losses can be as good as the best adhesive/polish connectors. For those with mechanical splices, the best way to terminate them is to verify the loss of the splice with a visual fault locator and "tweak" them as is done with mechanical splices.

Hints for field terminations
Here are a few things to remember when you are terminating connectors in the field. Following these guidelines will save you time, money and frustration.

Whatever you do, always follow the manufacturer's termination instructions closely.

Choose the connector carefully and clear it with the customer if it is anything other than an epoxy/polish type. Some customers have strong opinions on the types or brands of connectors used in their job.

NEVER take a new connector type in the field until you have installed enough of them in the office or lab so that you know you can put them on successfully. The field is no place to experiment or learn! One of the biggest cost factors installing connectors is yield – how many pass testing. The biggest factor in yield is the experience of the installer,

Have the right tools for the job. Make sure you have the proper tools and they are in good condition before you head out for the job. This includes all the termination tools, cable tools and test equipment. Do you know your test cables are good? Without that, you will test good terminations as bad every time. More and more installers are owning their own tools like auto mechanics, saying that is the only way to make sure the tools are properly cared for.

Dust and dirt are your enemies. It's very hard to terminate or splice in a dusty place. Try to work in the cleanest possible location. Use lint-free wipes (not cotton swaps or rags made from old T-shirts!) to clean every connector before connecting or testing it. Don't work under heating vents, as they are blowing dirt down on you continuously. Put covers on connectors and patch panels when not in use. Keep them covered to keep them clean.

Don't overpolish. Contrary to common sense, too much polishing is just as bad as too little. The ceramic ferrule in most of today's connector is much harder than the glass fiber. Polish too much will cause undercutting of the fiber and you create a concave fiber surface not convex as it should be, increasing the loss. A few swipes is all it takes.

Change polishing film regularly. Polishing builds up residue and dirt on the film that can cause problems after too many connectors and cause poor end finish. Check the manufacturers' specs.

Inspect and test, then document. It is very hard to troubleshoot cables when you don't know how long they are, where they go or how they tested originally! So keep good records, smart users require it and expect to pay extra for good records.

Do You Have To Terminate In The Field?

Many manufacturers offer prefabricated fiber optic cabling systems for both premises and outside plant systems. In fact, the largest application for prefabricated systems is fiber to the home (FTTH) where it saves a tremendous amount of time in installation and cost. Using prefab systems requires knowing precisely where the cable will be run so cable lengths can be specified. Using CAD systems and design drawings, a complete fiber optic cabling system is designed to the customer's specifications and built in a factory using standard components. Early prefabricated systems (some are still available) simply terminated cables with standard connectors like STs or SCs and protected them inside a plastic pulling boot with a pulling loop attached to the fiber strength members. The cable would be placed with the boot in place then removed to connect into patch panels.

The factory-assembled cables usually have connection lower loss than direct field terminations, on a par with spliced-on pigtails. Costs also involve tradeoffs, as factory systems are more expensive for the components but installation time is much less. In new facilities, considering prefabricated systems is always a good idea, but all factors should be considered before making a decision.

Managing and Protecting Terminations

Connections can be made in many types of hardware including racks of patch panels or wall-mounted boxes. The proper types of hardware must be chosen appropriate to the installation and will be covered in more detail in the installation chapter.

While connectors are designed to be rugged enough to be handled and those terminating jacketed cables are fairly rugged, connectors still need some protection from damage and dust or dirt. OSP terminations are sometimes in pedestals where exposure to environmental dust is possible. Ideally, fiber optic connectors should be installed in patch panels or boxes with some sealing to keep dust out, but this may be impossible, especially at connections to equipment. Whenever these connectors are accessed, they should be cleaned carefully. Experience has shown that the connections to equipment transceivers can become contaminated with dust too, so they may need cleaning.

Since multifiber cables have many terminations where fibers may be accessed for testing or changing configurations, interconnection points require managing the terminations which includes identifying every connector/ fiber end and keeping records of where it goes.

Review Questions

True/False
Indicate whether the statement is true or false.

_____1.   Most singlemode field terminations are made by fusion splicing a factory-made pigtail onto the cable.

_____2.   The SC and LC connectors have different size ferrules and cannot be mated.

Multiple Choice
Identify the choice that best completes the statement or answers the question.

_____3.   The loss of a fiber optic connector is defined as _____?
A. The calculated loss due to geometric misalignment
B. The loss of the connector mated to another connector
C. One-half the loss of a mated pair of connectors
D. The loss of a statistical sample of connectors

_____4.   Field terminations of singlemode fibers are generally done by _____ ?
A. Adhesive/polish method
B. Heat-cured anaerobic adhesive
C. Prepolished/splice connectors with mechanical splices
D. Fusion splicing a factory terminated pigtail onto the fiber

_____5.   Factory terminations, such as used for making patchcords, generally use what method of attaching the connector to the cable?
A. Epoxy/polish
B. Anaerobic adhesive
C. Prepolished/splice
D. Any of the above

_____6.   From a reliability standpoint, _____ is the best method to join two fibers.
   A. Mechanical splicing
   B. Fusion splicing
   C. Adhesive/polish connectors
   D. Factory terminations

_____7.   The difference between a fiber optic connector and a splice is
_____.
   A. Connectors are larger than splices
   B. Connectors are demountable, while splices are permanent
   C. Connectors require adhesives
   D. Splices need expensive tools

_____8.   Which one of the following performance requirements are not shared by connectors and splices?
   A. Low loss
   B. Low back reflection
   C. Repeatability
   D. Durability under repeated matings

_____9.   In singlemode connectors, _____ is as important as low loss.
   A. Ease of field termination
   B. Low reflectance
   C. Low cost
   D. Compatibility with many cable types

_____10.   Both mechanical splices and prepolished/splice connectors require a good _____ to have low loss.
   A. Field polishing technique
   B. Cleave on the fiber being terminated
   C. Fiber loss
   D. Cable design

_____11.   Physical contact (PC) polish on connectors is designed to reduce
_____.
   A. Loss
   B. Reflectance
   C. Loss and reflectance
   D. Polishing time

_____12.   Preparing cables for splicing in splice closures requires

_____.
A. Leaving the proper length of buffer tubes from the cable
   entrance in the closure to the splice tray
B. Leaving the proper length of fiber to splice and fit the splice in
   the splice tray
C. Securing the cable properly at the closure entrance
D. All of the above

_____13.   Individual splice loss on concatenated cables can be verified by

_____ .
A. OTDR testing
B. Insertion loss testing
C. Visual fault location
D. Visual inspection

Matching

Identify the following connectors:

_____12.   ST

_____13.   SC

_____14.   LC

_____15.   MTP

Additional Study

Read the Connector Identifier page on the FOA Online Reference Guide to learn about more styles of connectors.

Read the "Virtual Hands-On" pages on the FOA Online Reference Guide to see detailed explanations of how epoxy/polish, anaerobic/polish, HotMelt/Polish, and prepolished/splice connectors are made and how singlemode terminations are polished.

Read the Fusion Splice and Mechanical Splice pages on the FOA Online Reference Guide to learn more detail about these splices.

Read the "Virtual Hands-On" pages on the FOA Online Reference Guide to see detailed explanations on how fusion splices are made on single and ribbon fibers and how mechanical splices are made.

Review manufacturers' websites for connector datasheets and application notes.

Lab Projects

Terminate jacketed simplex cables and/or 900 micron buffered fibers with connectors using several methods and styles of connectors. Inspect each connector and test for loss when finished.

Splice single and/or ribbon fibers with a fusion splicer. Test with an OTDR (see Testing Chapter) and compare OTDR test results with the estimate provided by the splicer.

Splice single fibers with mechanical splices. Optimize with a visual fault locator. Test loss with an OTDR or loss test set. Splice several times using different cleavers to see how this affects loss.

Chapter 8
Fiber Optic Testing

Objectives: From this chapter you should learn:
What parameters need to be tested
What instruments are used for fiber optic testing
How to perform basic fiber optic testing
Measurement uncertainty in fiber optic testing
How to troubleshoot problems

Fiber Optic Tests

After all fiber optic cables are installed, spliced and terminated, they must be tested. For every fiber optic cable plant, you need to test for continuity and polarity, end-to-end insertion loss and then troubleshoot any problems on every fiber in every cable. If it's a long outside plant cable with intermediate splices, you will probably want to verify the individual splices with an OTDR test also, since that's the only way to ensure that each splice is good. If you are the network user, you may also be interested in testing transmitter and receiver power, as power is the measurement that tells you whether the system is operating properly.

Testing is the subject of the majority of industry standards, as there is a need to verify component and system specifications in a consistent manner. A list of TIA and ISO fiber optic standards is on the FOA website. Most of these tests relate to manufacturing testing to verify component performance and are not relevant to installation testing. Perhaps the most important test is insertion loss of an installed fiber optic cable plant performed with a light source and power meter (LSPM) or optical loss test set (OLTS) which is required by all international standards to ensure the cable plant is within the loss budget before acceptance of the installation.

Testing fiber optic components and cable plants requires making several tests and measurements with the most common tests listed below. Some tests involve installer inspection and judgment, such as visual inspection or tracing while some use sophisticated instruments that provide direct measurements. Optical power, required for measuring source power, receiver power and, when used with a test source, loss or attenuation, is the most important parameter and is required for almost every fiber optic test. Backscatter measurements made by an OTDR are the next most important measurements, especially for testing outside plant installations and troubleshooting. Measurement of geometrical parameters of fiber and bandwidth or dispersion are essential for fiber manufacturers but not relevant to field testing. Troubleshooting installed cables and networks is required in every installation.

Visual Inspection

Visual Tracing
Continuity checking with a visual fiber tracer can trace a path of a fiber from one end to another through many connections, verifying continuity, correct connections and duplex connector polarity. A visual fiber tracer looks like a flashlight or a pen-like instrument with a light bulb or LED source that mates to a fiber optic connector. Attach the fiber to test to the visual tracer and look at the other end of the fiber to see the light transmitted through the core of the fiber. If there is no light at the far end, go back to intermediate connections to find the bad section of the cable.
A good example of how a visual tracer can save time and money is testing fiber on a reel before you install it to make sure it hasn't been damaged during shipment. First look for visible signs of damage to fiber on the reel (like cracked or broken reels, kinks in the cable, etc.). During testing, visual tracers help also identify the next fiber to be tested for loss with the test kit. When connecting cables at patch panels, use the visual tracer to make sure each connection is the right two fibers! To make certain the proper fiber is connected between the transmitter and receiver, use the visual tracer in place of the transmitter and your eye instead of the receiver to verify the connection. Follow all rules for eye safety when working with visual tracers.

Visual Fault Location
A higher power version of the fiber tracer called a visual fault locator (VFL) uses a visible laser that can also find faults. The red laser light is powerful enough for continuity checking or to trace fibers for several kilometers, identify splices in splice trays and show breaks in fibers or high loss connectors. You can see the loss of light at a fiber break by the bright red light from the VFL, even through the jacket of many yellow or orange simplex cables (not with black or gray jackets, of course.) It's most important use is finding faults in short cables or near the connector where OTDRs cannot find them.
You can also use the VFL to visually verify and optimize mechanical splices or prepolished-splice type fiber optic connectors. By visually minimizing the light lost you can get the lowest loss splice. No other method will assure you of high yield with those connectors.

VFLs need a warning on eye safety. VFLs use visible light. The power level is high and you should not be looking directly at it. You will find it quite uncomfortable to look directly at the output of a fiber illuminated by a VFL, so when tracing fibers, look to the side of the fiber to see if VFL light is present.

Visual Connector Inspection by Microscope
Fiber optic inspection microscopes are used to inspect connectors to confirm proper polishing and find faults like scratches, polishing defects and dirt. They can be used both to check the quality of the termination procedure and diagnose problems. A well made connector will have a smooth, polished, scratch free finish and the fiber will not show any signs of cracks, chips or areas where the fiber is either protruding from the end of the ferrule or pulling back into it.

The magnification for viewing connectors can be 30 to 400 power but it is best to use a medium magnification. If the magnification is too low, critical details may not be visible. Inspecting with a very high magnification may cause the viewer to be too critical, rejecting good connectors. Multimode connectors should use magnifications in the range of 100-200X and singlemode fiber can use higher magnification, up to 400X. A better solution is to use medium magnification, but inspect the connector three ways: viewing directly at the end of the polished surface with coaxial or oblique lighting, viewing directly with light transmitted through the core, and viewing at an angle with lighting from the opposite angle or with quite oblique lighting.

Viewing directly allows seeing the fiber and the ferrule hole, determining if the ferrule hole is of the proper size, the fiber is centered in the hole and a proper amount of adhesive has been applied. Only the largest scratches may be visible this way, however. Adding light transmitted through the core will make cracks in the end of the fiber, caused by pressure or heat during the polish process, visible.

Viewing the end of the connector at an angle, while lighting it from the opposite side at approximately the same angle or using low-angle lighting and viewing directly will allow the best inspection for the quality of polish and possible scratches. The shadowing effect of angular viewing or lighting enhances the contrast of scratches against the mirror smooth polished surface of the glass.

One needs to be careful in inspecting connectors, however. The tendency is to sometimes be overly critical, especially at high magnification. Only defects over the fiber core are generally considered a problem. Chipping of the glass around the outside of the cladding is not unusual and will have no effect on the ability of the connector to couple light in the core on multimode fibers. Likewise, scratches only on the cladding should not cause any loss problems.

The best microscopes allow you to inspect the connector from several angles, either by tilting the connector or having angle illumination to get the best picture of what's going on. Check to make sure the microscope has an easy-to-use adapter to attach the connectors of interest to the microscope.

Video readout microscopes are now available that allow easier viewing of the end face of the connector and some even have software that analyzes the finish. While they are much more expensive than normal optical microscopes, they will make inspection easier and greatly increase productivity.

Remember to check that no power is present in the cable before you look at it in a microscope to protect your eyes! The microscope will concentrate any power in the fiber and focus it into your eye with potentially hazardous results. Some microscopes have filters to stop the infrared radiation from transmitters to minimize this problem.

Optical Power

Practically every measurement in fiber optics refers to optical power. The output of a transmitter or the input to receiver are "absolute" optical power measurements, that is, you measure the actual value of the power. Loss is a "relative" power measurement, the difference between the power coupled into a component like a cable, splice or a connector and the power that is transmitted through it. This difference in power level before and after the component is what we call optical loss and defines the performance of a cable, connector, splice, or other component.

Whenever tests are performed on fiber optic networks, the results are displayed on an instrument readout. Power measurements are expressed in "dB," the measurement unit of power and loss in optical fiber measurements. Optical loss is measured in "dB" while optical power is measured in "dBm." Loss is a negative number (like -3.2 dB) as are many power measurements. Measurements in dB can sometimes be confusing.

In the early days of fiber optics, source output power was usually measured in milliwatts, a linear scale, and loss was measured in dB or decibels, a logarithmic scale. Over the years, all measurements migrated to dB for convenience causing much confusion. Loss measurements were generally measured in dB since dB is a ratio of two power levels, one of which is considered the reference value. The dB is a logarithmic scale where each 10 dB represents a ratio of 10 times. The actual equation used to calculate dB is dB = 10 log (measured power / reference power).

Thus 10 dB is a ratio of 10 times (either 10 times as much or one-tenth as much), 20 dB is a ratio of 100, 30 dB is a ratio of 1000, etc. When the two optical powers compared are equal, dB = 0, a convenient value that is easily remembered. If the measured power is higher than the reference power, dB will be a positive number, but if it is lower than the reference power, it will be negative. Thus measurements of loss are typically expressed as a negative number.

Measurements of optical power such as the output of a transmitter or input to a receiver are expressed in units of dBm. The "m" in dBm refers to a reference power of 1 milliwatt. Thus a source with a power level of 0 dBm has a power of 1 milliwatt. Likewise, -10 dBm is 0.1 milliwatt and +10 dBm is 10 milliwatts.

To measure loss in a fiber optic system, we make two measurements of power, a reference measurement before the component we are testing and a loss measurement after the light passes through the component. Since we are measuring loss, the measured power will be less than the reference power, so the ratio of measured power to reference power is less than 1 and the log is negative, making dB a negative number. When we set the reference value, the meter reads "0 dB" because the reference value we set and the value the meter is measuring is the same. Then when we measure loss, the power measured is less, so the meter will read "- 3.0 dB" for example, if the tested power is half the reference value. Although meters measure a negative number for loss, convention is the loss is expressed as a positive number, so we say the loss is 3.0 dB when the meter reads - 3.0 dB.

Instruments that measure in dB can be either optical power meters or optical loss test sets (OLTS). The optical power meter usually reads in dBm for power measurements or dB with respect to a user-set reference value for loss. While most power meters have ranges of +3 to -50 dBm, most sources are in the range of +10 to -10 dBm for lasers and -10 to -20 dBm for LEDs. Only lasers used in CATV or long-haul telephone systems have powers high enough to be really dangerous, up to +20 dBm; that's 100 milliwatts or a tenth of a watt.

It is important to remember that dB is for measuring loss, dBm is for measuring power and the more negative a number is, the higher the loss. Set your zero reference before measuring loss and check it occasionally while making measurements.

Calibration of Power Measurements
Calibrating fiber optic power measurement equipment requires setting up a reference standard traceable to a national standards lab like the National Institute of Standards and Technology in the US for comparison purposes while calibrating every power meter or other instrument. The NIST standard for all power measurements is an ECPR, or electrically calibrated pyroelectric

radiometer, which measures optical power by comparing the heating power of the light to the well-known heating power of a resistor. Calibration is done at 850, 1300 and 1550 nm. Sometimes, the wavelength of lasers at 1310 nm is used by manufacturers as the calibrated wavelength on a power meter, but the standard for power meter calibration is 1300 nm. To conveniently transfer their laboratory standard to fiber optic power meter manufacturers calibration laboratories, NIST currently uses a laboratory optical power meter which is sent around to labs as a transfer standard.

Meters calibrated in this manner have an uncertainty of calibration of about +/- 5%, compared to the NIST primary standards. Limitations in the uncertainty are the inherent inconsistencies in optical coupling, about 1% at every transfer, and slight variations in wavelength calibration. NIST is working continuously with instrument manufacturers and private calibration labs to try to reduce the uncertainty of these calibrations.

Recalibration of instruments should be done annually, however experience has shown that the accuracy of meters rarely changes significantly during that period, as long as the electronics of the meter do not fail. The calibration of fiber optic power meters requires considerable investment in capital equipment so meters must be returned to the original manufacturer or private calibration labs for calibration.

Understanding FO Power Meter Measurement Uncertainty

Much attention has been paid to developing transfer standards for fiber optic power measurements. The US NIST in Boulder, Colorado and standards organizations of most other countries have worked to provide good standards to work from. We can now assure traceability for our calibrations, but even so the errors involved in making measurements are not ignorable. Even when fiber optic power meters are calibrated within specifications, the uncertainty of a measurement may be as great as +/- 5% (about 0.2 dB) compared to standards. Understanding power meter errors and their probable causes will insure a realistic viewpoint on fiber optic power measurements.

The first source of error is optical coupling. Light from the fiber is expanding in a cone. It is important that the detector to fiber geometry be such that all the light from the fiber hits the detector, otherwise the measurement will be lower than the actual value. But every time light passes through a glass to air interface, such as the window on the detector, a small amount of the light is reflected and lost. Finally, the cleanliness of the optical surfaces involved can cause absorption and scattering. The sum total of these potential errors will be dependent on the connector type, wavelength, fiber size and NA.

Beyond the coupling errors, one has errors associated with the wavelength calibration. Semiconductor detectors used in fiber optic instruments (and systems too) have a sensitivity that is wavelength dependent. Since the actual source wavelength is rarely known, there is an error associated with the spectral sensitivity of the detector. By industry convention, the three cardinal wavelengths (850, 1300 and 1550 nm) are used for all power measurements, not the exact source wavelength.

Another source of error exists for high and low level measurements. At high levels, the optical power may overload and saturate the detector, causing the measurement to be in error. At low levels, the inherent detector noise adds to the signal and becomes an error. If the signal is 10 dB above the noise floor (10 times the noise), the offset error is 10% or 0.4 dB.

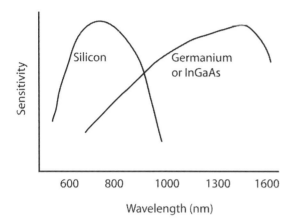

Instrument Resolution vs. Measurement Uncertainty

Considering the uncertainty of most fiber optic measurements, instrument manufacturers have provided power and loss meters with a measurement resolution that is usually much greater than needed. The uncertainty of optical power measurements is about 0.2 dB (5%), loss measurements are more likely to have uncertainties of 0.2-0.5 dB or more, and optical return loss measurements have a 1 dB uncertainty.

Instruments which have readouts with a resolution of 0.01 dB are generally only appropriate for laboratory measurements of very low component losses or changes caused by environmental changes. Within the laboratory, a resolution of 0.01 dB can be extremely useful, since one often measures the loss of connectors or splices that are under 0.10 dB or changes in loss under environmental stress that are under 0.1 dB. Stability of sources and physical stress on cables limits measurement uncertainty to about 0.02 to 0.05 dB per day, but 0.01 dB resolution can be helpful in determining small changes in component performance.

Field measurements have higher uncertainty because more components are measured at once and losses are higher. Practically, measurements are better when the instrument resolution is limited to 0.1dB. Readings will be more likely to be stable when being read and more indicative of the measurement uncertainty.

Fiber Optic Power Meters

Measuring power requires a power meter with an adapter that matches the fiber optic connector on the cable being tested, and if you are testing a transmitter, a known good fiber optic cable (of the right fiber size, as coupled power is a function of the size of the core of the fiber) and a little help from the network electronics to turn on the transmitter. Remember when you measure power, the meter must be set to the proper wavelength and range (usually dBm, sometimes microwatts, but never "dB" - that's a relative power range used only for testing loss.) Refer to the instructions that come with the test equipment for setup and measurement instructions.

To measure power, attach the meter to the cable attached to the source that has the output you want to measure. That can be at the receiver to measure receiver power, or using a patchcord or reference test cable (tested and known to be good) that is attached to the transmitter to measure output power. Turn on the transmitter/source and give it a few minutes to stabilize. Set the power meter for the matching wavelength and note the power the meter measures. Compare it to the specified power for the system and make sure it's enough power but not too much.

Optical Loss or Insertion Loss

Optical loss is the primary performance parameter of most fiber optic components. For fiber, it's the loss per unit length or attenuation coefficient. For connectors, it's connection loss when mated to another connector. For cables, it's the total loss of the components of the cable, including connectors, fiber, splices and any other components in the cable run being tested. We'll use cables to illustrate insertion loss then look at other components.

Loss of a cable is the difference between the power coupled into the cable at the transmitter end and what comes out at the receiver end. Testing for loss requires measuring the total amount of optical power lost in a cable (including fiber attenuation, connector loss and splice loss) with a fiber optic light source and power meter (LSPM) or optical loss test set (OLTS.) Loss testing is done at wavelengths appropriate for the fiber and its usage. Generally multimode fiber is tested at 850 nm and optionally at 1300 nm with LED sources. Singlemode fiber is tested at 1310 nm and optionally at 1550 nm with laser sources.

Most loss testing is done on cable assemblies, either patchcords or installed cable plants. But fiber manufacturers test every fiber for loss to calculate its attenuation coefficient. Connector manufactures test many connectors to obtain an average value of the loss the connector will have when terminated on fibers. Other component manufacturers also test the loss of their components to verify their performance.

The insertion loss measurement is made by mating the cable being tested to known good reference cables with a calibrated launch power that becomes the "0 dB" loss reference. Why do you need reference cables to measure loss? Testing with reference cables on each end simulates a cable plant with patchcords connecting to transmission equipment. You need a cable to measure the output power of the source for calibration of the "0 dB" loss reference.

Also, in order to measure the loss of the connectors on the end of a cable you must mate them to a similar, known good, connector. This is an important point often not fully understood. When we say connector loss, we really mean "connection" loss - the loss of a mated pair of connectors. Thus, testing connectors requires mating them to reference connector which must be high quality connectors themselves to not adversely affect the measured loss when mated to an unknown connector.

In addition to a power meter, you need a test source (light source) to measure loss. The test source should be compatible with the type of fiber being tested (generally a LED for MM or laser for SM) and wavelength (850, 1300, 1550 nm) that will be used on the fiber optic cable you are testing. If you are testing to some standards, you may need to add some mode conditioning, like a mandrel wrap, to meet the standard launch conditions.

Fiber Optic Test Sources

A fiber optic test source must be chosen for compatibility with the type of fiber in use (singlemode or multimode with the proper core diameter) and the wavelength desired for performing the test. Most sources are either LED's or lasers of the types commonly used as transmitters in actual fiber optic systems, making them representative of actual applications and enhancing the usefulness of the testing. Some laboratory tests, such as measuring the attenuation of fiber over a range of wavelengths requires a variable wavelength source, which is usually a tungsten lamp with a monochromator to vary the light source wavelength.

Typical wavelengths of sources are 650 or 665 nm (plastic fiber), 820, 850 and 870 nm (short wavelength multimode fiber) and 1300 (long wavelength multimode fiber) or 1310 nm and 1550 nm (long wavelength singlemode fiber). LED's are typically used for testing multimode fiber and lasers are used for singlemode fiber, although there is some crossover. High speed LANs which use multimode fiber may be tested with VCSELs like the system sources and short singlemode jumper cables may be tested with LEDs. The source wavelength can be a critical issue in making accurate loss measurements on long links, since the attenuation coefficient of the fiber is wavelength sensitive. Thus all test sources should be calibrated for wavelength in case corrections for wavelength variations are required.

Test sources almost always have fixed connectors. Hybrid test jumpers with connectors compatible with the source on one end and the connector being tested on the other must be used as reference cables. This may affect the type of reference setting mode used for loss testing.

Source-related factors affecting measurement accuracy are the stability of the output power and the modal distribution launched into multimode fiber. Source stability is mainly a factor of the electronic circuitry in the source. Industry standards have requirements on the modal output of test sources for multimode fiber that are important to the manufacturers of the test sources. Various standards have called for mode scramblers, filters and strippers to adjust the modal distribution in the fiber to approximate actual operating conditions. Today, most standards call for sources to meet output requirements and for a mode conditioner to be used in testing. The effects of mode power distribution on multimode measurements are covered in the chapter on optical fiber.

Reference Cables
Loss testing requires one or two reference cables, depending on the test performed and the appropriate mating adapters for the connectors. Reference cables are typically 1-2 meters long, with fiber and connectors matching the cables to be tested. The accuracy of the measurement will depend on the quality of the reference cables, since they will be mated to the cable under test. The quality and cleanliness of the connectors on the launch and receive cables is one of the most important factors in the accuracy of loss measurements. Always test reference cables by the patchcord or single ended method shown below to make sure they are in good condition before you start testing other cables.
Standards groups have not been able to successfully specify the quality of reference cables in terms of tightly toleranced components like the fiber and connectors. Standards which call for special reference quality test cables now specify cables with low loss connections. The best recommendation for qualifying reference cables is to choose cables with low loss, tested "single-ended" per cable test standard FOTP-171 as described below.

Only the highest quality mating adapters should be used for testing, as they are a factor in loss also. Inexpensive adapters generally have plastic mating sleeves to align the connector ferrules which wear out quickly, causing high loss with even good connectors. Use only mating adapters with metal or preferably ceramic mating sleeves which are specified for both multimode and singlemode connectors.

Testing Loss

There are two methods that are used to measure insertion loss with a light source and power meter, a "patchcord test" also called "single-ended loss," per TIA standard FOTP-171, and an "installed cable plant test" or "double-ended loss" per TIA standard OFSTP-14 (multimode) and OFSTP-7 (singlemode). The difference between the two tests is that single-ended loss testing uses only a launch cable and tests only the connector attached to the launch cable plus the fiber and any other components in the cable. Single ended testing is primarily used for testing patchcords or short cables since it can test each connector individually.

Double-ended loss testing uses a launch cable and receive cable attached to the meter and measures the loss of the connectors on both ends of the cable under test.

Single-ended testing is generally used on patchcords to allow testing the connectors on each end of a short cable individually to ensure both are good and allowing finding which connector might be bad if there is a problem. Double-ended testing is used with an installed cable plant to ensure the cable plant has been properly installed and to compare the test results to loss budget calculations.

Single-ended loss is measured by mating the cable you want to test to the reference launch cable and measuring the power out the far end with the meter. When you do this you measure only the loss of the connector mated to the launch cable and the loss of any fiber, splices or other connectors in the cable you are testing. Since you are aiming the connector on the far end of the cable at a detector on the power meter instead of mating it to another connector, it effectively has no loss so it is not included in the measurement. This method is described in FOTP-171 and is shown in the drawing. An advantage to this test is you can troubleshoot cables to find a bad connector since you can reverse the cable to test the connectors on the each end individually. When the loss is high, the bad connector is mated to the reference cable.

In a double-ended loss test, you attach the cable to test between two reference cables, one attached to the source and one to the meter. This way, you measure the losses of the connectors on each end, plus the loss of all the cable or cables, including connectors and splices, in between. This is the method specified in OFSTP-14 (multimode, the singlemode test is OFSTP-7), the standard test for loss in an installed cable plant.

Setting "0 dB" Reference For Loss Testing

In order to measure loss, it is first necessary to set a reference launch power for loss which becomes the 0 dB value. Correct setting of the 0 dB reference power is critical to making good loss measurements.

For single-ended testing, the reference power for 0 dB is set at the end of the reference cable. Simply attach the power meter to the end of the cable, measure the output power and, with most meters, set that as the reference for loss measurements. The meter will then read the loss of each cable tested directly.

There are three methods of setting the reference for a double-ended test, using one, two or three reference cables, and the method chosen will affect the measured loss. Why are there three methods? The three methods developed because of the variations in connector styles and how test equipment is made.

One Cable Reference

Most fiber optic connectors are constructed so that the fiber is held in a protruding ferrule, called a "plug" style connector. Two plug connectors are mated using a mating adapter that holds the ferrules in alignment and allows them to meet in the center. If connectors like these are being tested and the test equipment has interfaces that fit those connectors, the single cable reference can be used. This method is the simplest method and generally considered the method of choice as no connections are included when setting the 0 dB reference.

After setting a reference, the launch cable is detached from the meter, but not the source. The launch reference cable should never be removed from the source after setting the reference to ensure the launch power remains constant. The receive cable is attached to the meter and then both reference cables are attached to the cable to test. The loss reading will include both connections to the cable under test and the loss of the fiber and any other components in the cable itself.

Two Cable Reference

If the test equipment has an interface for a different style of connector, so the connectors on the cables being tested cannot be attached to the instruments, a two cable reference method can be used. Reference cables must be hybrid cables with connectors on one end to match the interfaces of the instruments and the other end to mate to the connectors on the cable to be tested. The 0 dB reference is set by attaching both reference cables to the instruments and connecting the other ends with a mating adapter. After setting the reference, the two cables are disconnected at the middle and the cable to be tested inserted in between them.

The loss reading will include both connections to the cable under test and the loss of the fiber and any other components in the cable itself *less the loss of the connection between the two reference cables when setting the reference.* Thus loss measured using the two cable reference will be lower than the one cable reference by the connection included when setting the reference. The uncertainty of this connection loss included in the reference also adds to the uncertainty of the loss measurement of any cables tested in this manner.

Three Cable Reference

OFSTP-14
3 Cable
Reference

Some fiber optic connectors are "plug" and "jack" style connectors where one has a protruding ferrule while the other has a jack or receptacle. Some have alignment pins that are only on one side, like the MTP connector where pins are used on the jack side. They are generally used with plugs on both ends of patchcords and jacks or receptacles on the permanently installed cables terminated in racks or outlets.

Either of these two styles of connectors can only be mated to an appropriate style of connector, making it hard to do a one or two cable reference. The solution is a three cable reference, where the hybrid cables attached to the instruments for reference cables are terminated in plugs and a third cable terminated in jacks is inserted between them to create a 3 cable reference. After setting the reference, the two reference cables are disconnected from the third cable at the middle and the cable to be tested inserted in between them in place of the reference cable.

As before, the loss reading will include both connections to the cable under test and the loss of the fiber and any other components in the cable itself *less the loss of the two connections between the third reference cable and the two reference cables when setting the reference.* Since the third cable is usually only a short length of fiber with connections on each end, the loss of the fiber is ignorable. The loss measured using the three cable reference will be lower than the one cable reference by the two connections included when setting the reference. The uncertainty of these two connection losses included in the reference also adds to the uncertainty of the loss measurement of any cables tested in this manner.

While this three cable method has the highest uncertainty, it is the only method that works for any connectors and any test equipment. Therefore, it has become the preferred method in several international standards.

Choosing a Reference Method

Some reference books and manuals show setting the reference power for loss using only a launch reference cable, both a launch and receive cable mated with a mating adapter or even three reference cables. Industry standards, in fact, include all three methods of setting a "0dB loss" reference. The two or three cable reference methods are acceptable for some tests and are the only way you can test some connectors, but it will reduce the loss you measure by the amount of loss between your reference cables when you set your "0dB loss" reference. Also, if any of the reference cables are bad, setting the reference with the cables does not reveal that problem. Then you could begin testing with bad launch cables making all your loss measurements wrong. This means that it is very important to inspect and test reference cables to ensure they are in good condition.

Modal Effect on Multimode Loss Measurements

If you measure the attenuation of a long graded-index multimode fiber in EMD (or with EMD simulated launch conditions) and compare it to a normal fiber with "overfill launch conditions " (that is the source fills all the modes equally), you will find the difference is about 1 dB/km, and this figure is called the "transient loss". Thus, the EMD fiber measurement gives an attenuation that is 1 dB per Km less than the overfill conditions. Fiber manufacturers use the EMD type of measurement for fiber because it is more reproducible and is representative of the losses to be expected in long lengths of fiber. Some standards call for using a higher attenuation coefficient when estimating cable plant loss than the tested attenuation coefficient of most fibers would justify, because cables covered in this standard are much shorter than EMD lengths. Likewise, when testing cables with connectors, the loss measured depends on the mode power distribution in the fiber. An EMD measurement can give optimistic results, since it effectively represents a situation where one launches from a smaller diameter fiber of lower NA than the receive fiber, yielding lower connector loss. The difference in connector loss caused by modal launch conditions can be dramatic. Using the same pair of connectors, it is possible to measure several tenths of a dB more with a fully filled launch than with a EMD simulated launch.

Most testing standards for cables with multimode fibers call for some method of controlling mode power distribution. Manufacturers use sophisticated methods that analyze the output power of the test source coupled into a reference cable. More practical field test methods call for a specification on source modal output followed by a mandrel wrap on the launch cable to remove higher order modes.

You should refer to relevant standards to determine the proper type of mode filter that should be used. If you are using patchcords or cables that are made with bend-insensitive fiber, the dimensions of a modal wrap may be different and you should use the recommendations of the manufacturer of the fiber.

What Loss Should You Get When Testing Cables?
Before testing, preferable during the design phase, you should calculate a
loss budget (see the chapter on design) for the cable plant to be tested to
understand the expected measurement results. Besides providing reference
loss values to test against, it will confirm that the network transmission
equipment will work properly on this cable. While it is difficult to generalize,
here are some guidelines:

-For each connector, figure 0.3-0.5 dB loss for adhesive/polish connectors,
0.75 for prepolished/splice connectors (0.75 max from TIA-568)
-For each splice, figure 0.2 dB (0.3 max from TIA-568)
-For multimode fiber, the loss is about 3 dB per km for 850 nm sources, 1 dB
per km for 1300 nm. This roughly translates into a loss of 0.1 dB per 100 feet
for 850 nm, 0.1 dB per 300 feet for 1300 nm.
-For singlemode fiber, the loss is about 0.5 dB per km for 1310 nm sources,
0.4 dB per km for 1550 nm. This roughly translates into a loss of 0.1 dB per
600 feet for 1310 nm, 0.1 dB per 750 feet for 1310 nm.
So for the loss of a cable plant, calculate the approximate loss as:

(0.5 dB X # connectors) + (0.2 dB x # splices) + fiber loss on the total length
of cable

Troubleshooting Hints
Most problems with high cable loss are caused by bad or dirty connectors,
high loss splices or stress loss caused during installation. Connectors can
be inspected with a microscope for dirt, scratches cracks, or other damage.
Visual fault locators can check for continuity, proper connections and, if the
cable jacket permits, high loss bends or breaks.
If you have high loss in a cable, reverse it and test in the opposite direction
using the single-ended method if possible. Since the single ended test only
tests the connector on one end, you can isolate a bad connector this way: it's
the one at the launch cable end mated to the launch cable on the test when
you measure high loss.
High loss in the double ended test should be isolated by retesting single-
ended and reversing the direction of test to see if the end connector is bad.
If the loss is the same, you need to either test each segment separately to
isolate the bad segment or, if it is long enough, use an OTDR.

OTDR testing

OTDRs are an essential test tool for most OSP installation and restoration.

OTDRs are used during installation to check cable before installation for shipping damage and after installation for damage caused by the installation process. Each fiber splice is checked by an OTDR before the splice is placed in a splice tray and the closure is sealed. After a cable run is concatenated, the OTDR will inspect the complete cable and every fiber in it and keep a record of the cable for future reference in case of changes in the network or comparison for restoration. During restoration, OTDRs can be used to locate problems like a cable cut or compare the current data to the installed data for comparison and determination of problems.

OTDRs are fiber optic instruments that can take a snapshot of a fiber, showing the location of splices, connectors, faults, etc. OTDRs are powerful test instruments for fiber optic cable plants, if one understands how to properly set the instrument up for the test and interpret the results. When used by a skillful operator, OTDRs can locate faults, measure cable length and verify splice loss. Within limits, they can also measure the loss of a cable plant. About the only fiber optic parameters they don't measure is optical power at the transmitter or receiver. There is a lot of information in the OTDR trace, as shown in the actual trace below.

OTDRs are almost always used on outside plant cables to verify the loss of each splice as it is made and find stress points or damage caused by installation. They are also widely used as OSP troubleshooting tools since they can pinpoint problem areas such as loss caused by stress placed on a cable during installation. Most ODTRs lack the distance resolution for use on the shorter cables typical of premises networks.

OTDRs are available in versions for standardized fiber optic systems, singlemode or multimode, at the appropriate wavelengths. In order to use an OTDR properly, it's necessary to understand how it works, how to set the instrument up properly and how to analyze traces. OTDRs offer an "auto

testing" option, but using that option without understanding the OTDR and   ,
manually checking its work often leads to problems.

How OTDRs Work

Unlike sources and power meters which measure the loss of the fiber optic
cable plant directly, the OTDR works indirectly. The source and meter
duplicate the transmitter and receiver of a fiber optic transmission link, so the
measurement correlates well with actual system loss.

The OTDR, however, uses backscattered light of the fiber to imply loss. The
OTDR works like RADAR, sending a high power laser light pulse down the
fiber and looking for return signals from backscattered light in the fiber itself
or reflected light from connector or splice joints. The amount of backscattered
light is very small, so the OTDR sends out many pulses and averages to
result.

At any point in time, the light the OTDR sees is the light scattered from the
pulse passing through a region of the fiber. Only a small amount of light
is scattered back toward the OTDR, but with wider test pulses, sensitive
receivers and signal averaging, it is possible to make measurements over
relatively long distances. Since it is possible to calibrate the speed of the
pulse as it passes down the fiber, the OTDR can measure time, calculate the
pulse position in the fiber and correlate what it sees in backscattered light
with an actual location in the fiber. Thus it can create a snapshot of the fiber, a
display at any point in the fiber.

Since the pulse is attenuated in the fiber as it passes along the fiber and
suffers loss in connectors and splices, the amount of power in the test pulse
decreases as it passes along the fiber in the cable plant under test. Thus the
portion of the light being backscattered will be reduced accordingly, producing
a picture of the actual loss occurring in the fiber. Some calculations are
necessary to convert this information into a display, since the process occurs
twice, once going out from the OTDR and once on the return path from the
scattering at the test pulse.

There is a lot of information in an OTDR display. The slope of the fiber
trace shows the attenuation coefficient of the fiber (loss per length) and
is calibrated in dB/km by the OTDR. The drop in the fiber trace across a
connector or splice allows measuring loss in dB. The peak caused by the
reflectance of a connector or mechanical splice can be measured also. While
some users measure the end-to-end loss of a fiber optic cable plant with an
OTDR, it requires a receive cable on the far end of the cable being tested to
test connectors on both ends and does not measure the same way as a light
source and power meter (or the system transmitter and receiver) so it may not
correlate with the system loss.

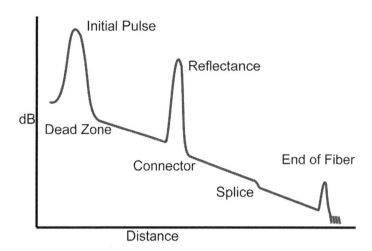

Note the large initial pulse on the OTDR trace above. That is caused by the high-powered test pulse reflecting off the OTDR connector and overloading the OTDR receiver. The recovery of the receiver causes the "dead zone" near the OTDR. To avoid problems caused by the dead zone, it is necessary to always use a launch cable of sufficient length when testing cables. Connectors and splices are called "events" in OTDR jargon. Both should show a loss, but connectors and mechanical splices will also show a reflective peak so you can distinguish them from fusion splices. Also, the height of that peak will indicate the amount of reflection at the event, unless it is so large that it saturates the OTDR receiver. Then the peak will have a flat top and tail on the far end, indicating the receiver was overloaded. The width of the peak shows the distance resolution of the OTDR, or how close it can detect events. OTDRs can also detect problems in the cable caused during installation. If a fiber is broken, it will show up as the end of the fiber much shorter than the cable or a high loss splice at the wrong place. If excessive stress is placed on the cable due to kinking or too tight a bend radius, it will look like a splice at the wrong location. Nothing helps troubleshooting with an OTDR more than having good documentation so one knows what the OTDR should be showing at locations along the fiber.

Making Measurements With The OTDR
All OTDRs display the trace on a screen and provide two or more markers to place at points on the screen to measure loss and distance. This can be used for measuring loss of a length of fiber, where the OTDR will calculate the attenuation coefficient of the fiber, or the loss of a connector or splice.

Attenuation Coefficient   Splice Loss   Reflectance

Fiber Attenuation Coefficient

To measure the length and attenuation of the fiber, we place the markers on either end of the section of fiber we wish to measure. The OTDR will calculate the distance difference between the two markers and give the distance. It will also read the difference between the power levels of the two points where the markers cross the trace and calculate the loss, or difference in the two power levels in dB. Finally, it will calculate the attenuation coefficient of the fiber by dividing loss by distance and present the result in dB/km, the normal units for attenuation. If the fiber segment is noisy or does not look straight, the OTDR can average the measurement with a method called least squares analysis (LSA).

Splice or Connector Loss

The OTDR measures distance to the event and loss at an event - a connector or splice - between the two markers. To measure splice loss, move the two markers close to the splice to be measured, having each about the same distance from the center of the splice. The OTDR will calculate the dB loss between the two markers, giving you a loss reading in dB.

Measurements of connector loss or splices with some reflectance will look very similar, except you will see a peak at the connector, caused by the back reflection of the connector. The OTDR can also use a least squares method to reduce noise effects and remove the error caused by the loss of the fiber between the two markers.

Reflectance

To measure reflectance, the OTDR measures the amount of light that's returned from both backscatter in the fiber and reflected from a connector or splice. Calculating reflectance is a complicated process involving the baseline noise of the OTDR, backscatter level and power in the reflected peak. Like all backscatter measurements, it has a fairly high measurement uncertainty, but an OTDR has the advantage of showing where reflective events are located so they can be corrected if necessary.

Comparing Traces

Comparing two traces in the same window is useful for confirming data collection and contrasting different test methods on the same fiber. Comparisons are also used to compare fiber traces during troubleshooting or restoration with traces take just after installation to see what has changed. All OTDRs offer this feature, where you can copy one trace and paste it on another to compare them.

OTDR Measurement Uncertainty

Like all instruments, OTDRs cannot measure with perfect accuracy. Some of the measurement uncertainty with OTDRs is due to what is actually being measured. For example, when measuring the length of a fiber optic cable or the distance to a fault, the OTDR measures time and calculates distance based on the speed of light in the fiber or inversely the index of refraction of the fiber which determines the speed. Not all fibers have the same index of refraction, depending on the type of fiber and the manufacturer, and it is usually different for different wavelengths.

Group Index of Refraction (IOR) – Single Mode Fiber

Manufacturer	IOR @ 1310nm	IOR @ 1550nm
Lucent Std. Single Mode	1.468	1.468
Lucent TrueWave and TrueWave-RS	1.471	1.470
Lucent AllWave	1.466	1.467
Corning SMF-28	1.4675	1.4681
Corning SMF-LS	1.471	1.470
Corning E-LEAF	N/A	1.469
Alcatel SMOF	1.464	1.4645

The difference is only about 0.5% between the highest and lowest index of refraction, but that can mean an difference of 50 meters at 10 km, a significant error if one is trying to locate a fault.

The other problem with OTDR distance measurements is the difference between fiber length and cable length. Fiber is loosely fitted in buffer tubes and the buffer tubes are helically wound around the cable so the fiber will not be stressed when the cable is pulled.

But with this cable construction, the fiber length is about 1% longer than the cable length, a difference of 100 meters at 10 km. Since the OTDR measures fiber length, not cable length, this provides another error in measuring cable length, distance to an event like a splice or locating events in a long cable run.

If the actual cable length is known, and it can sometimes be read off the cable jacket or might have been recorded in the documentation when the cable was installed, one can use that to calibrate OTDR distances to actual cable distance. If OTDR traces are taken from both ends of a cable to an event or a fault, the relative distance to the event or fault can be estimated by using the ratio of the two measurements.

The biggest source of measurement uncertainty that occurs when testing with an OTDR is a function of the backscatter coefficient of the fibers being tested, the amount of light from the outgoing test pulse that is scattered back toward the OTDR. The backscattered light used for measurement is not a constant, but a function of the attenuation of the fiber and the diameter of the core of the fiber.

Same or Equal Fibers   High Loss to Low Loss Fiber   Low Loss to High Loss Fiber

If you look at two different fibers spliced or connected together in an OTDR, any difference in backscatter from each fiber is a major source of error. If both fibers are identical, such as splicing a broken fiber back together, the backscattering will be the same on both sides of the joint, so the OTDR will measure the actual splice loss. However, if the fibers are different, unequal backscatter coefficients will cause a different percentage of light to be sent back to the OTDR.

If the fiber nearer the OTDR has more scattering (shown in the OTDR trace as attenuation) than the one after the connection, the percentage of light scattered back to the OTDR from the test pulse will go down, so the measured loss on the OTDR will include the actual loss plus a loss error caused by the lower backscatter level, making the displayed loss greater than it actually is. Looking the opposite way, from a low attenuation fiber to a high attenuation fiber, we find the backscatter goes up, making the measured loss less than it actually is. In fact, if the change in backscatter is greater than the splice loss, this shows a gain, a major confusion to new OTDR users.

While this error source is always present, it can be practically eliminated by taking readings both directions and averaging the measurements, and many OTDRs have this programmed in their measurement routines. This is the only way to test inline splices for loss and get accurate results.

OTDR "Ghosts"

If you are testing short cables with highly reflective connectors, you will likely encounter ghosts. These are caused by the reflected light from the far end connector reflecting back and forth in the fiber until it is attenuated to the noise level. Ghosts are very confusing, as they seem to be real reflective events like connectors, but will not show any loss. The best way to determine if a reflection is real or a ghost is to compare it to cable plant documentation. You can eliminate ghosts by reducing the reflections, for example using index matching fluid on the end of the launch cable.

OTDR Limitations

The limited distance resolution of the OTDR makes it very hard to use in a premises or building environment where cables are usually only a few hundred meters long. Most OTDRs have a great deal of difficulty resolving features in the short cables typical of a premises cable plant and is likely to show "ghosts" from reflections at connectors, confusing the OTDR user. On very long cables, the OTDR will show increased noise further from the instrument. Using wider test pulses and more signal averaging will increase the distance capability of the OTDR.

Using The OTDR Correctly

When using an OTDR, there are a few cautions that will make testing easier and more understandable. Always use a long launch cable, which allows the OTDR to settle down after the initial pulse and provides a reference cable for testing the first connector on the cable. If testing the final connector on the cable is desired, a receive cable on the far end of the cable plant is required.

The OTDR operator must carefully set up the instrument for each cable. Again, good documentation will help setting up the test parameters. Always start with the OTDR set for the shortest pulse width for best resolution and a range at least 2 times the length of the cable you are testing. Make an initial trace and see how you need to change the test parameters to get better results. Some users are tempted to use the OTDR's autotest function. More problems are caused by novices using autotest than any other issue in using OTDRs. Never use autotest until a knowledgeable technician has set up the OTDR properly and verified that autotest gives acceptable results.

Testing Long Haul, High Speed Fiber Optic Networks

One of the big advantages of fiber optics is its capability for long distance high speed communications. Attenuation at long wavelengths is lower. Singlemode fiber has extremely high bandwidth. Fibers can be fusion spliced with virtually no loss. High-powered lasers and fiber amplifier regenerators mean long distances are easily obtained.

However over very long distances, new factors in fiber performance become important. Chromatic dispersion, the dispersion caused by light of different wavelengths, and polarization mode dispersion, caused by the polarization in fibers, become factors limiting fiber links. Even the variation of fiber attenuation with wavelength can become an issue when networks using wavelength-division multiplexing are implemented. All 3 factors may need testing on long distance networks to ensure proper link performance. (See Chapter 5 on fiber for descriptions of these fiber characteristics.)

Chromatic Dispersion in the Cable Plant
As with any other component, optical fiber performance parameters can vary from batch to batch, so a long concatenated cable plant with many different fibers will have a end-to-end chromatic dispersion which is an integration of the CD of all the individual fibers. Therefore fiber in long distance links will probably be tested for CD after installation or before upgrading a link to higher bit rate electronics.

Testing Chromatic Dispersion
There are several methods used for testing CD in fibers. All involve testing at a variety of wavelengths using several discrete sources of various wavelengths, a tunable laser or a broadband source with a monochromator in the receiver and measuring the relative speeds of the signals. The data taken at discrete wavelengths is then analyzed to calculate the dispersion in terms of ps/nm/km.

Test methods use phase delay or time of flight and generally require access to both ends of the fiber as well as a second fiber for synchronization of the two test instruments at either end. However, an OTDR test method is also used, since the OTDR measures time to convert to distance. Since the speed of light is different at various wavelengths, the OTDR would measure different distances on the same fiber at different wavelengths. Traces are taken at several discrete wavelengths and CD can be calculated from the difference in the distance data (or round trip time of the test pulse) obtained from the traces. This allows CD testing in the field from one end of the fiber.

All these methods have international standards for the test methods, instruments and data analysis.

Standards	Description
IEC 60793-1-42	Measurement methods and test procedures—chromatic dispersion
ITU-T G.650.1	Definitions and test methods for linear, deterministic attributes of singlemode fiber and cable
TIA FOTP-175-B	Chromatic dispersion measurement of single-mode optical fibers
GR-761-CORE	Generic criteria for chromatic dispersion test sets

Phase Shift Method

Pulse Delay Method

OTDR Test Method

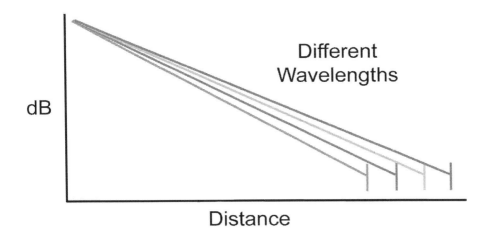

dB

Different Wavelengths

Distance

Polarization Mode Dispersion

PMD is a complex issue in installed optical fiber. In a long concatenated fiber, each fiber can have different waveguide and material birefringence characteristics caused by the random characteristics of each fiber in the link and variations of the stress on the fiber. Variations are particularly noticeable in aerial fiber, where the PMD may vary considerably according to temperature and wind speed buffeting the fiber!
PMD causes pulse broadening and/or jitter in the received electrical signal, potentially causing errors in the reception of the signals. Since the PMD can vary over time, an extra margin of 1 to 3 dB is often added to the power budget to accommodate variation in PMD.
PMD is an important issue as data rates on long distance links increases to 40 Gb/s and 100 Gb/s. Unfortunately, there are no reliable compensation schemes for PMD, so the only solution is to test links to be upgraded for PMD using one or more of the standardized test methods.

Testing PMD
PMD is generally tested for fibers during manufacture or when being cabled. In the field, it is common to test PMD on newly installed fibers which are intended for operation at high speeds, generally above 2.5 Gb/s or when upgrading fibers installed some time in the past. Since PMD varies over time, a single test becomes an average and tests at a later time may be done for comparison.
There are a number of commonly used test methods for PMD, some of which are limited to the manufacturing environment, while others can be used in the field. Essentially, all the test instruments have a source which can vary the polarization of the test signal and a measurement unit that can analyze polarization changes.

Here are descriptions of the methods and relevant standards.

Description	Test Method	Standards
PMD for single-mode optical fibers by the Fixed Analyzer method	Extrema Counting (EC) Fourier Transform (FT)	FOTP-113
PMD measurement for single-mode optical fibers by Stokes parameter measurements	Jones Matrix Eigen-analysis (JME) Poincaré Sphere Analysis (PSA)	FOTP-122
PMD measurement for single-mode optical fibers and cable assemblies by Interferometry	Traditional Interferometry(TINTY) General Interferometry (GINTY)	FOTP-124
Guideline for PMD and DGD measurement in single-mode fiber optic components and devices		FOTP-196
Measurement methods and test procedures—polarization mode dispersion	Fixed Analyzer measurement method (EC / FT) Stokes evaluation method (JME / PSA) Interferometry method (TINTY)	IEC 60793-1-48
Portable PMD test sets used for analyzing single-mode fiber		GR-2947-CORE
Definitions and test methods for statistical and nonlinear attributes of single-mode fiber and cable	Stokes parameter evaluation technique (JME & PSA) State of Polarization method (SOP) Interferometric methods (TINTY & GINTY) Fixed Analyzer technique (EC / FT / Cosine Fourier Analysis)	ITU-T G.650.2

PMD testing is not an easy, reproducible, accurate test. The measurement uncertainty can be as high as 10-20%, as shown by testing done within international standards committees. These committees have concluded that all these measurement techniques are permissible, that there are factors in making these measurements that are not well understood, and the methods of data analysis are not without question.

All this uncertainty of PMD measurements has the effect of making comparisons between tests and test methods difficult. Variations are particularly high on tests of older fiber links. Presentations of field have even shown that variations in PMD can be correlated to wind speed for aerial cables.

PMD testing needs to be done on long links but the data must be analyzed intelligently to be of real use.

Spectral Attenuation

With the development of low water peak fibers, the possibility of transmission from 1260 to 1675 nm has been considered. This results from careful manufacturing of the fiber to reduce the water in the fiber (in the form of OH-ions) that causes higher spectral attenuation at around 1244 and 1383 nm. Since one may want to use available fibers of unknown spectral attenuation for CWDM which uses lasers from 1260 to 1670 nm in 20 nm windows, it becomes necessary to test for spectral attenuation to verify the usability. At the water peaks, legacy fibers may have attenuation coefficients around 2 dB/km while low water peak fibers may be as low as 0.4 dB/km.

Testing spectral attenuation is done per TIA/EIA-455-61 or IEC 61300-3-7 with broadband sources like LEDs and a spectrum analyzer on the receiving end of the fiber. Calibration is done with a short fiber length, the instrument calculates the spectral attenuation on a long length being tested. The measurement of spectral attenuation uses instruments similar to those used for CD testing by the phase shift method, so some instruments do both measurements at one time.

The FOA wishes to acknowledge the invaluable reference materials on CD, PMD and SA in the JDSU Reference Guides to Fiber Optic Testing. These highly recommended books can be downloaded from the JDSU website, jdsu. com.

Other Testing

Manufacturers of fiber optic components do extensive testing to qualify their component designs, verify manufacturing procedures and test the products before shipment to customers. Fibers are tested for dimensions (core and cladding size, ovality and concentricity,) performance (attenuation coefficient, bandwidth or dispersion,) physical characteristics (strength, flexibility, etc.) and ability to withstand environmental conditions (temperature, humidity, and many more, including over long times.) Cables add even more stringent environmental tests.

Connectors and splices are tested in large batches to determine average losses expected in normal installations. Environmental testing mirrors that for cables, but may add tests for special applications like vibration for use on vehicles, ships or aircraft. Transceivers, WDMs, fiber amplifiers and other fiber optic components will have testing for both fiber-related performance and electrical performance. Most of these tests have been standardized to allow fair comparison among various manufacturers' products.

There are other field tests for cable plants that are becoming more common on long singlemode cables, polarization mode dispersion (PMD) and chromatic dispersion (CD). These become important for very long distances at very high bit rates. They are highly specialized and require complicated instrumentation, beyond the scope of this book.

Review Questions

True/False
Indicate whether the statement is true or false.

_____1.   Cables tested with an OTDR do not require insertion loss testing with a source and meter or OLTS.

_____2.   Connectors at each end of the cable plant should not be counted when calculating the cable plant loss.

_____3.   The OTDR should never be used without a "launch cable" which is also called a "pulse suppressor."

Multiple Choice
Identify the choice that best completes the statement or answers the question.

_____4.   Cable plant loss should be estimated during the _____ phase.
       A. Design
       B. Installation
       C. Testing
       D. Troubleshooting

_____5.   The standard method of testing installed singlemode cables in a cable plant is described in _____.
       A. FOTP-34
       B. ISO 11801
       C. FOTP-57
       D. OFSTP-7

_____6.   What test instrument(s) are used for insertion loss testing?
           A. OLTS or light source and power meter
           B. VFL
           C. OTDR

_____7.   Singlemode fiber optic cables are tested with _____
           sources at _____ and _____ wavelengths.
           A. LED, 650, 850 nm
           B. LED, 850, 1300 nm
           C. Laser, 980, 1400 nm
           D. Laser, 1310, 1550 nm

_____8.   What type of source is used for testing multimode fibers?
           A. LED
           B. VCSEL
           C. Laser

_____9.   How many methods are included in standards for setting the "0
           dB' reference for loss testing?
           A. One
           B. Two
           C. Three
           D. Four

_____10.   Patchcords can be tested to verify the connectors on each end
           individually by _____?
           A. Single-ended testing
           B. Double-ended testing
           C. OTDRs
           D. Visual fault locators

_____11.   Reference cables must match the _____ of the cables
           being tested.
           A. Fiber size and type
           B. Fiber size and connector type
           C. Connector type
           D. Fiber size and loss specification

_____12.   The total loss of the fiber in the cable plant is calculated
           by multiplying the attenuation coefficient of the fiber by the
           _____.
           A. Length
           B. Number of links
           C. Number of connectors
           D. Number of splices

_____13.   The principle of operation of OTDRs is similar to _____ .
A. Power meters and sources
B. Radar
C. Mirrors
D. Lenses

_____14.   OTDRs are used in outside plant cables to _____ .
A. Verify splice loss
B. Measure length
C. Find faults
D. All of the above

_____15.   In long distance applications, OTDR distance measurement
accuracy is limited by their _____ .
A. Output power
B. Distance capability
C. Calibration of fiber index of refraction
D. Software

_____16.   Chromatic dispersion can be tested using an OTDR because
_____ .
A. An OTDR can measure the round trip time differences at
each wavelength
B. Chromatic dispersion affects backscatter
C. The OTDR receiver is sensitive to the wavelength of light
D. OTDRs test at multiple wavelengths

_____17.   In long distance applications intended for wavelength division
multiplexing, a _____ test is used to verify fiber performance
over all wavelengths.
A. Dispersion
B. Spectral attenuation
C. OTDR
D. VFL

Additional Study And Projects
Testing is one of the more extensive subjects in fiber optics. The FOA Online Reference Guide has many pages of information on testing. We recommend you read all of them, but these first:
Five Different Ways to Test Fiber Optic Cables According to International Standards
Differences in OTDR and Insertion Loss Measurements
All the pages under "Testing & Troubleshooting Fiber Optic Systems"

Lab Exercises
Measure optical power with a fiber optic power meter. Change the calibration wavelength to another wavelength to see the difference in calibration.
Use a light source and power meter to measure loss of a fiber optic cable. Test using each of the methods for setting a 0 dB reference and see how the loss changes. Determine the effects of mandrel wraps on launch cable by testing a cable plant with a light source and power meter using a plain launch reference cable and then using different mandrel wraps.
Use an OTDR to learn how to set up the instrument and analyze traces. Measure fiber attenuation, loss of a splice or connector and reflectance. See how the measurement changes when measuring loss with the two point and LSA methods. Test the same cable plant with a light source and power meter and with an OTDR using only a launch cable then both launch and receive cables. How does the measured loss differ with the methods?

Chapter 9
Fiber Optic Network Design

Objectives: From this chapter you should learn:
What is involved in fiber optic network design
What a designer needs to know
How a project develops from idea to installation
How to choose equipment and components for the network
How to create a loss budget for the design
How to plan for and complete an installation

What Is Fiber Optic Network Design?

Fiber optic network design refers to the specialized processes leading to a successful installation and operation of a fiber optic network. It includes determining the type of communication system(s) which will be carried over the network, the geographic layout (premises, campus, outside plant (OSP, etc.), the transmission equipment required and the fiber network over which it will operate. Designing a fiber optic network usually also requires interfacing to other networks which may be connected over copper cabling and wireless. Next to consider are requirements for permits, easements, permissions and inspections. Once we get to that stage, we can consider actual component selection, placement, installation practices, testing, troubleshooting and network equipment installation and startup. Finally, we have to consider documentation, maintenance and planning for restoration in event of a future outage.
The design of the network must precede not only the installation itself, but it must be completed to estimate the cost of the project and, for the contractor, bid on the job. Design not only affects the technical aspects of the installation, but the business aspects also.

Working With Others
Designing a network requires working with other personnel involved in the project, even beyond the customer. These may include network engineers usually from IT (information technology) departments, architects and engineers overseeing a major project and contractors involved with building the projects. Other groups like engineers or designers involved in aspects of project design such as security, CATV or industrial system designers or

specialized designers for premises cabling may also be overseeing various parts of a project that involves the design and installation of fiber optic cable plants and systems. Even company non-technical management may become involved when parts of the system are desired to be on exhibit to visitors.

Qualifications For Fiber Optic Network Designers

It's the job of the designer to understand not only the technology of communications cabling, but also the technology of communications, and to keep abreast of the latest developments in not only the technology but the applications of both.

Designers should have an in-depth knowledge of fiber optic components and systems and installation processes as well as all applicable standards, codes and any other local regulations. They must also be familiar with most telecom technology (cabled or wireless), site surveys, local politics, codes and standards, and where to find experts in those fields when help is needed. Obviously, the fiber optic network designer must be familiar with electrical power systems, since the electronic hardware must be provided with high quality uninterruptible power at every location. And if they work for a contractor, estimating will be a very important issue, as that is where a profit or loss can be determined!

Those involved in fiber optic project design should already have a background in fiber optics, such as having completed a FOA CFOT certification course, and may have other training in the specialties of cable plant design and/or electrical contracting. It's also very important to know how to find in-depth information, mostly on the web, about products, standards, codes and, for the OSP networks, how to use online mapping services like Google Maps. Experience with CAD systems is a definite plus.

Copper, Fiber or Wireless?

While discussions of which is better – copper, fiber or wireless – has enlivened cabling discussions for decades, it's becoming moot. Communications technology and the end user market, it seems, have already made decisions that generally dictate the media and many networks combine all three. The designer of cabling networks, especially fiber optic networks, and their customers today generally have a pretty easy task deciding which media to use once the communications systems are chosen.

The Communications System

Before one can begin to design a fiber optic cable plant, one needs to establish with the end user or network owner where the network will be built and what communications signals it will carry. The contractor should be familiar with premises networks, where computer networks (LANs or local area networks) and security systems use structured cabling systems built around well-defined industry standards. Once the cabling exits a building, even for short links for example in a campus or metropolitan network, requirements for fiber and cable types change. Long distance links for telecommunications, CATV or utility networks have other, more stringent requirements, necessary to support longer high speed links, that must be considered.

But while the contractor generally considers the cabling requirements first, the real design starts with the communications system requirements established by the end user. One must first look at the types of equipment required for the communications systems, the speed of the network and the distances to be covered before considering anything related to the cable plant. The communications equipment will determine if fiber is necessary or preferable and what type of fiber is required.

Outside Plant Networks

Telephone networks are mainly outside plant (OSP) systems, connecting buildings over distances as short as a few hundred meters to hundreds or thousands of kilometers. Data rates for telecom are typically 2.5 to 10 gigabits per second using very high power lasers that operate exclusively over singlemode fibers. The big push for telecom is now taking fiber directly to a commercial building or the home, since the signals are now too fast for traditional twisted copper pairs.

CATV also uses singlemode fibers with systems that are either hybrid fiber-coax (HFC) or digital where the backbone is fiber and the connection to the home is on coax. Coax still works for CATV since it has very high bandwidth itself. Some CATV providers have discussed or even tried some fiber to the home, but have not seen the economics become attractive yet.

Besides telecom and CATV, there are many other OSP applications of fiber. Intelligent highways are dotted with security cameras and signs and/or signals connected on fiber. Security monitoring systems in large buildings like airports, government and commercial buildings, casinos, etc. are generally connected on fiber due to the long distances involved. Like other networks, premises applications are usually multimode while OSP is singlemode to support longer links.

Metropolitan networks owned and operated by cities can carry a variety of traffic, including surveillance cameras, emergency services, educational systems, telephone, LAN, security, traffic monitoring and control and sometimes even traffic for commercial interests using leased bandwidth on dark fibers or city-owned fibers. However, since most are designed to support longer links than premises or campus applications, singlemode is the fiber of choice.

For all except premises applications, fiber is the communications medium of choice, since its greater distance and bandwidth capabilities make it either the only choice or considerably less expensive than copper or wireless. Only inside buildings is there a choice to be made, and that choice is affected by economics, network architecture and the tradition of using copper inside buildings. Next, we'll look at the fiber/copper/wireless choices in more detail.

Premises Networks

Premises cable systems are designed to carry computer networks based on Ethernet which currently may operate at speeds from 10 megabits per second to 10 gigabits per second. Other systems may carry security systems with digital or analog video, perimeter alarms or entry systems, which are usually low speeds, at least as far as fiber is concerned. Premises telephone systems can be carried on traditional twisted pair cables or, as is becoming more common, utilize LAN cabling with voice over IP (VoIP) technology.

Premises networks are usually short, often less than the 100 meters (about 330 feet) used as the limit for standardized structured cabling systems that allow twisted pair copper or fiber optic cabling, with backbones on campus networks used in industrial complexes or institutions as long as 500 m or more, requiring optical fiber.

Premises networks generally operate over multimode fiber. Multimode systems are less expensive than singlemode systems, not because the fiber is cheaper (it isn't) nor because cable is cheaper (the same), but because the large core of multimode fiber allows the use of cheaper LED or VCSEL sources in transmitters, making the electronics much cheaper. Astute designers and end users often include both multimode and singlemode fibers in their backbone cables (called hybrid cables) since singlemode fibers are very inexpensive and it provides a virtually unlimited ability to expand the systems.

Premises networks will include a entrance facility where outside plant and premises communications systems meet. This facility must include not only cabling connections but compatible communications equipment. Since it is indoors, it must consider issues for building and electrical codes, such as the common requirement that bare OSP cables can only come 50 feet (about 15 meters) before being terminated in fire-rated cables unless it is in conduit.

Cabling Design

Long Distance and Outside Plant Cabling

Other than telco systems that still use copper for the final connection to the home, practically every cable in the telephone system is fiber optic. CATV companies use a high performance coax into the home, but it connects to a fiber optic backbone. The Internet backbone is all fiber. Most commercial buildings in populous areas have direct fiber connections from communications suppliers. Cities use SM fiber to connect municipal buildings, surveillance cameras, traffic signals and sometimes offer commercial and residential connections, all over singlemode fiber. Even cellular antenna towers along highways and on tall buildings usually have fiber connections. Remote areas such as central Africa depend on satellite communications since cables are too expensive to run long distances for the small amounts of traffic involved.

Designing long distance or outside plant applications generally means choosing cabling containing singlemode (SM) fiber over all other media. Most of these systems are designed to be used over distances and speeds that preclude anything but SM fiber. Occasionally other options may be more cost effective, for example if a company has two buildings on opposite sides of a highway, a line-of-sight or radio optical wireless network may be easier to use since they have lower cost of installation and are easier to obtain relevant permits.

The choice of the actual singlemode fiber, however, can depend on the application. Depending on the length of the link, the wavelength of the transmitters, data rate of the transmission and if CWDM or DWDM are planned, different types of fiber may be optimal. Refer to Chapter 5 on fiber for more details.

Premises Cabling

The desire for mobility, along with the expansion of connected services, appears to lead to a new type of corporate network. Fiber optic backbone with copper to the desktop where people want direct connections and multiple wireless access points, more than is common in the past, for full coverage and maintaining a reasonable number of users per access point is the new norm for corporate networks.

Most building management systems use proprietary copper cabling, for example thermostat wiring and paging/audio speaker systems. Security monitoring and entry systems, certainly the lower cost ones, still depend on coax copper cable, although high security facilities like government and military installations often pay the additional cost for fiber's more secure nature.

Surveillance systems are becoming more prevalent in buildings, especially governmental, banking, or other buildings that are considered possible security risks. While coax connections are common in short links and structured cabling advocates say you can run cameras limited distances on Cat 5E or Cat 6 UPT like computer networks, fiber has become a much more common choice. Besides offering greater flexibility in camera placement because of its distance capability, fiber optic cabling is much smaller and lightweight, allowing easier installation, especially in older facilities like airports or large buildings that may have available spaces already filled with many generations of copper cabling.

When these premises communications systems connect to the outside world, it is generally to singlemode optical fiber. The entrance facility and equipment room must accommodate the equipment needed to make those connections.

Use of Cabling Standards

Many documents relating to cable plant design focus on industry standards for both communications systems and cable plants. US standards come from the TIA or Telcordia while worldwide standards may come from ISO/IEC or ITU.

It is important to realize why and by whom these standards are written. These standards are written by manufacturers of products to ensure that various manufacturers' products work together properly. Whenever users specify standards for any project, it is important that the contractor/installer understand what standards are being referenced and ensure that such standards are relevant to the job being done.

Choosing Transmission Equipment

Choosing transmission equipment is the next step in designing a fiber optic network. This step will usually be a cooperative venture involving the customer, who knows what kinds of data they need to communicate, the designer and installer, and the manufacturers of transmission equipment. Transmission equipment and the cable plant are tightly interrelated. The distance and bandwidth will help determine the fiber type necessary and that will dictate the optical interfaces on the cable plant. The ease of choosing equipment may depend on the type of communications equipment needed. Telecom has been standardized on fiber optics for 30 years now, so they have plenty of experience building and installing equipment. Since most telecom equipment uses industry conventions, you can usually find equipment for telecom transmission that will be available for short links (usually metropolitan networks, maybe up to 20-30 km), long distance and then really long distance like undersea runs. All run on singlemode fiber, but may specify different types of singlemode.

Shorter telecom links will use 1310 nm lasers on regular singlemode fiber, often referred to as G.652 fiber, it's international standard. Longer links will use a dispersion-shifted fiber optimized for operation with 1550 nm lasers

(G.652 fiber). For most applications, one of these will be used. Most telco equipment companies offer both options.

Most CATV links are AM (analog) systems based on special linear lasers called distributed feedback (DFB) lasers using either 1310 nm or 1550 nm operating on regular singlemode fibers. As CATV moves to digital transmission, it will use technology more like telecom, which is already all digital.

The choices become more complex when it comes to data and CCTV because the applications are so varied and standards may not exist. In addition, equipment may not be available with fiber optic transmission options, requiring conversion from copper ports to fiber using devices called media converters.

In computer networks, the Ethernet standards, created by the IEEE 802.3 committee, are fully standardized. You can read the standards and see how far each equipment option can transmit over different types of fiber, choosing the one that meets your needs. Most network hardware like switches or routers are available with optional fiber optic interfaces, but PCs generally only come with UTP copper interfaces that require media converters. An Internet search for "fiber optic media converters" will provide you with dozens of sources of these inexpensive devices. Media converters will also allow the choice of media appropriate for the customer application, allowing use with multimode or singlemode fiber and may even offer transceiver options for the distance that must be covered by the link.

CCTV is a similar application. More cameras now come with fiber interfaces since so many CCTV systems are in locations like big buildings, airports, or areas where the distances exceed the capability of coax transmission. If not, video media converters, usually available from the same vendors as the Ethernet media converters, are readily available and also inexpensive. Again, choose converters that meet the link requirements set by the customer application, which in the case of video, not only includes distance but also functions, as some video links carry control signals to the camera for camera pan, zoom and tilt in addition to video back to a central location.

What about industrial data links? Many factories use fiber optics for its immunity to electromagnetic interference. But industrial links may use proprietary means to send data converted from old copper standards like RS-232, the ancient serial interface once available on every PC, SCADA popular in the utility industry, or even simple relay closures. Many companies that build these control links offer fiber optic interfaces themselves in response to customer requests. Some of these links have been available for decades, as industrial applications were some of the first premises uses of fiber optics, dating back to before 1980.

Whatever the application, it's important for the end user and the cabling contractor to discuss the actual application with the manufacturer of the transmission hardware to ensure getting the proper equipment. While the telecom and CATV applications are cut and dried and the data (Ethernet) applications covered by standards, it is our experience that not all manufacturers specify their products in exactly the same way.

One company in the industrial marketplace offered about fifteen different fiber optic products, mainly media converters for their control equipment. However, those fifteen products had been designed by at least a dozen different engineers, not all of whom were familiar with fiber optics and especially fiber jargon and specifications. As a result, one could not compare the products to make a choice or design them into a network based on specifications. Until their design, sales and applications engineers were trained in fiber optics and created guidelines for product applications, they suffered from continual problems in customer application.

The only way to make sure you are choosing the proper transmission equipment is to make absolutely certain the customer and equipment vendor – and you – are communicating clearly what you are planning to do.

Planning The Route

Having decided to use fiber optics and chosen equipment appropriate for the application, it's time to determine exactly where the cable plant and hardware will be located. One thing to remember – every installation will be unique. The actual placement of the cable plant will be determined by the physical locations along the route, local building codes or laws and other individuals involved in the designs. As usual, premises and outside plant installations are different so we will consider them separately.

Premises and campus installations can be simpler since the physical area involved is smaller and the options fewer. Start with a good set of architectural drawings and, if possible, contact the architect, contractor and/or building manager. Having access to them means you have someone to ask for information and advice. Hopefully the drawings are available as CAD files so you can have a copy to do the network cabling design in your computer, which makes tweaking and documenting the design so much easier.

If the building is still in the design stage, you may have the opportunity to provide inputs on the needs of the cable plant. Ideally, that means you can influence the location of equipment rooms, routing of cable trays and conduits, availability of adequate conditioned power and separate data grounds, sufficient air-conditioning and other needs of the network. For pre-existing buildings, detailed architectural drawings will provide you with the ability to route cabling and network equipment around the obstacles invariably in your way.Outside plant (OSP) cabling installations have enormous variety depending on the route the cable must take. The route may cross long lengths of open fields, run along paved rural or urban roads, cross roads, ravines, rivers or lakes, or, more likely, some combination of all of these. It could require buried cables, aerial cables or underwater cables. Cable may be in conduit, innerduct or direct buried, aerial cables may be self-supporting or lashed to a messenger. Longer runs often include crossing water, so the cable may be underwater or be lashed across a bridge with other cables.

Site Visits
And as soon as possible, you must visit the site or route where the network will be installed. Outside plant routes need to be driven or walked every foot of the way to determine the best options for cable placement, obstacles to be avoided or overcome, and to determine what local entities may have input into the routing. Often cities or other governments will know of available conduits or rules on using utility poles that can save design time and effort.
For installations inside current buildings, you should inspect every area to be absolutely certain you know what the building really looks like and then mark up drawings to reflect reality, especially all obstacles to running cabling and hardware and walls requiring firestopping that are not on the current drawings. Take pictures if you can. For buildings under construction, a site visit is still a good idea, just to get a feeling of what the final structure will be like and to get to know the construction managers you will be working with. They may be the best source of information on who the local authorities are who will be inspecting your work and what they expect.

With all those options on OSP installations, where do you start? With a good map. Not just a road map or a topographical map, but satellite images overlaid on roads is much better, like "Google Maps" can provide. Creating a route map is the first step, noting other utilities along the route on that map, and checking with groups that document the current utilities to prevent contractors from damaging currently installed pipes and cables.
Once you have marked up maps, the real "fun" begins: finding out whose permission you need to run your cabling. OSP installs are subject to approval by local, state and federal authorities who will influence heavily how your project is designed. Some cities, for example, ban aerial cables. Some have already buried conduit which you can use for specific routes. Since many

municipalities have installed city-owned fiber networks, they may have fiber you can rent, rather than go through the hassle of installing your own. Unless you are doing work for a utility that has someone who already has the contacts and hopefully easements needed, you may get to know a whole new set of people who have control over your activities. And you have to plan for adequate time to get approval from everyone who is involved.

Call Before You Dig

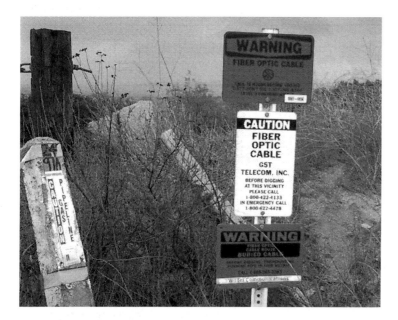

Digging safely is vitally important. The risk is not just interrupting communications, but the life-threatening risk of digging up high voltage or gas lines. Some obstacles may be found during site visits, where signs like these are visible. There are several services that maintain databases of the location of underground services that must be contacted before any digging occurs, but mapping these should be done during the design phase and double-checked before digging to ensure having the latest data.
If all this sounds vague, it is. Every project is different and requires some careful analysis of the conditions before even beginning to choose fiber optic components and plan the actual installation. Experience is the best teacher.

Choosing Components

Choosing Components For Outside Plant Installations
The choice of outside plant fiber optic (OSP) components begins with developing the route the cable plant will follow. Once the route is set, one knows where cables will be run, where splices are located and where the cables will be terminated. All that determines what choices must be made on cable type, hardware and sometimes installation methodology.

Cables

When choosing components, most projects start with the choice of a cable. Cable designs are optimized for the application type. In OSP installations, cables may be underground, direct buried, aerial or submarine (or simply underwater.)

Underground cables are generally installed in conduit which is usually a 4 inch (10 cm) conduit with several innerducts for pulling cables. Here cables are designed for high pulling tension and lubricants are used to reduce friction on longer pulls. Automated pulling equipment that limits pulling tension protects the cables. Very long runs or those with more bends in the conduit may need intermediate pulls where cable is pulled, figure-8ed and then pulled to the next stage or intermediate pulling equipment is used. Splices on underground cables are generally stored above ground in a pedestal or in a vault underground. Sufficient excess cable is needed to allow splicing in a controlled environment, usually a splicing trailer, and the storage of excess cable must be considered in the planning stage.

Direct buried cable is placed underground without conduit. Here the cable must be designed to withstand the rigors of being buried in dirt, so it is generally a more rugged cable, armored to prevent harm from rodent chewing or the pressures of dirt and rocks in which it is buried. Direct burial is generally limited to areas where the ground is mostly soil with few rocks down to the depth required so trenching or plowing in cable is easily accomplished. Splices on direct buried cables can be stored above ground in a pedestal or buried underground. Sufficient excess cable is needed to allow splicing in a controlled environment, usually a splicing trailer, and the storage of excess cable must be considered.

Aerial installations go from pole to pole, but the method of securing cables can vary depending on the situation. Some cables are lashed to messengers or other cables, such as CATV where light fiber cables are often lashed to the heavy coax already in place. Cables are available in a "8" configuration with an attached steel messenger that provides the strength to withstand tension on the cable. Some cables are made to directly be supported without a messenger, called all-dielectric sefl-supporting cables that use special hardware on poles to hold the cables. Optical ground wire is used by utilities for high voltage distribution lines. This cable is an electrical cable with fibers in the middle in a hermetically-sealed metal tube. It is installed just like standard electrical conductors. Splices on aerial cables can be supported on the cables or placed on poles or towers, Most splices are done on the ground, although it is sometimes done in a bucket or even on a tent supported on the pole or tower. Hardware is available for coiling and storing excess cable.

Sometime OSP installations involve running cables across rivers or lakes where other routes are not possible. Special cables are available for this that are more rugged and sealed. Even underwater splice hardware is available. Landings on the shore need to be planned to prevent damage, generally by burying the cable close to shore and marking the landing. Transoceanic links are similar but much more complex, requiring special ships designed for cable laying.

Since OSP applications often use significant lengths of cables, the cables can be made to order, allowing optimization for that particular installation. This usually allows saving costs but requires more knowledge on the part of the user and more time to negotiate with several cable manufacturers.

To begin specifying the cable, one must know how many fibers of what type will be included in each cable. It's important to realize that fiber, especially singlemode fiber used in virtually all OSP installations, is cheap and installation is expensive. Installation of an OSP cable may cost a hundred times the cost of the cable itself. Choosing a singlemode fiber is easy, with basic 1300 nm singlemode (called G.652 fiber) adequate for all but the longest links or those using wavelength-division multiplexing. Those may need special fiber optimized at 1500-1600 nm (G.653 or G.654). For premises and campus cable plants, OM3 type laser-optimized 50/125 multimode fiber is probably the best choice for any multimode OSP runs, as its lower attenuation and higher bandwidth will make most networks work better.

Including more fibers in a cable will not increase the cable cost proportionally; the basic cost of making a cable is fixed but adding fibers will not increase the cost much at all. Choosing a standard design will help reduce costs too, as manufacturers may have the cable in stock or be able to make your cable at the same time as others of similar design. The only real cost for adding more fibers is additional splicing and termination costs, still small with respect to total installed cost. And remember that having additional fibers for future expansion, backup systems or in case of breaks involving individual fibers can save many future headaches.

Common traits of all outside plant cables include strength and water or moisture protection. The necessary strength of the cable will depend on the installation method (see below.) All cables installed outdoors must be rated for moisture and water resistance. Until recently, most people chose a gel-filled cable, but now dry-water blocked cables are widely available and preferred by many users. These cables use water-absorbing tape and power that expands and seals the cable if any water enters the cable. Installers especially prefer the dry cables as it does not require the messy, tedious removal of the gel used in many cables, greatly reducing cable preparation for splicing or termination.

OSP cable construction types are specifically designed for strength depending on where they are to be direct buried, buried in conduit, placed underwater or run aerially on poles. The proper type must be chosen for the cable runs. Some applications may even use several types of cable. Having good construction plans will help in working with cable manufacturers to find the appropriate cable types and ordering sufficient quantities. One must always order more cable than route lengths, to allow for service loops, preparation for termination and excess to save for possible restoration needs in the future.

Like cable types, cable plant hardware types are quite diverse and should be chosen to match the application type and cable types being used. With so many choices in hardware, working with cable manufacturers is the most expeditious way to chose hardware and ensure compatibility. Besides cable compatibility, the hardware must be appropriate for the location, which can be outdoors, hung on poles, buried, underwater, inside pedestals, vaults or buildings, etc. Sometimes the hardware will need to be compatible with local zoning, for example in subdivisions or business parks. The time consumed in choosing this hardware can be lengthy, but is very important for the long term reliability of the cable plant.

Splicing And Termination Hardware
Splicing and termination are the final category of components to be chosen. Most OSP singlemode fiber is fusion spliced for low loss, low reflectance and reliability. Multimode fiber, especially OM2, 3 and 4, is also easily fusion spliced, but if only a few splices are necessary, mechanical splicing may provide adequate performance and reliability.

Finished splices are placed in a splice tray and placed in a splice closure outdoors or optionally in trays on patch panels indoors. They are sealed to prevent moisture reaching the splices and are designed to be re-entered for repair or re-routing fibers. Splice closures are available in hundreds of designs, depending on the placement of the closure, for example underground in a manhole or vault, above ground in a pedestal, buried underground or mounted on a pole. Closures must also be chosen by the number and types of cables being spliced and whether they enter at both ends or only one. The numbers of cables and splices that a closure can accommodate will determine the size of the closure, and those for high fiber count cables can get quite large.

Splice trays generally hold twelve single fiber fusion splices but may hold fewer ribbon or mechanical splices. Each splice tray should securely hold the splice and have a cover to protect the fibers when stacked in the closure. Singlemode fibers are best terminated by fusion spicing factory-made pigtails onto fibers in the cable and protecting the splices in a closure or patch panel tray. If termination is done directly on multimode OSP cables, breakout kits will be necessary to sleeve fibers for reliability when connectors are directly attached. This takes more installation time than splicing pre-terminated pigtails on the cables, as is common with singlemode fiber cables, and may not save any costs. Even complete preterminated outside cable plant systems are becoming available, reducing the time necessary for termination and splicing. Talk to the cable manufacturers to determine feasibility of this option. Outdoor terminations are sometimes housed in pedestals or equipment housings such as those used for local phone switches or traffic control systems. Some of these closures may not be fully sealed from dust and moisture, in which case it is recommended that the fiber connections be inside a more protective housing to prevent future unreliability.

Choosing the proper components for OSP installations can take time, but is important for system operation. Once components are chosen, the materials lists are added to the documentation for purchase, installation and future reference.

Choosing Components For Premises Installations

Premises cabling and outside plant cabling will coexist in the entrance facility or the equipment room where the two are connected. The choice of premises fiber optic components are affected by several factors, including the choice of communications equipment, physical routing of the cable plant and building codes and regulations. If the design is a corporate network (LAN), the design will probably include a fiber optic backbone connecting computer rooms to wiring closets. The wiring closets house switches that convert the fiber backbone to UTP copper for cable connected desktops and either copper or fiber to wireless access points. Some desktops, especially in engineering or design departments, may require fiber to the desktop for it's greater bandwidth. Extra cables or fibers may be needed for security systems (alarms, access systems or CCTV cameras) and building management systems also.

Design of the fiber optic cable plant requires coordinating with everyone who is involved in the network in any way, including IT personnel, company management, architects and engineers, etc. to ensure all cabling requirements are considered at one time, to allow sharing resources.

As in OSP design, consider the fiber choice first. Most premises networks use multimode fiber, but many users now install hybrid cables with singlemode fibers for future expansion. The 62.5/125 micron fiber (OM1 fiber) that has been used for almost two decades has mostly been superceded by the new 50/125 laser-optimized fiber (OM3), as it offers substantial bandwidth/distance advantages.

Virtually all equipment will operate over 50/125 OM3 fiber just as well as it did on 62.5/125 OM1 fiber, but it's always a good idea to check with the equipment manufacturers to be sure. Remember in the design documentation to include directions to mark all cables and patchpanels with aqua-colored tags, indicative of OM3 fiber.

Cable in premises applications is generally either distribution or breakout cable. Distribution cables have more fibers in a smaller diameter cable, but require termination inside patch panels or wall mounted boxes. Breakout cables are bulky, but they allow direct connection without hardware, making them convenient for industrial use. Fiber count can be an issue, as backbone cables now have many fibers for current use, future expansion and spares, making distribution cables the more popular choice. The cable jacket must be fire-retardant per the NEC, generally OFNR-rated (Riser) unless the cable in air-handling areas above ceilings, where OFNP (plenum) is needed. Cable jacket color for OM3 cables can be ordered in aqua for identification as both fiber optics and OM3 50/125 fibers.

If the cable is going to be run between buildings, indoor/outdoor designs are now available that have dry water-blocking and a double jacket. The outer jacket is moisture-resistant for outdoor use but can be easily stripped, leaving the fire-rated inner jacket for indoor runs.

Fiber optic connector choices are also changing. STs and even SCs are succumbing to the success of the smaller LC connector. Since most fast (gigabit and above) equipment uses LC connectors, using them in the cable plant means only one connector needs to be supported. The LC offers another big advantage for those users who are upgrading to OM3 fiber. The LC connector is incompatible with SC and ST connectors, so using it on 50/125 fiber cable plants prevents mixing 50 and 62.5 fibers with high fiber mismatch losses.

Premises fiber optic cables need to be run separately from copper cables to prevent crushing. Sometimes they are hung carefully below copper cable trays or pulled in innerduct. Using innerduct can save installation time, since the duct (which can be purchased with pull tapes already inside) can be installed quickly without fear of damage and then the fiber optic cable pulled quickly and easily. Some applications may require installing fiber optic cables inside conduit, which requires care to minimize bends, provide intermediate pulls to limit pulling force or use fiber optic cable lubricants.

The hardware necessary for the installation will need to be chosen based on where the cables are terminated. Premises runs are generally point-to-point and are not spliced. Wherever possible, allow room for large radii in the patch panels or wall-mounted boxes to minimize stress on the fibers. Choose hardware that is easy to enter for moves, adds and changes but lockable to prevent intrusion.

In premises applications, it's worth considering a preterminated system. These use backbone cables terminated in multifiber connectors and preterminated patch panel modules. If the facility layout is properly designed, the cable manufacturer can work with you to create a "plug and play" system that needs no on-site termination and the cost may be very competitive to a field-terminated system.

Creating A Materials List

For every installation, a complete materials list must be created listing each component needed and quantities required. This list will be used by the installation crew, but first it will be used to estimate the cost of the project. It is very important to list every component. Some components can be estimated based on other quantities. Ducts for example will be ordered in lengths similar to the cable pulled into them. Each fiber needs termination on both ends of the cable plant. Splice trays and closures must be ordered according to the numbers of fibers in the cables.

You should include extra quantities for installation. Every splice point, for example, needs 10-20 meters extra cable for splicing in a splice trailer, stripping for the splice and service loops. Extra cable should also be ordered to be kept for possible future restoration. Extra connectors or pigtails are needed to replace those improperly installed during installation. Some contractors routinely order 2-5% more than they estimate is necessary for the job.

While ordering more components than necessary can be costly, it's less expensive than being short during the actual installation, especially for special order items like cables or patchcords. Excess components should be packed and stored as part of a restoration kit.

Cable Plant Link Loss Budget Analysis

Loss budget analysis is the calculation and verification of a fiber optic system's operating characteristics. This encompasses items such as routing, electronics, wavelengths, fiber type, and circuit length. Attenuation and bandwidth are the key parameters for budget loss analysis. The designer should analyze link loss early in the design stage prior to installing a fiber optic system to make certain the system will work over the proposed cable plant.

Both the passive and active components of the circuit can be included in the budget loss calculation. Passive loss is made up of fiber loss, connector loss, and splice loss. Don't forget any couplers or splitters in the link. If the system electronics are already chosen, active components such as wavelength, transmitter power, receiver sensitivity, and dynamic range can be considered. If the electronics are not known, industry generic or standard loss values can be used for the loss budget. Prior to system turn up, test the insertion loss of the cable plant with a source and power meter to ensure that it is within the loss budget.

The idea of a loss budget is to insure the network equipment will work over the installed fiber optic link. It is normal to be conservative over the specifications. Don't use the best possible specs for fiber attenuation or connector loss to allow some margin for installation and component degradation over time.

The best way to illustrate calculating a loss budget is to show how it's done for a typical cable plant, here a 2 km hybrid multimode/singlemode link with 5 connections (2 connectors at each end and 3 connections at patch panels in the link) and one splice in the middle. See the drawings below of the link layout and the instantaneous power in the link at any point along it's length, scaled exactly to the link drawing above it.

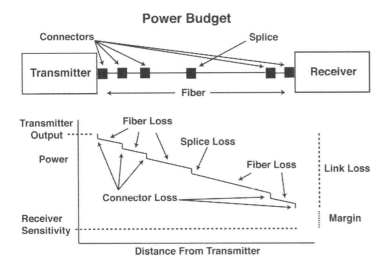

Cable Plant Passive Component Loss

Step 1. Calculate fiber loss at the operating wavelengths

Cable Length (km)	2.0	2.0	2.0	2.0
Fiber Type	Multimode		Singlemode	
Wavelength (nm)	850	1300	1300	1550
Fiber Atten. (dB/km)	3 [3.5]	1 [1.5]	0.4 [1/0.5]	0.3 [1/0.5]
Total Fiber Loss (dB)	6.0 [7.0]	2.0 [3.0]	0.8 [2/1]	0.6 [2/1]

(All specifications in brackets are maximum values per EIA/TIA 568 standard. For singlemode fiber, a higher loss is allowed for premises applications, 1 dB/km for premises, 0.5 dB/km for outside plant.)

Step 2. Connector Loss

Multimode connectors will have losses of 0.2-0.5 dB typically. Singlemode connectors, which are factory made and fusion spliced on will have losses of 0.1-0.2 dB. Field terminated singlemode connectors may have losses as high as 0.5-1.0 dB. Let's calculate it at both typical and worst case values.

Connector Loss	0.3 dB (typical adhesive/polish connector)	0.75 dB (prepolished/ splice connector and TIA-568 max acceptable)
Total # of Connectors	5	5
Total Connector Loss	1.5 dB	3.75 dB

(All connectors are allowed 0.75 max per EIA/TIA 568 standard)
Many designers and technicians forget when doing a loss budget that the connectors on the end of the cable plant must be included in the loss budget. When the cable plant is tested, the reference cables will mate with those connectors and their loss will be included in the measurements.

Step 3. Splice Loss
Multimode splices are usually made with mechanical splices, although some fusion splicing is used. The larger core and multiple layers make fusion splicing abut the same loss as mechanical splicing, but fusion is more reliable in adverse environments. Figure 0.1-0.5 dB for multimode splices, 0.3 being a good average for an experienced installer. Fusion splicing of singlemode fiber will typically have less than 0.05 dB (that's right, less than a tenth of a dB!)

Splice Loss	0.3 dB
Total # splices	1
Total Splice Loss	0.3 dB

(For this loss budget calculation, all splices are allowed 0.3 max per EIA/TIA 568 standard)

Step 4. Total Cable Plant Loss
Add together the fiber, connector and splice losses to get the total link loss of the cable plant.

	Best Case [TIA 568 Max]		Best Case [TIA 568 Max]	
Wavelength (nm)	850	1300	1300	1550
Total Fiber Loss (dB)	6.0 [7.0]	2.0 [3.0]	0.8 [2/1]	0.6 [2/1]

Total Connector Loss (dB)	1.5 [3.75]	1.5 [3.75]	1.5 [3.75]	1.5 [3.75]
Total Splice Loss (dB)	0.3 [0.3]	0.3 [0.3]	0.3 [0.3]	0.3 [0.3]
Other (dB)	0	0	0	0
Total Link Loss (dB)	7.8 [11.05]	3.8 [7.05]	2.6 [6.05/5.05]	2.4 [6.05/5.05]

These values of cable plant loss should be the criteria for testing. Allow +/- 0.2 -0.5 dB for measurement uncertainty and that becomes your pass/fail criterion.

Equipment Link Loss Budget Calculation

Link loss budget for network hardware depends on the dynamic range, the difference between the sensitivity of the receiver and the output of the source into the fiber. You need some margin for system degradation over time or environment, so subtract that margin (as much as 3dB) to get the loss budget for the link.

Step 5. Data From Manufacturer's Specification for Active Components (Typical 100 Mb/s multimode digital link using a 1300 nm LED source.)

Operating Wavelength (nm)	1300
Fiber Type	MM
Receiver Sensitivity (dBm@ required BER)	-31
Average Transmitter Output (dBm)	-16
Dynamic Range (dB)	15
Recommended Excess Margin (dB)	3

Step 6. Loss Margin Calculation

Dynamic Range (dB) (above)	15	15
Cable Plant Link Loss (dB @ 1300 nm)	3.8 (Typical)	7.05 (TIA)
Link Loss Margin (dB)	11.2	7.95

As a general rule, the Link Loss Margin should be greater than approximately 3 dB to allow for link degradation over time. LEDs in the transmitter may age and lose power, connectors or splices may degrade or connectors may get dirty if opened for rerouting or testing. If cables are accidentally cut, excess margin will be needed to accommodate splices for restoration.

Project Documentation

Documentation of the cable plant is a necessary part of the design and installation process for a fiber optic network that is often overlooked. Documenting the installation properly during the planning process will save time and material in the installation. It will speed the cable installation and testing since the routing and terminations are already known. After component installation, the documentation should be completed with loss test data for acceptance by the end user. During troubleshooting, documentation eases tracing links and finding faults. Proper documentation is usually required for customer acceptance of the installation.

The documentation process begins at the initiation of the project and continues through to the finish. It must begin with the actual cable plant path or location. OSP cables require documentation as to the overall route, but also details on exact locations, e.g. on which side of streets, which cable on poles, where and how deep buried cables and splice closures lay and if markers or tracing tape is buried with the cable. Premises cables require similar details inside a building in order for the cable to be located anywhere in the path.

Most of this data can be kept in CAD drawings and a database or commercial software that stores component, connection and test data. Long outside plant links that include splices may also have OTDR traces which should be stored as printouts and possibly in computer files archived on disks for later viewing in case of problems. A computer with proper software for viewing traces must be available, so a copy of the viewing program should be on the disks with the files. If the OTDR data is stored digitally, a listing of data files should be kept with the documentation to allow finding specific OTDR traces more easily.

The Documentation Process
Documentation begins with a basic layout for the network. A sketch on building blueprints may work for a small building but a large campus, metropolitan or long distance network will probably need a complete CAD layout. The best way to set up the data is to use a facility drawing and add the locations of all cables and connection points. Identify all the cables and racks or panels in closets and then you are ready to transfer this data to a database.

Fiber optic cables, especially backbone cables, may contain many fibers that

connect a number of different links which may not all be going to the same place. The fiber optic cable plant, therefore, must be documented for cable location, the path of each fiber, interconnections and test results. You should record the specifications on every cable and fiber: the manufacturer, the type of cable and fiber, how many fibers, cable construction type, estimated length, and installation technique (buried, aerial, plenum, riser, etc.)
It will help to know what types of panels and hardware are being used, and what end equipment is to be connected. If you are installing a big cable plant with many dark (unused) fibers, some will probably be left open or unterminated at the panels, and that must be documented also. Whenever designing a network, it's a very good idea to have spare fibers and interconnection points in panels for future expansion, rerouting for repair or moving network equipment.
Documentation is more than records. All components should be labeled with color-coded permanent labels in accessible locations. Once a scheme of labeling fibers has been determined, each cable, accessible fiber and termination point requires some labeling for identification. A simple scheme is preferred and if possible, explanations provided on patch panels or inside the cover of termination boxes.

Protecting Records
Cable plant documentation records are very important documents. Keep several backup copies of each document, whether it is stored in a computer or on paper, in different locations for safekeeping. If a copy is presented to the customer, the installer should maintain their own records for future work on the project. One complete set on paper should be kept with a "restoration kit" of appropriate components, tools directions in case of outages or cable damage. Documentation should be kept up to date to be useful so that task should be assigned to one on-site person with instructions to inform all parties keeping copies of the records of updates needed. Access to modify records should be restricted to stop unauthorized changes to the documentation.

Planning for the Installation

Once the design of a fiber optic project is complete and documented, one might think the bulk of the design work is done. But in fact, it's just beginning. The next step is to plan for the actual installation. Planning for the installation is a critical phase of any project as it involves coordinating activities of many people and companies. The best way to keep everything straight is probably to develop a checklist based on the design during the early stages of the project.

The Project Manager

Perhaps the most important issue is to have a person who is the main point of contact for the project. The project manager needs to be involved from the beginning, understands the aims of the project, the technical aspects, the physical layout, and is familiar with all the personnel and companies who will be involved. Likewise all the parties need to know this person, how to contact them (even 24/7 during the actual install) and who is the backup if one is needed.

The backup person should also be involved to such a degree that they can answer most questions, may even be more technically savvy on the project, but may not have full decision-making authority. The backup on big jobs may well be the person maintaining the documentation and schedules, keeping track of purchases and deliveries, permits, subcontractors, etc. while the project manager is more of a hands-on manager.

Design Checklist

Planning for a project is critical to the success of the project. The best way is to develop a checklist before beginning the design process. The checklist below is comprehensive but each project will have some of its own unique requirements that need to be added. Not all steps need be done serially, as some can be done in parallel to reduce time required for designing the project. The designer must interface with many other people and organizations in designing a project so contacts for outside sources should be maintained with the design documentation.

Design process

- Link communications requirements
- Link route chosen, inspected, special requirements noted including inspections and permits
- Specify communications equipment and component requirements
- Specify cable plant components
- Determine coordination with facilities, electrical and other personnel
- Documentation completed and ready for installation
- Write test plan
- Write restoration plans

Contractor package for the install

- Documentation, drawings, bills of materials, instructions
- Permits available for inspection
- Guidelines to inspect workmanship at every step, test plan
- Daily review of progress, test data
- Safety rules to be posted on the job site(s) and reviewed with all supervisors and installation personnel

Requirements for completion of cable plant installation
- Final inspection
- Review test data on cable plant
- Instructions to set up and test communications system
- Final update of documentation
- Update and complete restoration plan, store components and documentation

Developing A Project Checklist

The final project checklist will have many items, all of great importance. Each item needs a full description, where and when it will be needed and who is responsible for it. See Chapter 10 for a recommended project installation checklist. Components like cables and cable plant hardware should indicate vendors, delivery times and where, when and sometimes how it needs to be delivered. Special installation equipment needs to be scheduled also, with notes of what is needed to be purchased and what will be rented. If the jobsite is not secure and the install will take more than a day, security guards at the jobsite(s) may need to be arranged.

A work plan should be developed that indicates what specialties are going to be needed, where and when. Outside plant installations (OSP) often have one crew pulling cable, especially specialty installs like direct burial, aerial or underwater, another crew splicing and perhaps even another testing. OSP installers often do just part of the job since they need skills and training on specialized equipment like fusion splicers or OTDRs and installation practices like climbing poles or plowing-in cables. Inputs from the installation crews can help determine the approximate time needed for each stage of the installation and what might go wrong that can affect the schedule.

And things will go wrong. All personnel working on the project should be briefed on the safety rules and preferably be given a written copy. Supervisors and workers should have contact numbers for the project manager, backup and all other personnel they may need to contact. Since some projects require working outside normal work hours, for example airports or busy government buildings where cabling is often done overnight, having a project manager available – preferably onsite – while the work is being done is very important.

During the installation itself, a knowledgeable person should be onsite to monitor the progress of installation, inspect workmanship, review test data, create daily progress reports and immediately notify the proper management if something looks awry. If the project manager is not technically qualified, having someone available who is technical is important. That person should have the authority to stop work or require fixes if major problems are found.

Facilities and Power/Ground issues

This chapter primarily focuses on the unique aspects of fiber optic cable plant design and installation, but this process cannot be done in a vacuum. Cable plants may require municipal permits, cooperation from other organizations to allow access through their property and construction disruptions. Any communications system requires not only the cable plant but facilities for termination at each end, placing communications equipment, providing power (usually uninterruptible data quality power) and a separate data ground. Inside the facility, connections must be made to the end users of the link. The large number of options involved in almost every project make it impossible to summarize the issues in a few sentences, so let's just say you must consider the final, complete design to gain cooperation and coordinate the final installation. One of the most valuable assets you can have when designing and installing a fiber optic project is an experienced contractor.

Developing A Test Plan

Every installation requires confirmation that components are installed properly. The installer or contractor wants to ensure the work is done properly so the customer is satisfied and callbacks for repair will not be necessary. Customers generally require test results as well as a final visual inspection as part of the documentation of a proper installation before approving payment. In our experience, however, there is often confusion about exactly what should be tested and how documentation of test results is to be done on fiber optic projects. These issues should be agreed upon during the design phase of the project. Project paperwork should include specifications for testing, references to industry standards and acceptable test results based on a loss budget analysis done during the design phase of the project.

The process of testing any fiber optic cable plant may require testing three times, testing cable on the reel before installation, testing each segment as it is installed, including verifying every splice as it is made using an OTDR and finally testing complete end to end loss of every fiber in the cable plant. Practical testing usually means testing only a few fibers on each cable reel for continuity before installation to ensure there has been no damage to the cable during shipment. Then each segment is tested as it is spliced and/or terminated by the installers. Finally the entire cable run is plugged together and tested for end-to-end loss for final documentation.

One should require visual inspection of cable reels upon acceptance and, if visible damage is detected, testing the cable on the reel for continuity before installing it, to ensure no damage was done in shipment from the manufacturer to the job site. Since the cost of installation usually is high, often much higher than the cost of materials, it only makes sense to ensure that one does not install bad cable, which would then have to be removed and replaced. It is generally sufficient to just test continuity with a fiber tracer or visual fault locator. However, long spools of cable may be tested with an

OTDR if damage is suspected and one wants to document the damage or determine if some of the cable needs to be cut off and discarded (or retained to get credit for the damaged materials.)

After cable installation, splicing and termination, each segment of the cable plant should be tested individually as it is installed, to ensure each splice, connector and cable is good. One should never complete splicing cables without verifying the splices are properly done with an OTDR before sealing the splice closure. Finally each end to end run (from equipment to equipment connected on the cable plant) should be tested for loss as required by all standards. Remember that each fiber in each cable will need to be tested, so the total number of tests to be performed is calculated from the number of cable segments times the number of fibers in each cable. This can be a time-consuming process.

Required vs. Optional Testing

Testing the complete cable plant requires insertion loss testing with a source and power meter or optical loss test set (OLTS) per TIA standard test procedure OFSTP-14 for multimode or OFSTP-7 for singlemode. The test plan should specify the "0 dB" reference method option (one, two or three reference cables) as this will affect the value of the loss. TIA 568 calls for a one cable reference, but this may not be possible with all combinations of test sets and cable plant connectors. The required test methods need to be agreed upon by the contractor and user beforehand.

OTDR testing is generally done on outside plant cables, but OTDR testing alone is not acceptable for cable plant certification. Long lengths of outside plant cabling which include splices should be tested with an OTDR to verify splice performance and look for problems caused by stress on the cable during installation.

While there are advocates of using OTDRs to test any cable plant installation, including short premises cables, it is not required by industry standards nor is it recommended for premises cabling. The shorter lengths of premises cabling runs and frequent connections with high reflectance often create confusing OTDR traces that cause problems for the OTDR autotest function and are sometimes difficult for even experienced OTDR users to interpret properly.

Coordinating Testing and Documentation

The Test Plan should be coordinated with the cable plant documentation. The documentation must show what links need testing and what test results are expected based on loss budget calculations. The Test Plan should also specify how the test data are incorporated into the documentation for acceptance of the installation and for reference in case of future cabling problems that require emergency restoration.

Planning for Restoration

About once a day in the USA, a fiber optic cable is broken by a contractor digging around the cable, as this photo shows. Premises cables are not as vulnerable, except for damage caused by clumsy personnel or during the removal of abandoned cables. Any network is susceptible to damage so every installation needs a restoration plan.

Efficient fiber optic restoration depends on rapidly finding the problem, knowing how to fix it, having the right parts and getting the job done quickly and efficiently. Like any type of emergency, planning ahead will minimize the problems encountered.

Documentation for Restoration
Documentation is the most helpful thing you can have when trying to troubleshoot a fiber network, especially during restoration. Start with the manufacturer's datasheets on every component you use: electronics, cables, connectors, hardware like patch panels, splice closures and even mounting hardware. Along with the data, one should have manufacturer's "help line" contact information, which will be of immense value during restoration. During installation, mark every fiber in every cable at every connection and keep records using cable plant documentation software or a simple spreadsheet of where every fiber goes. When tested, add loss data taken with an optical loss test set (OLTS) and optical time domain reflectometer (OTDR) data when available. Someone must be in charge of this data, including keeping it up to date if anything changes.

Equipment For Restoration

Testing and Troubleshooting
You must have available proper test equipment to troubleshoot and restore a cable plant. An OLTS should also have a power meter to test the power of the signals to determine if the problem is in the electronics or cable plant. Total failure of all fibers in the cable plant means a break or cut in the cable.

For premises cables, finding the location is often simple if you have a visual fault locator or VFL, which is a bright red laser coupled into the optical fiber that allows testing continuity, tracing fibers or finding bad connectors at patch panels.

For longer cables, an OTDR will be useful. Outside plant networks should use the OTDR to document the cable plant during installation, so during restoration a simple comparison of installation data with current traces will usually find problems. OTDRs can also find non-catastrophic problems, for example when a cable is kinked or stressed, so it only has higher loss, which can also cause network problems.

Tools and Components

Once you find the problem, you have to repair it. Repair requires having the right tools, supplies and trained personnel available. Besides the test equipment needed for troubleshooting, you need tools for splicing and termination, which may include a fusion splicer for outside plant cables. You also need components necessary for restoring the cable plant.

For every installation, a reasonable amount of excess cable and installation hardware should be set aside in storage for restoration. Some users store the restoration supplies along with documentation in a sealed container ready for use. Remember that the fiber optic patchcords that connect the electronics to the cable plant can be damaged also, but are not considered repairable. Just keep replacements available.

One big problem in restoring damaged cables is pulling the two cable ends close enough to allow splicing them together. You need several meters of cable on each end to strip the cable, splice the fibers and place them in a splice closure. Designing the cable plant with local service loops is recommended. If the cable ends are too short , or the damaged cable is underground or buried, you will have to splice in a new section of cable. Since the restoration cable must match the damaged cable or at least have a greater nuber of fibers, the best source of cable for restoration is cable leftover from the original installation. Manufacturers also can supply cable restoration kits that include cable and splice closures.

What else besides cables and cable plant hardware should be in a restoration kit? You should have a termination or mechanical splice kit and proper supplies. For splices, you need splice closures with adequate space for a number of splices equal to the fiber count in the cable. All these should be placed in a clearly marked box with a copy of the cable plant documentation and stored in a safe place where those who will eventually need it can find it fast.

Preparing Personnel

Personnel must be properly trained to use this equipment and do the troubleshooting and restoration. And, of course, they must be available on a moments notice. The biggest delay in restoring a fiber optic communications link is often the chaos that ensues while personnel figure out what to do. Having a plan that is known to the responsible personnel is the most important issue.

Major users of fiber optics have restoration plans in place, personnel trained and kits of supplies ready for use. It's doubtful that most premises users are ready for such contingencies. Users may find that the cost of owning all this expensive equipment is not economic. It may be preferable to keep an inexpensive test set consisting of a VFL and OLTS at each end of the link and having an experienced contractor on call for restoration.

Managing A Fiber Optic Project

Managing a fiber optic project can be easiest part of the installation if the design and planning have been done thoroughly and completely, or, if not, the hardest. But even assuming everything has been done right, things will still probably go wrong, so planning for the unexpected is also very important. Here are some guidelines for managing the project that can minimize the problems and help in their speedy solution.

On Site Management and Supervision
First, someone has to be in charge, and everyone involved must know they are the boss, including them. During the project, they must be readily available for consultation and updates. While this may sound obvious, sometimes the network user's representative has other responsibilities (like managing an IT department) and may not be able or willing to direct full attention to the project. Whoever is assigned the task of managing the project must be involved and available, preferably on the job site, full time. If necessary, delegate responsibility to the contracting construction supervisor with requirements for daily reports and personal updates.

Make certain that everyone responsible for parts of the project have appropriate documentation and have reviewed the installation plan. Everyone should have toured the relevant job sites and be familiar with locations. They must also know who to contact about questions on the sites, within the network user, the contractor and any outside organizations such as local governments or utilities. Everyone needs to have contact information for each other (cell phones usually, since email may be too slow and instant messaging will probably not be available to field workers.) The onsite supervisor should have a digital camera and take plenty of photos of the installation to be filed with the documentation for future reference and restoration.

Locations of components, tools and supplies should be known to all personnel. On larger jobs, managing equipment and materials may be a full time job. Special equipment, like splicing trailers or bucket trucks, should be scheduled as needed. Rental equipment should be double checked with the suppliers to ensure delivery to the job site on time. Contacts for vendor technical support should be noted on documentation for the inevitable questions arising during installation.

Contacts with Local Authorities
Outside plant installs may require local authorities to provide personnel for supervision or police for protection or traffic management on public job sites, so they must also become involved in the scheduling. If job inspections are required, arrangements should be made so that the job interruptions for inspections are minimized. Supervisory personnel must be responsible for job site safety and have appropriate contact information, including for public services like police, fire and ambulance.
If the project is large enough to last several days or more, daily meetings to review the day's progress are advisable. At a minimum, it should involve the onsite construction supervisor and the network user's person in charge of the project. As long as things are going well, such a meeting should be short. On longer projects, overnight security personnel at job sites should have contact information for the job manager who must be available 24/7 as well as public service contacts.

Continuous Inspection, Testing and Corrections
Inspection and testing of the installed cable plant should not be left until after the job is completed. Testing continually during installation can find and fix problems such as cable stresses or high termination losses before those problems become widespread. Each installer doing testing should have documentation with loss budget calculations and acceptable losses to use for evaluating the test results. Installers should be double-checking each other's work to ensure quality.
What do you do when (not if) things go wrong? Here judgment calls are important. When something happens, obviously it is the responsibility of the onsite supervisor to decide quickly if they can take care of it. If not, they must know who needs to be brought in and who needs to be notified. By reviewing progress regularly, disruptions can be minimized. Equipment failures, e.g. a fusion splicer, can slow progress, but other parts of the project like cable laying can continue, with splicing resumed as soon as replacement equipment is available. Problems with termination should be reviewed by an installer with lots of experience and the cure may require new supplies or turning termination over to more experienced personnel. Never hesitate to call vendor support when these kinds of questions or problems arise.
Following the completion of the install, all relevant personnel should meet, review the project results, update the documentation and decide if anything else needs to be done before closing the project.

Review Questions
True/False
Indicate whether the statement is true or false.

_____1.   Fiber optic network designers should have a knowledge of electrical power systems and hardware as well as communications design.

_____2.   The first consideration for any network is choosing the proper fiber optic cable type.

_____3.   Discussions of which is better – copper, fiber or wireless – are no longer relevant, as fiber is the only choice.

_____4.   It may be more cost effective for the fiber optic cabling in many projects to be custom designed and made.

_____5.   Testing a fiber optic installation may require testing three times, cable before installation, each segment as installed and a final test of end-to-end loss.

Multiple Choice
Identify the choice that best completes the statement or answers the question.

_____6.   Fiber optic network designers should have an in-depth knowledge of _____.
    A. Fiber optic components and systems
    B. Installation processes
    C. All applicable standards, codes and any other local regulations
    D. All of the above

_____7.   The first requirement that must be considered for a new fiber optic project is _____.
    A. The customer's communications system requirements
    B. Where the cable plant will be run
    C. Whether it will be multimode or singlemode fiber
    D. The customer's budget

_____8.   Fiber Optic Network design involves _____.
    A. Determining the types of communications systems involved
    B. Planning the routes for all cabling or wireless
    C. Choosing appropriate cabling and media
    D. All of the above

____9.   When choosing components, most projects will start with the
            choice of a _____ .
            A. Cable
            B. Splice type
            C. Connector
            D. Cable hardware

____10.   Most premises networks today should use _____
            multimode fiber but backbone cables can contain _____
            fibers for future expansion.
            A. OM1, OM3
            B. OM1, singlemode
            C. OM3, singlemode
            D. OM2, OM3

____11.   _____ of the cable plant is a necessary part of the design
            and installation process for a fiber optic network that is often
            overlooked.
            A. Planning
            B. Documentation
            C. CAD-CAM drawing
            D. OTDR testing

____12.   What is the most helpful information you can have when trying to
            troubleshoot a cabling network for restoration?
            A. Phone number of a fiber optic contractor
            B. Loss data on each fiber
            C. OTDR traces
            D. Documentation

Multiplc Response
*Identify one or more choices that best complete the statement or answer the
question.*

____13.   Metropolitan networks can involve which of the following
            systems?
            A. CCTV surveillance cameras
            B. Traffic monitoring
            C. Emergency services
            D. Educational systems

Additional Study And Projects

Read the sections on Designing Fiber Optic Networks on the FOA Online Reference Guide, including pages on LANs and FTTx.

Complete loss budgets for the example given in this chapter at other wavelengths for typical fiber optic systems.

Using case studies provided by the instructor, design several fiber optic networks on paper, noting special issues that can only be solved by field observations and conversations with users.

Chapter 10
Fiber Optic Network Installation

Objectives: From this chapter you should learn:
What is involved in a fiber optic installation
The role of the contractor and installer
How to prepare for the installation
What is involved in the installation process
How to verify the quality of the installation
Safety for fiber optic installations

Preparing For Installation

After the process of designing fiber optic networks is completed, the next step is to install it. What do we mean by the "installation process?" Assuming the design is completed, we're looking at the process of physically installing and completing the network, turning the design into an operating system. This chapter covers preparing for the installation, requirements for training and safety and then the actual installation process.
Since outside plant fiber optic networks can cover a broad range of installation types using varied components over different types of geography, it is impossible to cover the specifics of any one installation. This chapter should provide an overview of the various options available in OSP installations and general knowledge that should prepare those involved in any particular installation to understand how to proceed.

The Role of the Contractor in an Installation
To begin work on a fiber optic installation, the network owner or user must choose a contractor, perhaps the most important decision in the entire process. The fiber optic contractor should be able to work with the customer in each installation project through six stages: design, installation, testing, troubleshooting, documentation and restoration. The contractor must be experienced in fiber optic installations of the type involved and should be able to provide references for similar work.
One should be able to rely the contractor to not only do the installation but to assist in the design of the network and help choose components and vendors. Once the contractor has been given the assignment, they should be able to help the customer with the design, including choosing the right kinds of fibers,

cables, connectors and hardware for the installation. The contractor should know which components meet industry standards to ensure interoperability and what state of the art components will facilitate future expandability. The experienced contractor also should be able to help in the choice of vendors. Experience with particular product types and vendors will allow the contractor to assist the customer to choose products that make the installation faster and easier and often higher performance and more reliable. Should the customer choose components that are unfamiliar to the contractor, it is important that the contractor know early in the process so they may obtain proper training, often from the manufacturer, as well as any unique tools that may be required.

Generally, the customer is not as familiar with fiber optic technology and practice as an experienced contractor. The contractor may need to discuss certain choices with the customer where they believe alternatives may be better choices.

The actual installation process can involve more than just putting in cable, terminating and testing it. If the contractor is knowledgeable and experienced, the user may ask the contractor to purchase, receive, inspect and bring components to the work site also, which can be another good source of revenue for the contractor. Having full control of the materials process can also make life easier for the contractor, as they have a better chance to keep on schedule rather than depending on a customer who has many other priorities. Plus, they may have the latitude to choose components they are more familiar with, facilitating the actual installation process.

The technicians actually doing the installation should be trained and certified by organizations like The Fiber Optic Association (www.thefoa.org) and/or manufacturers of the products being installed. Certification provides a level of confidence that the installation techs are knowledgeable and have the skills needed for the work involved.

The final four requirements from the contractor, testing, troubleshooting, documentation and restoration, need to be discussed before the project ever begins. Every fiber optic project requires insertion loss testing of every link with a light source and power meter or optical loss test set according to industry standards. Some projects, like long outside plant links with splices, may also require OTDR testing. The contractor and customer must agree that testing includes troubleshooting problems and fixing them as well as documenting test results for every link.

Likewise, for the contractor, documentation must begin before the project starts so the scope of work is known to everyone and end only when the final test data is entered. Copies of the documentation, along with excess components left over from the installation, must be presented to the customer to facilitate future network restoration, should it be required.

The Contract

The contract for a fiber optic installation should include detailed requirements for the project, spelling out exactly what is to be installed, acceptable test results, and documentation to be provided. All this should be discussed between the customer and the contractor and agreed to in writing. They are not irrelevant details, as they are important to ensure the customer gets what they expect and the contractor knows what is expected of them when designing the network, estimating costs, doing the actual installation and providing proof of performance in order to show the work is completed and payment should be made.

Planning For The Project

Once the contracts are signed and a set of plans has been handed to the contractor, what's next? Planning the job is the first task. Proper planning is important to ensure the job is installed properly, on time and meets cost objectives, so the contractor can make a profit.

It is assumed you have a finished design for the project, know where and how everything will be installed and have any special requirements like permits ready. One can also assume you have a completion date, hopefully a reasonable one, to work toward. The first step then is to create a schedule which will be the centerpiece of the planning process.

In order to schedule a job, you need a lot of information, much of which can be acquired from estimates you did when bidding the job. When buyers price the components to be used on a job, they should get delivery times as well as prices. Some items used on fiber optic projects should be stock items, like connectors, patch panels or splice closures. Cables, however, may have to be made to order.

Many fiber optic cables are custom items, depending on the cable type, number and types of fibers and color coding. Custom cables will often be less expensive because they don't have extra fibers for specifications you don't need, for example, but they will have longer lead times since they must be made from scratch. Whenever specifying a fiber optic cable, always try to have a few extra fibers available, just in case fibers are damaged during installation.

The astute contractor tries to always use the same types of components on every job so they are familiar with not only the installation procedures but the typical costs, yield (i.e. number of connectors or splices that will pass testing first time) and any problems likely to be encountered.

If any components are not familiar to the installers, they need to learn how to install them correctly, either by experimenting in the office on off-time or getting manufacturers to train them. The need for training may also arise if new equipment types are required, such as outside plant cable placing tools or new types of test equipment. The cardinal rule of installation is never take an unfamiliar component or tool on the job; it's a recipe for disaster.

Buyers need to order the components when the job is acquired, scheduling delivery to the job site either to have everything available before the installation begins, or on a large job with an extended schedule, according to how long the installation of that component will take. Here you also need to plan on where the components will be delivered to, either a staging area in your warehouse, for example, or to the job site.

Components delivered to the job site may require security. Theft can be a problem with cable particularly, since many thieves think all cables contain copper and the price of copper makes cable worth stealing. But vandalism is another concern, requiring components be either locked up or if too large to put indoors like large spools of cable or fiber optic innerduct, may require on site overnight guards.

Next, one needs to schedule labor. Again, the estimates should tell you how many installers of what experience will be needed and how long they are expected to need to complete the installation. If any training is needed, additional time may need to be added to the schedule.

Having covered labor and materials in the schedule, the planning is almost done. Review the schedule with everyone involved to get them on board and start the processes, beginning with acquiring materials. Then add to the plan a review of safety rules for supervisors, installers and anyone expected to be on site. Also add notes to keep all scrap cable, connectors, etc. to package and present to the user in case they are needed for future restoration.

If the start date is not tomorrow (because the customer wanted it yesterday!) and you have other projects in the interim, pull out this schedule regularly to check if everything is on schedule to prevent any last minute surprises.

Installation Checklist

Planning for the installation is a critical phase of any project as it involves coordinating activities of many people and companies. The best way to keep everything straight is to develop a checklist based on the design. The checklist below is comprehensive but each project will have some of its own unique requirements that need to be added to the list.

Pre-install checklist:
- Main point of contact/project manager chosen
- Link communications requirements set
- Equipment and component requirements set and vendors chosen
- Link route chosen, permits obtained
- Cable plant components and vendors chosen
- Coordination with facilities and electrical personnel complete
- Documentation completed and ready for installation, preliminary restoration plans ready

- Test plan complete
- Schedule and start date set for installation, all parties notified
- Components ordered and delivery date set, plans made for receiving materials (time, place,) arrange security if left outside or on construction site
- Contractor/installer chosen and start date set
- Link route tour with contractor(s)
- Construction plans reviewed with contractor(s)
- Components chosen reviewed with contractor(s)
- Schedule reviewed with contractor(s)
- Safety rules reviewed with contractor(s)
- Excess materials being kept for restoration reviewed with contractor(s)
- Test plan reviewed with contractor(s)

Before starting the install:
- All permits available for inspection
- Sites prepared, power available
- All components on site, inspected, 24-hour security arranged if necessary
- Contractor available
- Relevant personnel notified
- Safety rules posted on the job site(s) and reviewed with all supervisors and installation personnel

During The Installation:
- Inspect workmanship at every step
- Daily review of process, progress, test data
- Immediate notification and solution of problems, shortages, etc.

After completion of cable plant installation:
- Inspect workmanship
- Review test data on cable plant
- Set up and test communications system
- Update and complete documentation
- Update and complete restoration plan
- Store restoration plan, documentation, components, etc.

Preparing For Outside Plant Installations

Outside plant (OSP) installations of fiber optic cables can be much more diverse than premises installations. OSP installs may include installing aerial cable, direct-buried cable, underground cable in conduit or installing conduit or innerduct and then pulling cable, or placing cable underwater. A single link may include several types of installation, for example aerial in one section, pulling in conduit on a bridge crossing and burying the rest of the cable. Cables may end when pulled into buildings or terminated at the top of poles where surveillance cameras or wireless access points are located. Splices where cables are concatenated can be placed in pedestals, buried underground or hung in aerial splice closures.

The diversity of OSP installation makes it extremely important for the contractor to know the route of the cable to be installed intimately. Like the estimator who should walk the route before beginning the estimating process, the contractor needs to see for themselves the actual situations they are going to encounter. That inspection allows them to determine what problems may be encountered, what special equipment may be needed and even double check that all the permits needed are in order. Long cable pulls in conduit may require lubricants or intermediate pulls where your installers need to know how to "figure 8" cable to prevent kinking, a procedure described later in this chapter.

Call Before You Dig

The old story about the most likely fiber optic communications system failure being caused by "backhoe fade" is not a joke – it happens every day. But it reminds us that digging safely is vitally important. The risk is not just interrupting communications, but the life-threatening risk of digging up high voltage cables or gas lines. There are several services that maintain databases of the location of underground services that must be contacted before any digging occurs, but mapping these should be done during the design phase and double-checked before digging to ensure having the latest data.

At the same time as the cable is installed, markers like these indicating its location and ownership can also be installed.

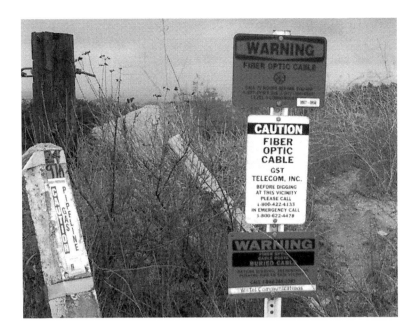

Pulling and Placing Cable

OSP installations fall into four broad categories, underground, direct buried, aerial and submarine (or underwater.) Each used different procedures, tools and even cables.

Underground Cables

Underground cables are pulled in conduit that is buried underground, usually 3-4 fcet (1-1.2 meters) deep to reduce the likelihood of accidentally being dug up. The process usually begins with digging a trench to bury the conduit which is generally 4 inch plastic pipe, sometimes with pre-installed innerduct (also called duct liner) with a pulling tape to facilitate the actual cable pulling process. Directional boring can also be used to avoid digging up the surface, for example in crossing streets or sidewalks. If the conduit and cables are all dielectric, a conductive marker tape may be buried about a foot above the conduit to assist in future cable location and as a warning to anyone digging in the vicinity of the cable.

Due to the disruptive nature of burying conduit, especially under roadways, many governments which grant permits for burying cable require the contractor to install extra conduits along the route to prevent having to dig again for any future cable installations. Since many cities have extensive conduits already buried for other services or may have required extra conduit to be buried during prior installations, conduit may be available for pulling new fiber optic cables.

Innerduct inside the conduit separates the cables and provides easier pulling of cables. Conduit can be purchased with innerducts installed, generally with pulling tapes also. If the innerduct does not have a pulling tape installed, a line may be blown through the duct to pull a stronger pulling tape or line through the duct.

Unless innerducts are installed in a conduit, only one cable can be installed in the conduit unless all the cables are pulled together. Pulling a cable into a conduit which already has several cables may cause tangling, increasing pulling tension and potentially damaging cables. Multiple cables may be pulled at once if the total cable fill and pulling tension does not exceed recommendations.

Innerduct or duct liners come in several types, including flexible tubes with corrugated or smooth interiors. Corrugated tubes with smooth liners have a greater tendency to flatten, limiting cable size, while corrugated interiors may be more fragile. A new type of duct liner is more like a fabric sleeve that lies flat until the cable is pulled through it, and takes up less space in the cable than rigid innerduct allowing space for more cables.

The length of cable that can be pulled will depend on many factors, including the type of cable, conduit or innerduct, temperature, and straightness of the run that affect the coefficient of friction. Except for short pulls, cables should be lubricated to reduce friction that increases pulling tension. Lubricants should be of a type approved by the cable manufacturer, not lubricants for copper communication or electrical cables, and applied per the lubricant and/ or cable manufacturer. Some lubricant manufacturers offer online calculators that will help in choosing and using lubricants.

Most cables can only be safely pulled by attachment of a swivel pulling eye to the strength members of the cable. Swivels are important to reduce twisting loads on the cable. For high tension loads, a breakaway swivel is used to prevent damage if pulling tension exceeds the cable specification. Some cables are rated for pulling by the jacket if a flexible wire mesh grip, commonly called a Kellems Grip, is used. These are also usually attached to the strength members of the cable. Later in this chapter are instructions for attaching pulling eyes.

Tension for pulling cables is often high enough that a powered capstan will be needed, probably for all but the shortest pulls. The capstan should be equipped with a monitor that can shut down pulling if a preset tension is exceeded. If tension becomes too high, the cause of excess friction needs to be found and fixed.

As with any cable installation, it is important to not bend the cable too tightly which may cause damage to the cable or its fibers. Standard cable guidelines are a minimal bend radius of 20 times the cable diameter under tension and

10 times the cable diameter after the pulling tension is removed. After pulling the cable may still have some tension at points, but if properly lubricated and carefully pulled, it should be minimal.

Cables can be pulled completely from one end if the length is short enough and there are no intermediate locations like manholes or vaults where the cable is to be pulled through, not spliced at that location. Devices exist to assist at midspan allowing pulling out of one conduit and into another at some locations, or the cable may be pulled to the location, laid on the ground in a figure 8 pattern to prevent twisting and then pulled through the next section. Alternately, cable can be pulled in one direction from an intermediate point, the remaining cable unspoiled in a figure 8 pattern, the flipped and pulled in the other direction. See the section on figure 8 cable pulls later in this chapter.

Cables can sometimes be installed by blowing special cable types into ducts called duct lines, micro-ducts or sub-ducts which have been installed in larger conduit or even pipes for carrying water, sewage or gas. High pressure compressed air provides an aerodynamic effect, floating the cable on the air stream and carrying it down the duct, allowing installation lengths as long as 2 km (6,500 feet.)

At any cable ends where splicing or termination is required, an extra 30-60 feet (10-20 meters) of cable should be left for splicing. Most splicing will be done in a trailer or tent on the ground and extra cable is needed to reach the splice location and have extra length to strip for splicing. Before beginning installation, check splice closure instructions for cable lengths required for splicing or midspan entry. Always allow extra length to cut off the pulling eye from the pulling end.

As with any cabling installation, work should be done in a neat and workmanlike manner. Cables should be neatly lashed in the proper locations in manholes or vaults, using cable ties but never tighten cable ties tightly as that can cause problems with the cable or fibers. Service loops should also be neatly lashed in place. At intermediate locations, it is extremely important to place identification tags on fiber optic cables to allow easy identification and prevent damage in the future if the cable is mistaken for a cable that is to be cut and removed.

Cables terminated inside premises need to be neatly installed. Conduit or cable trays should be used to protect the cables. Most building, fire or electrical codes limit the length of OSP cable that can be run indoors unless the cable is in conduit, so proper cable installation includes meeting appropriate building codes.

Buried Cables

If the geography allows, fiber optic cables of the appropriate types can be buried directly in the ground by plowing directly into the ground, directional boring or trenching and placing the cable in the trench. Where the ground is soft and relatively free of rocks and the land is flat and has no obstacles for the movement of heavy equipment, direct burial is a fast method of installation, allowing several miles/km of cables to be installed in a day. In more built-up areas, trenching may be easier because plowing requires big machinery and lots of room.

Heavy-duty cables can be buried directly or cables in ducts for extra protection can be installed using direct burial techniques. Cables can be supplied already in ducts for burial. An alternative technique is to bury duct and blow cables into the ducts as is done in underground installations.

Typically trunk cables in most areas are installed 3-4 feet deep (1-1.2 m), but in residential or urban areas, cables may be buried only 2 feet (0.6 m) deep. Some cables can be directly installed in sawn grooves in roads, but these are only buried a few inches deep, still within the roadway material and are filled with sealer. If the cable is all dielectric, a conductive marker tape may be buried about a foot above the conduit to assist in future cable location and as a warning to anyone digging in the vicinity of the cable.

Plowing cables can be done with large static plows or smaller vibratory plows, but they should be plows rated for pulling fiber optic cables. Plows for copper cables may not meet fiber requirements for cable support, bend radius, tension or vibration. Sometimes the cable plowing is proceeded by a ripping operation where a preliminary plowing is done to prepare the ground and find underground obstacles.

Plowing in cable requires careful feeding of the cable into the cable chute of the plow to reduce stress. A capstan feed is used on many plows to synchronize cable feed. The cable reel and feed chute should be isolated from vibration also.

Plowing in fiber optic cables is a process that demands care and experience. Needless to say the plow operator and crew need to know what they are doing and exercise great caution. Inexperienced personnel should work with an experienced crew to learn the proper procedures.

Trenching involves digging a trench with a backhoe or trencher, laying the cable and then filling the trench. All sizes of trenchers are available, and don't need to be fiber specific equipment unlike plows. The contractor needs to be careful about sharp objects or rocks in the trench or filler since they may damage the cable. If the ground is rocky, burying the cable in sand before filling the trench will provide protection.

Cables may also be buried by directional boring, a method often preferred when crossing roads or shallow waterways as it does not require digging up the surface. The size and length of the bore are related, as bigger bores can not be made over as long a length, and both may be determined by the type of ground encountered. Directional boring also requires exact knowledge of other buried utilities to prevent damage to them during the boring process. Buried cables may be spliced in closures which are buried along the cable route or placed above ground in a pedestal. At any cable ends where splicing or termination is required, an adequate length of cable must be left, typically an extra 30-60 feet (10-20 meters) of cable for splicing in a trailer or tent on the ground. Before beginning installation, check splice closure instructions for cable lengths required for splicing or midspan entry. Always allow extra length to cut off the pulling eye from the pulling end.

As with any cabling installation, work should be done in a neat and workmanlike manner. Cables should be neatly lashed in the proper locations in manholes or vaults, using cable ties but never tighten cable ties tightly as that can cause problems with the cable or fibers. Service loops should also be neatly lashed in place. At intermediate locations, it is extremely important to place identification tags on fiber optic cables to allow easy identification and prevent damage in the future if the cable is mistaken for a cable that is to be cut and removed.

Cables terminated inside premises need to be neatly installed. Conduit or cable trays should be used to protect the cables. Most building, fire or electrical codes limit the length of OSP cable that can be run indoors unless the cable is in conduit, so proper cable installation includes meeting appropriate building codes.

Aerial Cables

In many areas, cables are still installed on utility poles. Aerial cables are subject to continual tension as well as extra tension caused by temperature changes, wind and in some areas, the weight of ice. Most fiber optic cables do not have sufficient strength to allow direct aerial installation, but there are methods to install them aerially as well as special cables that are designed for aerial installation.

The simplest solution is to lash a regular OSP cable to a messenger, usually a metallic stranded cable used to support the cable but sometimes another cable if it has adequate strength. CATV overbuilds sometimes lash fiber cables to existing coax cables and even power cables can have fiber optic cables lashed to them. The messenger must be selected to have adequate strength to support the fiber optic cable over the span between support structures. Care must be taken when installing fiber optic cables with a messenger to accommodate length variations in the messenger, for example due to stretching in the wind or with temperature changes. Since optical fiber cables are designed not to stretch as that would stress the optical fibers, slack must be provided, usually at the supports, to reduce tension on the fiber optic cable when the messenger length changes. The National Electrical Safety Code and RUS provide guidelines for support structure design, but manufacturers should always be consulted about the proper support methods for the cables being chosen for aerial installation.

The first stage of a lashed aerial installation is installation of the support messenger cable. Typically the strand will be laid on the ground along the span, pulled onto the poles using pulleys, then have the tension adjusted and the messenger clamped securely. Lashing of the optical fiber cable to the messenger must be done separately on each span of the cable installation. The optical fiber cable can be pulled onto temporary support rings and lashed, or alternately, laid along the ground under the messenger and an aerial guide in front of the lasher used to position the cable next to the messenger for lashing. Some methods also use a truck that pays out the cable and pulls the lasher.

Cables with built in messengers, called figure 8 cables (not to be confused with the process of coiling cables on the ground called "figure 8-ing",) can be installed directly as the support structure is built into the cable. The cable is supported by clamping to the strength member of the cable in a manner similar to installing a messenger strand. One can also buy aerial conduit, a small fiber conduit with a messenger attached like a figure 8 cable and then an OSP fiber optic cable can be pulled into the conduit.

There is also a category of all dielectric self-supporting (ADSS) cables that are designed with more strength members and a thicker jacket to have adequate strength to withstand the rigors of aerial installation when installed with special hardware designed to grip the cable on the jacket properly without causing damage to the cable over long term high tension loading. As each manufacturer generally has their own hardware and procedures, they should be consulted during the design stage for proper cable plant design and placement procedures.

ADSS cables have two types of mounts, ends or dead-ends where the cable is supported against the tension caused by the installed cable, and pass-throughs where the cable can be attached to a pole but allowed to move within the assembly. Ends don't mean the end of the fiber optic cable, but a location where the cable is held firmly under tension. At a pole, two ends may be used to change directions of a cable, provide slack for tensioning or to allow ends to be brought to the ground for splicing. Tensioning can be done with a chain hoist with gage to set tension.

Another type of aerial cable is optical power ground wire (OPGW.) OPGW is a high voltage conductor with a hermetically sealed tube in the center which contains optical fibers. This cable is widely used throughout the world to provide communications as well as power. OPGW is installed in the same manner as high voltage cable but ends are brought to the ground and spliced or terminated, the coiled up on the tower. If communications equipment is required at that location, fiber optic cables are brought from the splices into a local facility housing the equipment. Installation of OPGW should be left to experienced utility personnel except for splicing which may be done by fiber installation personnel.

With all aerial cable installations where splicing or termination is required, an extra 30-60 feet (10-20 meters) of cable should be left for splicing. Even more may be required if splicing is done on the ground on cable installed on tall poles.

Whenever installing aerial cabling, careful planning is very important. Working high above the ground can be dangerous and working on poles may mean working in proximity to electrical power lines. If at all possible, have the power cables shut down before installing any other cables on utility poles. Be especially careful when installing metallic support hardware for fiber cables; the fiber cables may not be conductive but the hardware can be. Install the longest cables you can to reduce the number of locations for splicing. Have proper equipment and adequate numbers of properly trained personnel on the job site, and, if possible, local authorities who may have responsibility for the installation on their property.

Submarine/Underwater Cabling

Fiber optic cables sometimes need to be installed underwater. The best known of these installations are probably the transoceanic cables that provide worldwide telecom and Internet communications. Installing those cables is a very specialized process that requires special cable designs and custom cable-laying ships to pay out the cable over thousands of kilometer runs and place it on the ocean floor at great depths. Those applications, while interesting, are beyond the scope of this book.

Other underwater installations involve river or lake crossings where it is more cost effective to lay fiber cable under water than detour around the water, place the cable in conduit lashed to bridges or other structures or run the cable aerially. Underwater crossings may require special permits because of the jurisdiction of various environmental groups.

When cables are run underwater, there is always danger of the cable being snagged. For relatively shallow water, the cable should, if at all possible, be buried several feet under the bottom of the river or lake. For deeper water, special armored cables with one of more layers of wire armor should be used to prevent damage to the cable if snagged. Due to the specialized splice housings needed for underwater cables, running a single length across the water will be much easier and less costly.

Underwater installation brings its own safety hazards also. Experienced divers may be needed to assist in placing the cable and troubleshooting problems.

Hardware and Equipment

OSP installations may require installation of supporting structures before the cable installation can begin. New conduit or innerduct may need to be buried or conduit already in place may need to be checked, old cables removed and new innerduct installed. Some buried cables may even require the installation of pedestals, manholes or controlled-environment vaults for equipment as well as conduit.

Not only does the contractor need to consider all the hardware that may need to be installed, but they have to schedule the specialized equipment needed: trenchers or cable plows, backhoes, bucket trucks, cable winches, etc. and ensure that personnel are well-trained in their use.

Splicing Cables

Once the infrastructure is in place and the cable placed, the fiber optic splicing work begins. Now scheduling the availability of appropriate fiber optic equipment is the concern. If the cable is to be spliced outdoors, a splice trailer is normally used, unless splices are being made on a pole or in a bucket, where a tent may be required in bad weather.

The cable needs to be prepared for the splicing process. This involves processes appropriate to the cable type being installed, but usually includes removing the cable jacket, exposing proper lengths of buffer tubes to connect to splice trays, cutting back strength members to attach to the splice closure and cleaning all water-blocking gel or powder. Finally, the appropriate lengths of fiber are exposed and cleaned for splicing.

Care should be taken to ensure each fiber is carefully placed in the splice closure to prevent damage especially if the closure must be re-entered in the future and the closure needs to be sealed carefully to prevent long term degradation. And, as we always warn splicers, careful identification marking inside the closure makes identifying fibers much easier if a later problem requires re-entry.

Each splice needs to be verified with an OTDR test. Testing is done preferably as each splice is made and placed in the splice tray, so to be efficient, a splicer will be on the job site and a test tech will be working at the other end of the cable with an OTDR to verify each splice. Splicing machines give an estimate of splice loss but it's just that, and going back later, opening a splice closure and resplicing is an expensive proposition!

Midspan Entry
It is sometimes necessary to splice large fiber count cables to smaller cables at a location other than at the end of the larger cable. Rather than cutting the cable and splicing all the fibers, a midspan entry can be used to access only the fibers required for splicing to the smaller cable(s). In order to do a midspan entry, it is necessary to know what the manufacturer of the cable recommends for procedures and have the proper tools and other hardware required by the cable construction.

For midspan entry, the cable sheath, which includes the jacket and armor or other protective layers on the cable, must be removed from a length of the cable, typically about 2 meters (80 inches.) The sheath is first ring cut at the beginning and end of the section to be removed. Then at one end, the sheath is shaved off with a special tool or a utility knife to access the cable's rip cords. The rip cords are cut at the ringing point and used to cut the sheath all the way to the ring cut on the other end of the opening. When both rip cords are used, the cable sheath can be removed in two sections.

Next the strength members (aramid fibers) and binding tapes (and water-blocking tapes if the cable is a dry water-blocked design) are cut and removed. The central strength member and cable stiffener then needs to be cut, with ends left for securing to a splice closure as appropriate.

Entry to individual buffer tubes to access fibers to be spliced should be done with an appropriate midspan entry tool that shaves the tube for access without damaging the fibers. Inside the tube should be found a ripcord which is used to split the tub along the length required. Then the split tube is cut off at both ends.

The remaining buffer tubes can be placed in the storage section of a splice closure while the exposed fibers are spliced to other cables and stored in a splice tray. As with any splice closure, care must be taken to not damage fibers or kink buffer tubes during the process and to properly store all fibers and buffer tubes to allow reentry without harming any fibers if necessary.

Termination

Cables will be terminated inside facilities where they will connect to communications equipment. OSP cables generally do not meet NEC flammability requirements, so the cable entering a building must be terminated or spliced to indoor cables soon after entry, generally within 50 feet (16 meters) to meet fire codes. Some OSP cables have double jackets, an outer one for outdoors and an inner one rated for indoor use, so the outer jacket can be stripped off inside the building and the cable run to the equipment room. Cables terminated in pedestals or vaults do not have this requirement.

Generally singlemode OSP cables will be terminated by splicing pigtails onto each fiber and splices will be placed in a splice closure. Multimode fibers can be handled the same way or terminated directly onto the fibers. Most OSP cables will require installing a breakout kit which sleeves each fiber in a tube rugged enough for direct termination.

Preparing For Premises Fiber Optic Installations

Every outside plant cable project will include some premises cabling where the OSP cables are terminated, so every OSP contractor needs to be familiar with premises installation. Most building codes will require OSP cable, which is not fire-retardant, to be terminated a short distance after entering a building or be run in approved conduit. Before beginning installation of fiber optic cables and hardware in a premises installation, the site must be properly prepared for the installation of fiber optic cables, hardware and transmission equipment. During the design and planning stages, the site should have been inspected and all the hardware necessary for the cable plant included in the design.

Premises Support Structures

There are numerous structures used for the securing of fiber optic cable in premises installations making generalizations difficult. Cable may be hung on appropriate hangers, laid in cable trays or pulled into conduit or innerduct. Termination of the cables can be at racks in telecom rooms, in wall-mounted boxes or even wall outlets. Preparing for an install includes planning for storage of cable service loops behind racks such as shown here.
You must install support structures for fiber optic cable installations before

the installation of the fiber optic cable itself. These structures should follow the guidelines of appropriate standards such as TIA/EIA 569-A and NECA/ BICSI 568-2001. Allow for future growth in the quantity and size of cables when determining the size of the pathways. Follow all cable bend radius requirements and avoid pulling cables around hazards if possible. Sometimes new cables can be laid in existing cable trays. Do not install a fiber optic cable in a conduit or duct that already contains cabling, regardless of the cable type to prevent damage. Existing or new empty ductwork can be modified to accept several different installations by the proper placement of innerduct.

Premises support structures also include patch panels for terminations. They may be wall- or rack mounted and must be chosen appropriately for the cable types being used. Terminated simplex or zipcord cables can be terminated on open panels, but 900 micron tight-buffered fibers from distribution cables require closed termination panels for protection. If possible, the design of support structures should be such that adequate space is provided for termination of the cables and storage for service loops.

Fire Stopping

Premises cabling requires firestopping at all penetrations of walls and floors. Telecommunications firestopping must always comply with applicable codes and standards. All penetrations should be protected by type-approved firestops.

In most areas the breaching of a fire separation will require physical monitoring until it has been repaired. Check with the "Authority Having Jurisdiction" for specific requirements on the project before commencing work.

Electrical Systems
All fiber optic equipment will require proper power at the locations of the equipment. Power must be high quality power, protected for surges and spikes, and generally must have appropriate backup capacity to prevent loss of communications during power loss. Data equipment will require a separate ground and adequate power for year-round air conditioning. Consideration should be given to efficiency in cooling to reduce power consumption. Consult with the site owner, customer and appropriate user personnel to plan electrical power installation.

Grounding and Bonding

All conductive cabling and components must be grounded and bonded. Ground systems must be designed as specified by the NEC or other applicable codes and standards. Although most fiber optic cables are not conductive, any metallic hardware used in fiber optic cabling systems (such as wall-mounted termination boxes, racks, and patch panels) must be grounded. All conductive cables require proper grounding and bonding for applicable conductors.

Marking and Identifying Cables
Fiber optic cables should be specified with colored jackets per industry standards which identify the cables as fiber optic cables and indicate the type of fiber in the cable. All fiber optic cable terminations should be marked on racks or boxes where the cables terminate. Cables should be tagged with identification that they are fiber optic cables and proper handling is required.

Particular care should be taken in premises cabling upgrades. For nearly two decades, 62.5/125 micron multimode fiber has been the primary fiber for premises cabling. With the emergence of gigabit networks, laser-optimized 50/125 fiber has become more popular. Mixing the two fibers can result in excessive loss at connections that may cause systems to not operate properly. Color coding, marking and even using incompatible connectors (SC or ST on 62.5/125 and LC on 50/125 fiber) should be used whenever possible.

Removal of Abandoned Cables

Unless directed by the owner or other agency that unused cables are reserved for future use and the cables are marked accordingly, it may be required to remove abandoned optical fiber cable (cable that is not terminated at equipment other than a connector and not identified for future use with a tag) as required by the National Electrical Code or local codes.

At the discretion of the owner of the site, the contractor may be requested to remove other cables (e.g. copper communications or power cables) in addition. Removal of cables is much more time consuming than installation, as each cable must be identified and carefully removed to prevent damaging other cables. No cable should be cut for removal unless it is positively identified as one to be removed.

All cables removed should be recycled properly. Most communications cable has significant scrap value, not only for any copper conductors but for other metallic elements and even some plastics.

Equipping Installation Personnel

Equipping The Installer With Tools

As you near the time of the actual installation, it's time to determine how to outfit the crews who will do the work. Choosing the proper installation and test equipment is important, as it will affect the installation time and quality or even determine the profitability of the job. The frequency of problems caused by tools is appalling: their poor design, improper use, poor condition or the unfamiliarity with their use.

Installation tools include some big hardware like bucket trucks, trenchers, cable pullers or plows. The need for these will be established early in the planning stages. Many contractors do not own expensive equipment like this, finding it more cost effective to rent it as needed. If your crews are not familiar with a particular piece of equipment, subcontracting the work to someone who has both the equipment and an experienced crew may be much more cost effective, as mistakes in their operation can be disastrous – both costly and dangerous.

Outside plant cables and premises singlemode cables will generally require fusion splicing for concatenation of long cable runs and splicing on pigtails for termination. Since fusion splicers have become less costly, more contractors have purchased them. Other contractors who have fewer projects that require splicing prefer to rent them, knowing they are getting a splicer that is a newer model with the latest technology that has been recently serviced. The downside of a rental unit is your installers may not be familiar with that model and require some training or time to familiarize themselves with it. If you own your splicer, it's assumed your crews are familiar with its operation and need only to inspect the unit to ensure it's working properly and the arc electrodes are in good condition.

Most contractors own termination equipment for multimode fiber as it is used on most jobs. Generally contractors have a preferred method of termination, either adhesive/polish or prepolished/splice types. Either type requires dedicated toolkits. For epoxy or Hot Melt terminations, the appropriate curing ovens will be required, and the two are quite different; the Hot Melt oven is much hotter. If you use epoxy or anaerobic adhesives from your stock, check the expiration dates on all of them to make sure they are fresh. Also check for other consumables like wipes, isopropyl alcohol, cable gel cleaner and of course, connectors.

Prepolished splice connectors have been getting better and easier to use. Newer termination kits include a quality cleaver like those used with fusion splicers and a visual fault locator to verify the internal splice. Since newer kits can now produce connectors that have lower losses, around 0.5 dB, a new kit with the latest connectors and perhaps some training could be a good investment.

When checking out the termination kits, pay particular attention to the condition of the tools. Of course missing tools will need replacement, but hopefully that was done when the kits were inspected after the last job. However, tools like jacket strippers, fiber strippers and cleavers can wear out or be damaged, so its important to check their operation with some sample fibers to see if they are working properly.

It's mandatory to check out every piece of equipment you intend to take to a job site to ensure its proper operation and let the installation crew reacquaint themselves with its operation. This process needs to be done with enough time to have the unit serviced or replaced and restock any consumable supplies. It should also be obvious that one never puts back on the shelf any equipment that has had problems in the field. It should immediately be replaced or sent out for repair to be ready for the next job.

Let me caution you on another problem we have seen recently with tools. Several recent complaints of poor quality tools, especially fiber strippers, have led us to believe that poor quality imports are becoming more common. In one case, the tools appear to have been counterfeit, branded with a well-known American name. I suggest you purchase tools only from reputable sources and inspect them on receipt to ensure they work properly.

Finally, as the equipment is checked out and readied for use, make certain that appropriate safety equipment is packed with the tools. Everyone who works with fiber needs safety glasses and clean, unscratched ones will make seeing those hair-thin fibers much easier. Black work mats for splicing and termination also help the installer see the fibers and find fiber scraps for easier cleanup.

Equipping The Installer With Test Equipment
Installers also need test equipment. There are many options in the sophistication and cost of fiber optic test equipment. Proper selection can reduce both equipment costs and testing labor costs. The types and quantities of test equipment required will also vary by job type.
All installation techs should all carry a visual tracer or visual fault locator. The tracer is a visible flashlight or LED source used with multimode fiber to check continuity and trace fibers to ensure proper connections. A visual fault locator is a visible laser source with higher power that can be used with either singlemode or multimode fiber for tracing, but will also allow finding some faults like stress or breaks in most simplex or zipcord cables or plain buffered fibers. Either visual tracers or fault locators are inexpensive but invaluable during the installation and troubleshooting process.
Every fiber in a fiber optic cable plant requires loss testing with a light source and power meter, also called an optical loss test set (OLTS.) The OLTS will confirm that the fiber was installed and terminated properly, by testing end-to-end loss and comparing it to the loss budget created during the design phase. Big jobs may require more than one set to finish the job in a timely manner. Loss testers come in several configurations, including a separate light source and power meter usually sold as a test kit, an OLTS which is a single instrument that includes both the light source and power meter, and modules for converting copper testers to an OLTS. The individual light source and power meter are usually the cheapest solution, especially for small jobs, since the meter and source can be separated to be carried by two techs to each end of the cable being tested. If an OLTS is used, two will be needed to test a cable end-to-end, but it can test two fibers at one time, saving labor costs. The OLTS adapters for copper testers are usually not cheap, but they can take advantage of the sophisticated data handling of the expensive copper tester and produce complete reports. Contractors often choose these adapters if they have already invested in the copper testers.
Each loss test set needs reference test cables. These are just good 1-2 meter long fiber optic patchcords that match the fiber size and connectors of the cables being tested. The reference cables do not have to be special cables, just ones that have been tested to have low loss. Bad patchcords will give bad test results, causing good fibers to fail testing. Reference cables need to be tested frequently to ensure they are still in good condition and have low loss. It makes good sense for each test set to have several sets of reference

cables as they wear out or get damaged and need replacement.
Long outside plant runs with intermediate splices will require OTDR testing.
OTDRs also are good troubleshooting tools for long cable plants but are
generally not designed to be used on short cables such as those common
in premises applications. OTDRs are expensive, complicated instruments.
Unless you use one often, it's hard to justify the cost. Users not familiar with
the quirks of interpreting OTDR data cause many problems, failing good
cables and passing bad ones, often with expensive consequences. OTDRs
can be rented but considering the number of problems we see caused by
inexperienced users, subbing OTDR testing to an experienced contractor
could also be a wise move.
OTDRs need reference cables too, especially a long launch cable, sufficiently
long enough to allow the OTDR to settle down from the overload caused by
the test pulse. For singlemode fiber, a 1 km launch cable is recommended.
100 meters is adequate for most multimode OTDRs. New standards are
calling for a cable on the other end of the cable under test to allow testing the
connector on the far end, where 100 meters length is usually adequate.
The most important thing to remember about test equipment is to know how
to use it and always check it out before taking it to a job site. Batteries should
be replaced or recharged, reference cables tested and most importantly, the
user spends a few minutes refreshing their memory of how the instrument is
used. On the job site is not the place to find that the equipment is not ready
for use.

Training and Safety

Fiber Optic Training
The #1 Rule Of Fiber Optic Installation is never, ever, try to install a new type
of component or undertake a new type of application without proper training.
Not having the knowledge or skills related to that component or application
makes it virtually impossible to ensure success on the job and mistakes can
be very expensive. At the FOA, we have lots of examples of installations that
went wrong with terrible consequences.
No one can know everything nor can any training course possibly cover all
the aspects of fiber optics, all types of components and applications. Anyway,
the technology is always advancing, making it important to continue gaining
knowledge from all available sources. Much of the technical knowledge
needed can be obtained from websites like the FOA Online Reference
Guide, but what about the skills needed for working with actual fiber optic
components for installation, testing, troubleshooting and restoration? Those
skills can only come from training and experience.

Getting More Training

What kinds of training are necessary for success as a fiber optic contractor or installer and where can you obtain that training? There are many options for further training but first you need to figure out what your needs are, what training should include and who can provide appropriate training. As a general rule, all training in fiber optics that is aimed at installers must include sufficient hands-on activities with the relevant equipment, tools and components for the student to develop skills appropriate for that activity.

Fiber optic techs with some experience can often learn how to install many new component types or how to operate new equipment on their own. On websites of the FOA and many manufacturers, there is tutorial information on most installation subjects as well as the FOA "virtual hands-on" tutorials (VHO) on how it's done, step-by-step. Most manufacturers have good instructions and often tutorials online to help. Given proper tools and applications information, the astute tech should be able to learn new processes in a short time. The secret, of course, is to do this in a quiet, clean office environment before trying it on a customer's site with them looking over your shoulder!

Sometimes, it's better to take a course. Many FOA-approved schools offer advanced or specialist courses in termination, splicing, testing, fiber to the home, etc. that provide several days of intensive training, furnishing tools, equipment and supplies, as well as instructors who are familiar with the processes being taught. Manufacturers also offer product specific training, but one should try to get trained by applications engineers not sales personnel who may not have the depth of knowledge needed to adequately train installers.

Learning to install new components

There are hundreds of different types of fiber optic components that manufacturers have developed for specific applications or to simplify the job of the installer. Many of these components are unique to that manufacturer and may require special tools and installation processes. Examples are prepolished/splice connectors like the Corning Unicam, 3M HotMelt connectors, splice closures, all dielectric self-supporting cables, optical power ground wire, prefabricated cabling systems, etc.

Generally, one should go directly to the manufacturer for training like this unless an independent trainer has been trained and is recommended by the manufacturer and has the proper tools and components to teach the processes required. Some manufacturers offer short introductory courses on their new products which includes limited hands-on time, and such training may be ideal for those interested in learning more about that product before committing to purchasing all the tools and components necessary to use it. Follow-on comprehensive training can be done after making those purchases.

Learning to use new equipment
Some of the equipment necessary for fiber optic installation is complicated
and may be difficult to learn how to use without proper instruction on the
same piece of equipment. Examples are automated fusion splicers, especially
ribbon splicers, cable pulling or plowing equipment and OTDRs.
Some of these pieces of equipment are quite complex and have peripheral
products that must be used properly in conjunction with them to achieve
the expected results. Ribbon splicers, for example, use ribbon strippers and
cleavers, both of which are critical to achieving consistently good splices. All
automated splicers have unique programming features so one needs to learn
how to operate the splicer unit itself as well as how to make splices using it.
OTDRs are also complicated devices and learning to use them has two parts
- learning how to operate the OTDR with all its options and interpreting the
data it takes in testing a fiber (the trace or signature as it is called). While all
OTDR manufacturers offer "automatic testing" options, one cannot afford to
trust them in all uses, as they can easily become confused by artifacts like
ghosts. The user should always manually check the OTDR trace to ensure
proper conclusions from test data.
Training needs to be done on the actual type and model of equipment of
interest, as different manufacturers' products or different models from the
same manufacturer may have unique features. To be effective, the training
must include two phases - how to set up and operate the equipment itself
and how to complete the processes for which it is intended. Generally
manufacturers offer training on these products and independent trainers may
use the same equipment or will be willing to train you on your equipment if
you have already purchased it.

Learning New Applications
A point we make often is that there are many different applications for fiber
optics and there are substantial differences in how those applications are
designed, installed and tested. Outside plant techs, for example, generally
terminate by splicing on factory-made pigtails, while premises techs terminate
directly on fibers with adhesive/polish or prepolish/splice connectors. FTTx
techs may only use prefab cable assemblies. Techs moving from one
application to another may require training as well as on the job training (OJT)
to understand the application and develop the appropriate skills.

Finding Appropriate Training
Whatever your interest, make sure the courses you take are appropriate for
your interests or you'll be wasting time and money. Here are some options to
consider:

Can you learn it yourself? Some of us just learn better on our own. Is
information on the topic readily available, for example on the FOA Online

Fiber Optic Reference Guide? Good videos can help too, especially with hands-on topics like cable pulling and termination. Can you get the right tools and components to use in developing the skills necessary? Is there someone you can call for assistance?

Does the manufacturer offer training? Does it cover what you need to know? Does it offer lots of practice with the equipment and components? Will you be certified as an approved installer for that manufacturer? That can help in getting business from customers of that manufacturer.

Do independent trainers like the FOA-Approved Schools offer training in this area? Does it cover what you need to know? Does the trainer have the latest version of the equipment needed for training? Will they train you on your equipment? Is the instructor experienced and well-versed on the products and technology? Can the trainer offer manufacturer certification as well as other certifications?

Where is the training being offered? Travel costs can add significantly to training costs.

Remember FOA-Approved schools often offer other types of classes than just CFOT certification classes. Check with your FOA school or the online list of FOA-Approved schools for more information.

Safety In Working With Optical Fiber

Safety
OSP safety is a very important issue, well beyond the usual fiber issues of protecting your eyes from fiber shards or working with potentially hazardous chemicals. Routes should be cleared with "One Call" or "Call before you dig" services to ensure no buried cables or pipes are in the proposed route. Installers working with cable-placing machinery need to be well trained in how to operate them safely. Aerial installations are particularly dangerous,

since poles usually have electrical cables nearby. Every OSP job should have posted safety procedures and all personnel briefed in their use.
Safety in the lab or on the job site must be the number one concern of everyone. Besides the usual safety issues for construction, generally covered under OSHA rules that should be familiar to all contractors and installers, fiber optics adds concerns for eye safety, chemicals, sparks from fusion splicing, disposal of fiber shards and more. Before beginning any installation, safety rules should be posted on the classroom wall, lab wall or on the job site and reviewed with all onsite personnel. All personnel must wear the usual construction safety gear plus everyone must wear eye protection whenever working with fiber.

Eye Safety
Many people are concerned that the most dangerous part of fiber optic work was the chance you might get your eyes harmed by laser light in the fiber. They had confused communications fiber optics with optical fibers coupled to the output of high powered lasers used to cut metal, burn warts off skin at the doctors or perhaps they have seen too many science fiction movies.
In fact, most fiber optic systems do not have sufficient power to cause harm to your eyes and the light coming out of a fiber is expanding so the farther you are away from the end of the fiber, the lower the exposure. Having said that, consider yourself warned. In more recent times, some fiber optic systems are carrying sufficient power to be dangerous and some fiber optic inspection techniques which might be used on operating systems increase the chance of harm. But that is not the biggest danger facing installers.
The key to understanding the power issue is understanding power levels, wavelength of the light and the nature of light transmission in optical fiber. Fiber optic medical laser systems used for surgery and laser machining systems certainly have enough power to cause harm to your eyes, as well as burn off warts or machine some types of materials. Those systems use very high power lasers, often CO_2 lasers, which emit radiation at a wavelength that is really heat not light, around 10 microns wavelength. This wavelength is readily absorbed by materials and can heat them quickly, cutting those materials easily.
Fiber optic communications systems use much less power. First of all, most sources used in fiber optics are optimized for modulation speed, not absolute power. Premises cabling with multimode fiber and LED sources has very low power levels, too low to be a hazard. Higher speed premises links use VCSEL lasers, which are still quite low in power levels, and generally harmless. Most telco links use lasers with power levels slightly more than VCSELs.
Two types of links have high power, as much as 100 times more than other communications systems, and they are CATV or video links at 1550 nm and telco long distance links using dense wavelength division multiplexing (DWDM.) The CATV or video links used in fiber to the home (FTTH - read

more) may use fiber amplifiers (read more) that boost the power to very high levels, potentially dangerous the eye. Telco DWDM links are used on extremely long distance links (read more). They not only use fiber amplifiers for boosting the power, but they have many different signals operating at different wavelengths carried in one singlemode fiber. Any one wavelength may not be a problem, but the sum of 16, 32 or 64 individual wavelengths can be very powerful.

The next issue is focusing the light from a fiber into your eye. Light exiting an optical fiber spreads out in a cone, the angle of which is determined by the transmission characteristics of the fiber as determined by the numerical aperture. As your eye gets further from the end of the fiber, the amount of radiation it receives is inversely proportional to the square of the distance; double the distance and cut the power by 1/4, ten times the distance reduces the power to about 1%. You do not have to be far away from the fiber for the power to be reduced to low, harmless levels.

Because the light is exiting the fiber in a cone-shaped beam, the eye cannot focus it on the retina. This is unlike the typical lab laser or laser pointer that shines a narrow, collimated beam that does not spread out; a beam your eye can easily focus on the retina, causing temporary blindness.

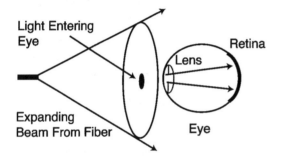

Finally, there is an issue of wavelength. Your eye cannot see many of the wavelengths used in fiber optics because the eye is sensitive to light in the blue to red region of the spectrum while fiber optic systems operate in the infrared. The liquid in your eye which is mostly water, which absorbs light in the infrared heavily. Light from most fiber optic sources will be absorbed by this liquid, so any potential harm is likely to come to the lens or cornea, not the retina.

While the expanding beam of the light exiting the fiber makes it less of an issue for direct viewing, using a fiber inspection microscope can be a problem. A microscope will focus virtually all the light back into the eye. Many microscopes used in fiber optics, therefore, have filters to absorb any infrared (IR) light that could be harmful. Be wary of inexpensive microscopes which may not have IR blocking filters.

To be certain fibers are safe to inspect or work with, always check fibers in an operating network with a fiber optic power meter to ensure no light is present before inspecting any connector with a microscope.

Bare Fiber Safety

Fiber optics installation, however, is not without risks. The more common problem is getting scraps of fiber in your eye when working with fiber. While few fiber optic systems have harmful levels of power, every termination and splice produces shards (scraps) of optical fiber which is potentially very harmful to your eyes and skin or may stick in your clothing and be carried to other locations where it may be harmful to others.

These shards of fiber are tiny, thin and often very sharp where they broke off the fiber. They can easily puncture your skin, burying themselves deep enough to be difficult to pull out, if only you could see them. Being transparent they practically disappear once imbedded in your skin. In most parts of your body, they merely become a nuisance, perhaps infecting or causing an irritating bump, until they eventually work themselves out.

Around your eye, however, they can be much more difficult to find and remove. The tears that wet your eyes make the transparent glass shards practically impossible to find and remove. The sharp ends of the fiber may cause it to imbed itself in the eye or surrounding tissue, making it even more difficult to remove. Unlike metallic particles, they cannot be removed with magnets,

It is imperative to follow procedures that minimize the dangers to the eye. Always wear protective eyewear with side shields, even if you normally wear glasses, to prevent any flying shards from getting near your eyes. Be extremely careful whenever handling fibers, especially when stripping fiber or scribing and breaking fiber extending out of an adhesive connector. Instead of breaking it, scribe it gently, then slide your fingers up the connector ferrule, grasping the fiber and pulling it off. Then dispose of it carefully.

Most cleavers used for splicing or terminating prepolished/splice connectors hold the fiber after cleaving, so the only problem is disposing of it. We recommend using disposable containers like those used for soups at carry-out restaurants. Use it for all your fiber scraps and then seal it and dispose of it properly.

You can also set up your workplace to make it easier to avoid problems. Use a black plastic mat for a work surface. The dark background will make it easier to see the fibers you are working with and handle them more carefully. Any broken fibers that fall on the mat are easily found for disposal.

Some techs like to place a length of double stick tape or a loop of black electrical tape on the mat and stick fibers to the adhesive surface, then dispose of the tape when finished. I prefer to simply use a disposable container and place every fiber scrap into that container rather than leave them exposed on the work surface.

Other Considerations for Safety

Chemicals: Fiber optic splicing and termination use various chemical cleaners and adhesives as part of the processes. Normal handling procedures for these substances should be observed. Even simple isopropyl alcohol, used as a cleaner, is flammable and should be handled carefully. Manufacturers will supply "material safety data sheets" (MSDS) on request or they may be found on the Internet.

Splicing hazards: Fusion splicers use an electric arc to make splices, so care must be taken to insure no flammable gasses are present in the space where fusion splicing is done.

No Smoking: Smoking should also not be allowed around fiber optic work. The ashes from smoking contribute to the dirt problems with fibers, in addition to the possible presence of combustible substances (and, of course, the health risks.)

Electrical Hazards: Installation of fiber optic cabling does not normally involve electrical hazards unless the cable includes conductors. However, these cables are often installed in proximity to electrical and conductive cables. Whenever you are near these cables, there is always a potential shock hazard. Be careful! If you are not familiar with electrical safety, we recommend you take a course on the NEC (National Electrical Code) and safety practices for installers!

Fiber Optic Installation Safety Rules

This is all very important, important enough to have a few workplace rules for all fiber optic techs that can prevent workplace accidents:

- Work on a black work surface as it helps to find fiber scraps.
- Wear disposable aprons to minimize fiber particles on your clothing. Fiber particles on your clothing can later get into food, drinks, and/or be ingested by other means.
- Always wear safety glasses with side shields and protective gloves. Treat fiber optic splinters the same as you would treat glass splinters.
- Never look directly into the end of fiber cables until you are positive that there is no light source at the other end. Use a fiber optic power meter to make certain the fiber is dark. When using an optical tracer or continuity checker, look at the fiber from an angle at least 6 inches away from your eye to determine if the visible light is present..
- Only work in well ventilated areas.
- Contact lens wearers must not handle their lenses until they have thoroughly washed their hands.
- Do not touch your eyes while working with fiber optic systems until your hands have been thoroughly washed.
- Keep all combustible materials safely away from electrical devices including splicers, testers and curing ovens.

- Put all cut fiber pieces in a properly marked container for disposal.
- Thoroughly clean your work area when you are done.
- Do not smoke while working with fiber optic systems.
- Keep all food and beverages out of the work area. If fiber particles are ingested they can cause internal hemorrhaging.

Installing Fiber Optic Cable

Receiving Fiber Optic Cabling and Equipment on Site
Fiber Optic equipment and components are subject to damage by improper handling or storage and must be handled accordingly.

Receipt
Fiber optic cable, equipment and supplies should be scheduled for delivery to the work site as closely to the time of use as possible to minimize possible damage from other construction, weather or theft. Coordinating deliveries can be difficult so delivery to a staging area offsite or providing a locked storage container onsite should be arranged. When initially received, all fiber optic components should be carefully inspected for damage and tested for continuity or loss if damage is suspected. Ensure that all components and parts have been shipped, received, match quantities ordered (e.g. fiber optic cable contains the number and type of fiber ordered and is the length ordered), and that any discrepancies or damaged goods are noted, the supplier notified and replaced as required.

Handling Fiber Optic Cables
Handle reels of fiber optic cable with care. All reels, regardless of size or length, should have both ends of the cable available for continuity testing. A fiber tracer or visual fault locator and bare fiber adapters can be used for continuity testing.
The cable reels should be moved carefully to avoid damage to the cable. Move small, lightweight spools of fiber optic cable by hand. Move larger reels with appropriate lifting equipment or using two or more installers skilled in the moving operation. Lifting equipment should only move reels with a matched set of slings or chokers, attached to an appropriately sized piece of pipe inserted into the hole in the center of the reel. Slings and chokers should never be attached around the spooled cable area of the reel.

Storage
All equipment and cabling should be stored in a clean and dry location, protected from harsh environments such as extremes of cold and heat. Due to the value of the cable and potential for theft, all components should be in secure storage with guards provided when or where necessary.

General Guidelines For Installing Fiber Optic Cable
Fiber optic cables are installed in so many different applications that generalizing on how to install fiber is very difficult, so this book will try to cover universal concerns and mention specifics where appropriate.
Fiber optic cable may be installed indoors or outdoors using several different installation processes. Outdoor cable may be direct buried, pulled or blown into conduit or innerduct, or installed aerially between poles. Indoor cables can be installed in raceways, cable trays above ceilings or under floors, placed in hangers, pulled into conduit or innerduct or blown though special ducts with compressed gas. The installation process will depend on the nature of the installation and the type of cable being used.
Installation methods for wire and optical fiber communications cables are similar. Fiber cable is designed to be pulled with much greater force than copper wire if pulled correctly, but excess stress on the cable may harm the fibers, potentially causing eventual failure. Particular care should be taken during installation to prevent exceeding the bend radius or kinking the cable which can harm the fibers.

Installation Guidelines
Follow the cable manufacturer's recommendations as no one knows how to handle cable as well as the company which made it. Fiber optic cable is often custom-designed for the installation and the manufacturer may have specific instructions on its installation.
Check the cable length to make sure the cable being pulled is long enough for the planned cable run. Try to complete the installation in one pull if possible. Prior to any installation, assess the route carefully to determine the methods of installation and obstacles likely to be encountered.

Pulling Tension
Cable manufacturers install special strength members, usually aramid yarn (Dupont Kevlar), to absorb the stress of pulling the cable. Fiber optic cable should only be pulled by these strength members unless the cable design allows pulling by a grip on the jacket. Any other method may put stress on the fibers and harm them.
Swivel pulling eyes should be used to attach the pulling rope or tape to the cable to prevent cable twisting during the pull.
Cables should not be pulled by the jacket unless it is specifically approved by the cable manufacturers and an approved cable grip, often called a "Kellems Grip," is used. These grips are usually tied to the strength members also.
Tight buffer cable can be pulled by the jacket in premises applications if a large (~40 cm, 8 in.) spool is used as a pulling mandrel. Wrap the cable around the spool 5 times and hold gently when pulling.
Do not exceed the maximum pulling tension rating. Consult the cable manufacturer and suppliers of conduit, innerduct, and cable lubricants for

guidelines on tension ratings and lubricant use.
When pulling long lengths of cable in conduit or innerduct (up to
approximately 3 miles or 5 kilometers in the outside plant, hundreds of
meters in premises cabling), use proper cable lubricants but make certain
it is compatible with the cable jacket. If possible, use an automated puller
with tension control and/or a breakaway pulling eye. On very long OSP runs
(farther than approximately 2.5 miles or 4 kilometers), pull from the middle out
to both ends or use an automated fiber puller at intermediate point(s) for a
continuous pull.
When laying loops of fiber on a surface during a pull, use "figure-8" loops to
prevent twisting the cable.

Twisting Cable
Do not twist the cable. Twisting the cable can stress the fibers. Tension on
the cable and pulling ropes can cause twisting. Use a swivel pulling eye to
connect the pull rope to the cable to prevent pulling tension causing twisting
forces on the cable.

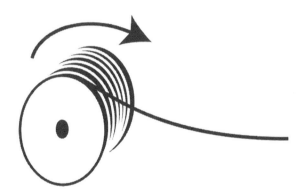

Roll the cable off the spool instead of spinning it off the spool end to prevent
putting a twist in the cable for every turn on the spool. When laying cable
out for a long pull, use a "figure-8" on the ground to prevent twisting. The
figure 8 puts a half twist in on one side of the 8 and takes it out on the other,
preventing twists.

Installing Swivel Pulling Eyes on Fiber Optic Cable
Cable manufacturers install special strength members, usually aramid yarn
(Dupont Kevlar), for pulling. Fiber optic cable should only be pulled by these
strength members unless the cable design allows pulling by the jacket. Any
other method may put stress on the fibers and harm them.
Swivel pulling eyes should be used to attach the pulling rope or tape to the
cable to prevent cable twisting during the pull.

Procedure For Installing Swivel Pulling Eyes:

Strip the cable jacket and cut back all fibers to the end of the jacket, leaving the aramid strength members only.

Separate the aramid yarn into two bundles and loop it through the swivel eve in opposite directions.

Tie knots in each bunch at the eye and loop the strength members back to the cable jacket.

Tape the strength members along the jacket and up to the pulling eye.

How To "Figure 8" Cable for Intermediate Pulls in OSP Installations

On very long OSP runs, typically longer than approximately 2.5 miles or 4 kilometers, it may be necessary to use an automated fiber puller at intermediate point(s) for a continuous pull or pull from the middle out to both ends (midspan pull.) When laying loops of fiber on a surface during a pull, use "figure-8" loops to prevent twisting the cable. The figure 8 puts a half twist in on one side of the 8 and takes it out on the other, preventing twists.

| Pull Cable, Lay On Ground in "8" | Flip Cable On Ground | Pull End To Next Point |

Use this procedure for pulling from one end:

Pull the cable out of the conduit or innerduct and lay on the ground in a large "figure 8" pattern. The size of the "8" will be determined by the size and stiffness of the cable, but 6-12 feet (2-4 m) is a common size. The end of the cable will be against the ground - you might want a tarp or plastic sheet to keep the cable clean. Pull slowly and carefully lay the cable in the figure 8 pattern to keep it from becoming kinked.

Using several installers, pick up the cable and flip it over so the end to be pulled to the next location is on top.
Attach the end to the pull rope with appropriate swivel pulling eyes and continue the pull.

For a midspan pull, use these directions:
This procedure eliminates having to flip the cable in the Figure 8 on the ground over.
Place the cable reel a mid point on the long span (ensuring the maximum pulling length in either direction would not be exceeded).
Pull the one end of cable through the conduit to one end of the span.
Roll the cable off the reel and Figure 8 the remaining cable on the ground.
The end on the cable will be on the top of the figure 8.
Pull the second end of the cable through the conduit to the other end of the span.

Bend Radius
Do not exceed the cable bend radius. Fiber optic cable can be broken when kinked or bent too tightly, especially during pulling. If no specific recommendations are available from the cable manufacturer, the cable should not be pulled over a bend radius smaller than twenty (20) times the cable diameter.
After completion of the pull, the cable should not have any bend radius smaller than ten (10) times the cable diameter.

Vertical Cable Runs
Drop vertical cables down rather than pulling them up whenever possible.
Support cables at frequent intervals to prevent excess stress on the jacket.
Support can be provided by cable ties (tightened snugly, not tightly enough to deform the cable jacket) or Kellems grips. Use service loops can to assist in gripping the cable for support and provide cable for future repairs or rerouting.

Installing Premises Cable in Cable Trays
Fiber optic cable is often installed in cable trays in premises applications.
Cable trays should not be shared with copper communications cables as their weight may harm the fiber cables. Likewise, large quantities of fiber cables in a tray may put too much pressure on the cables on the bottom. In applications where cable trays are used for copper communications cables, it may be possible to suspend lightweight fiber cables below the cable trays.

Use of Innerduct
It may be prudent to install critical indoor fiber optic cables inside bright orange "innerduct" to ease cable installation and protect it from future damage. Bright orange innerduct will identify fiber optic cable to any workers

at a later date and possible prevent damage. The additional initial cost of the innerduct may be offset by the simplification of the installation saving worker time.

Use Of Cable Ties
Fiber optic cables, like all communications cables, are sensitive to compressive or crushing loads. Cable ties used with many cables, especially when tightened with an installation tool, are harmful to fiber optic cables, causing attenuation and potential fiber breakage. When used, cable ties should be hand tightened to be snug but loose enough to be moved along the cable by hand. Then the excess length of the tie should be cut off to prevent future tightening. Hook-and-loop fastener ties are preferred for fiber optic cables, as they cannot apply crush loads sufficient to harm the cable.

Fire Stopping
Indoor cables will have to meet fire codes and pass inspection, so every cable that penetrates a fire-rated wall will have to be firestopped. All telecommunications firestopping must comply with applicable codes and standards. All penetrations must be protected by approved firestops. Fire stopping compounds
and devices shall be used whenever a fire separation has been breached by an installation. In most locals the breaching of a fire separation will require physical monitoring until it has been repaired. Check with the "Authority Having Jurisdiction" for specific requirements on the project before commencing work.

Grounding and Bonding
Conductive cables require proper grounding and bonding for applicable conductors. Although most fiber optic cables are not conductive, any metallic hardware used in fiber optic cabling systems (such as wall-mounted termination boxes, racks, and patch panels) must be grounded. Ground systems shall be designed as specified by the NEC and other applicable codes and standards. Most telecom rooms have a grounding bus bar which has a high quality building ground and connections to devices that require grounding.

Termination and Splicing

The processes of termination and splicing are covered in detail in Chapter 7. Terminations and splices in the field have no unusual requirements other than a need to find adequate dust-free space with moderate temperatures for working.

Splicing

Outside plant splicing is usually done in a special splicing trailer or truck. Inside the truck is a climate-controlled splicing lab with adequate bench space for working with the cables and splice closures. Sometimes, it's necessary to splice in the open, in a small tent or even in an aerial bucket. The installer has to be able to cope with the conditions found in the installation. In extremely cold conditions, a heated facility will probably be necessary as cables become stiff and equipment hard to operate. Hot climates may be easier on the processes but are equally uncomfortable for the installer.

Ideally splices should be tested with an OTDR as soon as they are made and before placing it in a splice tray. Fusion splicers give an estimate of splice loss, but it's just an estimate. The OTDR can confirm the quality of the splice, giving the installer an assurance that the splice is good and the splice closure will not have to be reopened to redo a bad splice.

Extreme care should be taken when placing splices in splice trays and arranging buffer tubes or fibers in the closure. One problem that occurs much too often is the fibers are broken as the trays and closure are assembled. Finding breaks in fibers inside the closure is difficult since they are too close to the splice to be resolved by an OTDR. If the splice is near enough to allow tracing with a visual fault locator, it may be found with visual inspection.

Cables must be secured to the splice closure and sealed properly. Generally loose tube cables will have the tubes extending from the entrance of the closure to the tray, where they are secured, then approximately 1 meter of bare fibers are organized in the tray after splicing. Care must be taken to properly bond electrical conductors such as the armor on some cables or center metallic strength members to the closure and at each end.

All closures must be sealed to prevent moisture entry. Closures must be properly secured, with the location being determined by the installation type, and excess cable properly coiled and stored. This may be in a pedestal or vault, on a pole or tower or buried underground.

Termination

Termination, at least, is generally done inside a building near the communications equipment, whether terminating outside cable plants or premises cables. The installer may still have problems with finding adequate space, for example in a telecom room with rows of patch panel and equipment racks. Hopefully, the cable installer has provided service loops for each cable to allow the cables to be brought to an open area for termination. Many installers use portable fold-up tables or rolling carts to create a workspace where they can reach the ends of the cables.

If the building is still under construction, dust can be a problem. Even in completed buildings, air conditioning systems can blow dust around. Be alert for dust and if working in a dusty environment is necessary, clean all the tools, polishing film and connectors as often as necessary.

If terminating singlemode cables by fusion splicing pigtails on each fiber, follow the same cautions on placing splices or fibers in cable trays and closures to prevent damage. For direct termination of 900 micron buffered multimode fibers in a distribution cable, allow adequate length to store excess fiber lengths and take care to avoid tight bends that can cause problems with loss of fiber failure in the future.

Like splices, each connector should be checked when the fiber termination is completed. Inspect every polished connector with a microscope to ensure polishing was done properly. If possible, test every prepolished/splice connector with a visual fault locator. After both ends of a fiber are terminated, end to end loss should be tested and documented. High loss connectors must be reterminated and it saves time to do it while the installer is already set up on the site.

Labeling and Documentation

It is usually the installer who terminates the cable that has the job of labeling each termination point. Ideally, the label has been created as part of the design of the cable plant and the installer only has to match the color codes of the fibers to the label, and, if not already placed, stick the label on the patch panel at the appropriate place. This is an important process, as the designation on each fiber will be used to record test data, connection to equipment and be followed during later moves, adds and changes. Doors to patch panels should be marked as to usage and include warnings regarding authorized entry.

Cleaning Up The Job Site

After terminating or splicing cables, the installer should carefully clean up the job site and leave it at least as clean as they found it, preferably cleaner. All scraps, especially fiber scraps which should be sealed in disposable containers, must be removed from the site.

Saving Excess Components

Any excess components should be saved for future use, especially restoration. Connectors and cables can be stored along with cable plant documentation so any restoration in the future will have compatible components for use in splicing or terminating cables.

Testing the Installed Fiber Optic Cable Plant

During the design phase, each cable run should have a loss budget calculated based on the component specifications. After installation, it is necessary to test each fiber in all fiber optic cables for verification of proper installation by comparing measured loss to the calculated loss from the loss budget.

Typically, the installer will perform the following tests:
Continuity testing to determine that the fiber routing and/or polarization is correct and documentation is proper.
End-to-end insertion loss using an OLTS power meter and source. Test multimode cables using TIA/EIA 526-14 Method B, and singlemode cables using TIA/EIA 526-7 unless connector-test equipment compatibility requires another reference method. Total loss should be less than the calculated maximum loss for the cable based on loss budget calculations using appropriate standards or customer specifications. If testing shows variances from expected losses, troubleshoot the problems and correct them.
Optional OTDR testing may be used to verify cable installation and splice performance. However, OTDR testing shall not be used to determine cable loss. Use of an OTDR in premises applications may be inappropriate if cables are short. An experienced OTDR technician should determine the appropriateness of the usage.
If the design documentation does not include cable plant length, and this is not recorded during installation, read the length from the distance markings on the cable jackets or test the length of the fiber using the length feature available on an OTDR or some OLTSs.

Continuity Testing
Perform continuity testing of optical fibers using a visual fiber tracer, visual fault locator, or OLTS power meter and source. Trace the fiber from end to end through any interconnections to ensure that the path is properly installed, and that polarization and routing are correct and documented.

Insertion Loss
Insertion loss refers to the optical loss of the installed fibers when measured with a test source and power meter (OLTS). Test multimode cables using TIA/EIA 526-14, preferably Method B (but always document the method used), and singlemode cables using TIA/EIA 526-7 (single mode).

Test multimode fiber at 850 and 1300 nm, and singlemode fiber at 1310 and 1550 nm, unless otherwise required by other standards or customer requirements.
Test reference test cables before testing to verify quality and clean them often.
Cabling intended for use with high speed systems using laser sources may be tested with appropriate laser sources to ensure that tests verify performance with that type
of source.

OTDR Testing
The optical time domain reflectometer (OTDR) uses optical radar-like techniques to create a picture of a fiber in an installed fiber optic cable. The picture, called a signature or trace, contains data on the length of the fiber, loss in fiber segments, connectors, splices and loss caused by stress during installation. OTDRs are used to verify the quality of the installation or for troubleshooting. However, OTDR testing alone shall not be used to determine cable loss.
OTDR testing should only performed by trained personnel, using certified equipment designed for the purpose. The technicians performing the tests should be trained not only in operation of the OTDR equipment, but also in the setup of OTDR test parameters and the interpretation of OTDR traces. OTDRs have limited distance resolution and may show confusing artifacts when testing short cables typical of premises applications. If OTDR testing of premises cables is desired, experienced personnel should evaluate the appropriateness of the tests.

Administration, Management, and Documentation

Documentation of the fiber optic cable plant is an integral part of the design, installation and maintenance process for the fiber optic network. Documenting the installation properly will facilitate installation, allow better planning for upgrading, simplify testing and future moves, adds and changes.
Unless the user specifies otherwise, documentation of the fiber optic cable plant should follow ANSI/TIA/EIA-606, Administration Standard for the Telecommunications Infrastructure of Commercial Buildings.
Fiber optic cables, especially those used for backbone cables, may contain many fibers that connect a number of different links going to several different locations with interconnections at patch panels or splice closures. The fiber optic cable plant should be documented as to the exact path that every fiber in each cable follows, including intermediate connections and every connector type. Documentation should also include insertion loss data and optional OTDR traces.

Review Questions
True/False
Indicate whether the statement is true or false.

_____1.   One should be able to rely the contractor to not only do the installation but to assist in the design of the network and help choose components and vendors.

_____2.   All metal components of the cabling system installed in a equipment or telecom room must be grounded and bonded.

_____3.   A single outside plant link may include several types of installation, including aerial, buried and underground.

Multiple Choice
Identify the choice that best completes the statement or answers the question.

_____4.   _____ will facilitate installation, allow better planning for upgrades and simplify testing.
A. Good workmanship
B. Low loss connectors
C. Safe workplace procedures
D. Proper documentation

_____5.   Outside plant cabling can be installed by _____
A. Pulling in underground in conduit
B. Direct burial
C. Aerial suspension
D. All of the above

_____6.   The protective gear every VDV installer must always wear is _____.
A. Eye protection
B. Plastic apron
C. Gloves
D. Shoe covers

_____7.   The fiberglass rod inside many fiber optic cables is for _____.
A. Increasing the pulling tension
B. Limit bend radius to preventing kinking
C. Winding the fibers around
D. Tying to messenger cables

_____8.   To prevent the cable from twisting when pulling it _____.
           A. Use a swivel eye
           B. Pull with braided rope
           C. Spin the cable off the spool
           D. Lubricate the cable

_____9.   On long pulls, at intermediate points, why do you lay the cable in
           a "figure 8'?
           A. Keep it from getting tangled with the pull rope
           B. Make it easier to spray on lubricant
           C. Keep workers from walking on it
           D. Prevent it from twisting

_____10.   Under pulling tension, the bend radius should not be less than

           _____.
           A. 5 times the cable diameter
           B. 10 times the cable diameter
           C. 20 times the cable diameter
           D. 50 times the cable diameter

_____11.   Underground cables are pulled in conduit that is buried
           underground, usually _____ deep to reduce the likelihood of
           accidentally being dug up. .
           A. 3-4 feet (1-1.2 meters)
           B. 1-2 feet (0.3-0.5 meter)
           C. 6-8 feet (2-2.5 meters)
           D. As deep as the local building codes allow

_____12.   Long cable pulls in conduit may require _____ or _____ and
           your installers need to know how to "figure 8" cable to prevent
           kinking.
           A. Heavy-duty mechanical pullers
           B. Trucks or tractors to pull the cable
           C. Lubricants
           D.   Intermediate pulls

_____13.   Most fiber optic cables do not have sufficient strength to allow
           direct aerial installation, but _____ or _____ can be used to
           install them aerially.
           A. Rubber clamps
           B. Pole-mounted grips
           C. Lashing to another cable
           D. Lashing to messenger strands

_____14.   Cable ties used on fiber optic cables _____.
A. Should be tightened firmly to prevent cable movement
B. Can be used to hang cables from J-hooks or cable trays
C. Should be rated for the weight of the cables
D. Can harm cables if too tight, so they should be hand-tightened

_____15.   Where the _____ is appropriate, direct burial installation allows for fast installation.
A. Local permit
B. Ground
C. Cost
D. Cable

_____16.   Aerial cables are subject to continual tension as well as extra tension caused by _____, _____ and in some areas _____.
A. Temperature changes
B. Wind
C. Rain
D. Weight of ice

_____17.   Each completed splice on an installed cable should be tested with an _____, preferably immediately after it is spliced.
A. OLTS
B. OTDR
C. VFL
D. CD test set

_____18.   If at all possible, _____ before installing any other cables on utility poles. .
A. Look for other installation options
B. Have the power cables shut down
C. Notify the proper authorities
D. Notify the owners of other cables

Additional Study And Projects

The *FOA/NECA 301 Fiber Optic Installation Standard* available from NECA (necanet.org) covers guidelines for installation concisely.

As part of a lab, build a complete fiber optic link using components typical of those used in real world applications. Include pulling or placing cable. terminations and splices.

Search for articles on fiber optic applications and review how projects are done.

Find websites for installation equipment manufacturers and review their videos or promotional instructions.

Appendix A
KSAs for CFOT + CFospT

The ability to perform any job requires certain abilities, knowledge and skills, commonly referred to as "KSAs." For the fiber optic technician, these KSAs have been determined from over 30 years of experience in actual installations. The FOA has developed this list to provide training organizations and instructors a list of topics that should be included in a basic training curriculum, as for CFOT certification and specialist training such as the CFospT for outside plant installation. For those working in the field who wish to become FOA-certified, it is a list of relevant topics for study, whether using a textbook or the FOA Online Reference Guide.

Knowledge

Fiber Optic Jargon
        Fiber optic terms
        Metric System

Fiber Optic Communications Systems
        How communications systems use light to transfer information
        OSP Systems: Telco including wireless antennas, CATV, Utility, Municipal networks, etc.
        Components and their functions in a datalink
                Sources: LED, Laser (FP, DFB, VCSEL)
                Detectors (photodiode, APD; Si, Ge, InGaAs)
        What determines how well a datalink transmits data

Optical Fiber
        Types of optical fiber
                SI MM , GI MM, SM
        Basic specifications that affect transmission
                Attenuation, dispersion
        Choosing the appropriate fiber for the system

Fiber Optic Cable
        Types of cables and their applications
                Tight buffer (simplex, zipcord, distribution, breakout)
                Loose tube (loose tube, ribbon)
        Specialty (OPGW, ADSS, underwater, air blown, flat saw-groove cable and conduit)
        Relevant specifications for applications
                Water blocking, pulling strength, armoring, etc.
        Choosing the proper cable for application

Conduit, innerduct, cable pullers, pulling eyes, lubricants, etc.

Termination and Splicing
    Uses
    Relevant performance
        Loss, reflectance, strength

    Splicing processes
        Mechanical
        Fusion
        Mass (ribbon) fusion
    Hardware, closures
    Fitting splices in trays, trays in closures, sealing, pressure testing
    Installing on Poles,
    Installing and racking cable

    Termination
    Connector types
        ST, SC, LC, MTP, etc.
    Termination processes
        Spliced-on pigtails
        Adhesive (epoxy, anaerobic, HotMelt)
        Prepolished splice
        Prefab systems
    Hardware

Testing
    Microscope inspection
    Visual tracing and fault location
    Fiber identification
    Insertion loss testing
    OTDR testing, setup for long cables
    Long haul SM testing for CD and PMD

Fiber Optic Network Design
    Evaluating communications system requirements
    Aerial, direct buried, pulled in conduit, submarine and other
    installations
    Designing the proper cable plant
    Layout
    Choosing components
    Loss budgets
    Documentation

Fiber Optic Installation
       Evaluating needs based on cable plant design
       Planning for the installation
              Safety
              Eye Safety
              Tool safety
              Chemical safety
              Disposal of materials
       Basic knowledge of Codes, standards, and Regulations
       Installation tools and equipment: cable pullers, plows, bucket trucks, splicing trailers, directional boring, etc.
       Performing the installation
       Documenting the cable plant

Skills

General Installation
       Using ladders, bucket trucks, etc.
       Climbing poles and towers for aerial installation

Fiber Optic Cable
       Attaching pulling eye and rope to a cable by strength members
       Pulling cable
       Preparing cable for splicing or termination (stripping cable and fiber)

Spicing
       Preparing cable for splicing
       Mechanical splicing
       Fusion splicing
       Fitting splices in trays, trays in closures, sealing

Termination
       Identifying connectors
       Preparing cables for termination
       Breakout kits on loose tube cable
       Installing connectors
       Inspecting connectors

Grounding
       Cables with metallic armor
       Enclosures
       Hardware on poles, etc

Distribution buildings

Testing
>Microscope inspection
>Visual tracing and fault location
>Insertion loss testing
>OTDR testing and troubleshooting
>PMD Testing
>CD Testing

Abilities

Good eyesight with color rendition
Good hand-eye coordination
Be able to use hand and power tools
Analytical skills
Follow directions
Patience
Work in adverse conditions

Appendix B
Fiber To The Home

Since the first installations of fiber optic networks in the late 1970s, the goal of the fiber optic industry has been to install fiber optics all the way to the home. From an economic standpoint, fiber was immediately cost effective in the long-distance networks. Compared to copper or digital radio, fiber's high bandwidth and low attenuation easily offset its higher cost. Compared to copper wire used in telephony, fiber could carry thousands of times more phone conversations hundreds of times further, making the cost of a phone connection over fiber only a few percent as much as transmitting over copper. It took only a few years before fiber optics dominated the long distance market. Crews buried cables underground or ran aerial cables on poles nonstop for a decade to upgrade long distance service. At the same time, technology was developed for submarine cables and by the late 1980s, all overseas communications expansion was done by fiber optics, replacing copper cables and satellites. Today, virtually all long distance communications is over the installed fiber optic network.

The next step was connecting local central offices, the link between subscribers and the switched phone network. Around the time the long distance networks were being completed, consumer use of the Internet took off. Metropolitan phone networks became overloaded quickly and fiber optics was ready to provide the expansion capability. The scope of metropolitan fiber optic installations was obvious to anyone driving around town, as it was hard to drive anywhere without encountering roads torn up for the installation of conduit and fiber optic splicing trucks blocking the roadways.

Then the telecom/Internet "bubble" burst in 2001. The Internet "bubble" that caused the telecom "bubble" and thereby the fiber optic "bubble" caused the downfall of a tremendous number of companies and left the industry with a glut of installed fiber capacity as well as fiber optic component manufacturing capacity. The cost of fiber optic components declined as supply outstripped demand, setting the stage for the next big application for fiber optics.

Many homes today are connected with aging, low- performance copper telephone wire that cannot support DSL connection speeds that allow the phone companies to compete with the cable modems used by CATV companies for broadband access. These aging phone lines not only cannot carry high bandwidth digital signals, they are extremely expensive to maintain just for POTS (plain old telephone service.) Savings in maintenance alone were projected by a Telcordia report to pay back the cost of installing fiber in under 20 years, irrespective of revenue from new services.

In addition, new network architectures have been developed that allow sharing expensive components for FTTH. A passive splitter that takes one input and broadcasts it to as many as 32 users cuts the cost of the links substantially by sharing, for example, one expensive laser and transmission equipment with up to 32 homes.

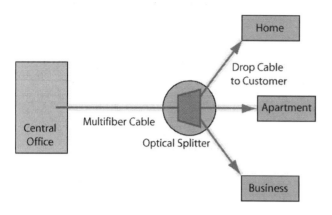

Each home needs to be connected to the local central office with singlemode fiber, perhaps through a local splitter. Every home will have a singlemode fiber link pulled or strung aerially to the phone company cables running down the street and a network interface device containing fiber optic transmitters and receivers will be installed on the outside of the house. The incoming cable needs to be terminated at the house, tested, connected to the interface and the service tested.

Fiber is now gaining acceptance in the final frontier of telephone networks, the "last mile"—the connection to the home. Phone companies are now realizing the only choice for upgrading the subscriber connection is fiber to the home (FTTH).Phone companies such as Verizon have committed billions of dollars to connecting millions of home with fiber in the near future.

Right now, Verizon is the leader in the US in FTTH with their FiOS program, but the US trails many other countries around the world in converting to FTTH. Progress requires massive capital investment and training lots of people to install FTTH, or FTTP (fiber to the premises as they call it.) Even the CATV companies are considering fiber to replace aging coax, since the price is right and performance unlimited.

Besides the telcos, several other groups are attempting to install FTTH. Municipalities: Some of the first FTTH systems were installed by cities - progressive ones like Palo Alto did it at the request of their high-tech citizens, some did it to entice businesses to move there, like Anaheim, some did it (or are trying to) because they were not pleased with the service of telcos or CATV companies. The latter often found the telcos or CATV companies to be formidable opponents who did not always play fair! Most municipal FTTx projects use rights of way available to the city through city-owned utilities. FTTH is a considered a battleground by telcos and CATV companies: Whenever a city or private company proposes to install FTTH, they can expect to have to deal with the legal, advertising and technical staff of the current telco or CATV company protecting their franchises.

Utilities: Owning rights of way to the home convinced some utilities to try

FTTH or FTTC. Ethernet over power lines is becoming a option for power companies who can use power lines for the final connection to the home. FTTx is even becoming real for rural customers through rural electrical cooperatives.

CLECs (Competitive Local Exchange Carriers) install their own networks and can then sell connections to anyone they pass, but mostly focus on businesses which spend much more money on communications than households.

Private companies: There are private companies that will build municipal FTTH networks under an agreement with the city, similar to CATV agreements. In addition, some contractors building large subdivisions or apartments are installing FTTH with the assumption that they can connect with telecommunications companies for services to resell.

Fiber To The Home Architectures

New network architectures have been developed to reduce the cost of installing high bandwidth services to the home, often lumped into the acronym FTTx for "fiber to the x". These include FTTC for fiber to the curb, also called FTTN or fiber to the node, FTTH for fiber to the home and FTTP for fiber to the premises, using "premises" to include homes, apartments, condos, small businesses, etc. Let's begin by describing these network architectures.

FTTC: Fiber To The Curb (or Node, FTTN)

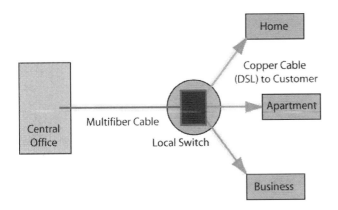

Fiber to the curb brings fiber to the curb, or just down the street, close enough for the copper wiring already connecting the home to carry DSL (digital subscriber line, or fast digital signals on copper.)

FTTC is less expensive than FTTH but depends on the quality of the copper wiring currently installed to the home and the length to reach from the node to the home. Newer homes that have good copper and are near where the DSL switch is located can expect good service. Homes with older copper or longer distances will have less available bandwidth.

However FTTC is easy to upgrade to FTTH.

FTTH Active Star Network

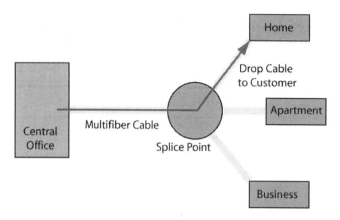

The simplest way to connect homes with fiber is to have a fiber link connecting every home to the phone company switches, either in the nearest central office (CO) or to a local active switch.

FTTH home run
The drawing above shows a home run connection from the home directly to the CO, while below, the home is connected to a local switch, like FTTC upgraded to fiber to the home.

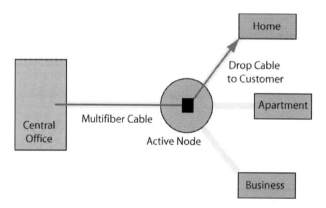

A home run active star network has one fiber dedicated to each home (or premises in the case of businesses, apartments or condos.) This architecture offers the maximum amount of bandwidth and flexibility, but at a higher cost, both in electronics on each end (compared to a PON architecture, described below) and the dedicated fiber(s) required for each home.

FTTH PON: Passive Optical Network

A PON system allows sharing expensive components for FTTH. A passive splitter that takes one input and splits it to broadcast to as many as 64 users cuts the cost of the links substantially by sharing, for example, one expensive laser with up to 32 homes. Because of all the splitters and since most systems are designed for AM video like CATV systems, non-reflective connectors (like the SC-APC angle-polished connector) are generally used.

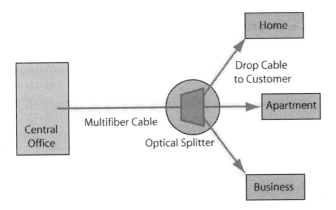

The splitter can be one unit in a single location as shown above or several splitters cascaded as shown below. Cascading is usually done when houses being served are clustered in smaller groups.

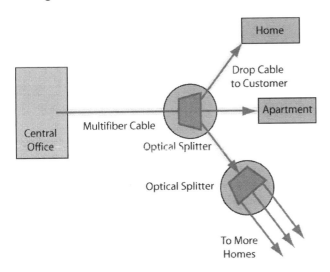

Each home needs to be connected to the local central office with singlemode fiber, through an optical splitter. Every home will have a singlemode fiber link pulled into underground conduit or strung aerially to the phone company cables running down the street. Verizon has pioneered installing prefabricated fiber links that require little field splicing.

Here is a fiber distribution system that has been spliced into cables connected to the local central office. The preterminated drop cable to the home connects to the closure on the pole and is usually lashed to the aerial telephone wire already connected to the home.

If the cable is underground, it will usually be pulled through conduit from connection to the distribution cable or the splitter to the home. Here a preterminated systems has two home drops connected to the distribution cable.

The splitter can be housed in a central office or a pedestal in the neighborhood near the homes served. Here is a typical pedestal that has connections to the CO, splitters and fibers out to each home in a sealed enclosure. The advantage of PONs is that this pedestal is passive - it does not require any power as would a switch or node for fiber to the curb.

A network interface device containing fiber optic transmitters and receivers will be installed on the outside of the house. The incoming cable needs to be terminated at the house, tested, connected to the interface and the service tested.

Below is the layout of a typical PON network with the equipment required at the CO, fiber distribution hub and the home. This drawing shows the location of the hardware used in creating a complete PON network and defines the network jargon.

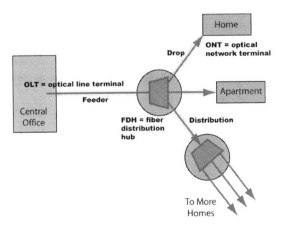

Triple Play Systems

Most FTTH systems are "triple play" systems offering voice (telephone), video (TV) and data (Internet access.) To provide all three services over one fiber, signals are sent bidirectionally over a single fiber using three separate wavelengths of light. Three different protocols are in use today, BPON, shown below, is the most popular, while EPON is used in some countries and GPON is predicted to become more popular in the future. Read more on PON protocols.

Downstream digital signals from the CO through the splitter to the home are sent at 1490 nm. This signal carries both voice and data to the home. Video on most current systems uses the same technology as CATV, an analog modulated signal, broadcast separately using a 1550 nm laser which may require a fiber amplifier to provide enough signal power to overcome the loss of the optical splitter. Upstream digital signals for voice and data are sent back to the CO from the home using an inexpensive 1310 nm laser. WDM couplers separate the signals at both the home and the CO.

As digital TV over the Internet (called IPTV for Internet-Protocol TV) becomes available, the separate 1550 nm TV signal will no longer be needed.

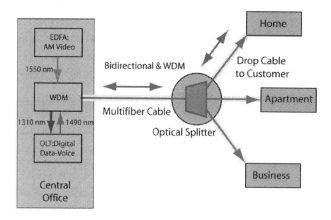

Fiber To The Home PON Types

Standards for PON Triple Play Systems

Most FTTH systems are so-called "triple play" systems offering voice (telephone), video (TV) and data (Internet access.) To provide all three services over one fiber, signals are sent bidirectionally over a single fiber using several wavelengths of light.

Type	Description	International Standard
BPON	Broadband PON	ITU-T G.983
GPON	Gigabit PON	TU-T G.984
EPON	Ethernet PON	IEEE 802.3ah (1 Gb/s) IEEE 802.3av (10Gb/s)

BPON uses ATM as the protocol. ATM is widely used for telephone networks and the methods of transporting all data types (voice, Internet, video, etc.) are well known. BPON operates at ATM rates of 155, 622 and 1244 Mb/s. Downstream digital signals from the CO through the splitter to the home are sent at 1490 nm. This signal carries both voice and data to the home. Video on most current systems uses the same technology as CATV, an analog modulated signal, broadcast separately using a 1550 nm laser which may require a fiber amplifier to provide enough signal power to overcome the loss of the optical splitter. Upstream digital signals for voice and data are sent back to the CO from the home using an inexpensive 1310 nm laser. WDM couplers separate the signals at both the home and the CO.

GPON, or gigabit-capable PON, uses an IP-based protocol and either ATM or GEM (GPON encapsulation method) encoding. Data rates of up to 2.5 Gb/s are specified and it is very flexible in what types of traffic it carries. GPON enables "triple play" (voice-data-video) and is the basis of most planned FTTP applications in the near future. In the diagram above, one merely drops the AM Video at the CO and carries digital video over the downstream digital link. EPON or Ethernet PON is based on the IEEE standard for Ethernet in the First Mile. It uses packet-based transmission at 1 Gb/s with 10 Gb/s under discussion. EPON is widely deployed in Asia. The system architecture is the same as GPON but data protocols are different.

RFOG: CATV's FTTH

CATV operators need something to combat their subscriber's clamoring for fiber to the home, which has lead to the development of RFOG, "RF over Glass." CATV standards have looked at PON architectures and the SCTE has proposed a standard for deploying a broadcast architecture of analog signals similar to PONs called RFoG for RF (radio frequency - i.e. FM) over Glass. RFOG is basically nothing more than an all-fiber HFC/cable modem system built with less expensive components now available thanks to the volume pricing of components used in FTTH. It's designed to operate over a standard telco PON (passive optical network) fiber architecture with short fiber lengths and including the losses of a FTTH PON splitter.

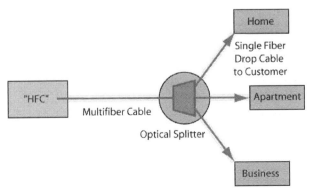

There is one interesting part of this approach. Now telcos and CATV companies can deliver the same services over the same cable plant using totally different technologies. But that means that office or apartment building owners, developers or even whole towns that might be considering installing FTTH infrastructure themselves and leasing the fiber to a service provider can have a choice of service providers. One cable network can support either CATV or telco systems – or even someone else for that matter. That opens up a big market for private fiber optic systems.

PONs in Premises Applications

The high volume of PON installations has led to a large amount of experience in installing and managing PONs and caused a big reduction in cost. PONs are now being used in corporate networks as LANs, phone systems and video systems, where they are similar to installations in multi-dwelling units or small residential areas.

Link Specifications for FTTx

Application	Parameter	TIA 492CAAB (OS2)		
	Nominal wavelength (nm)	1270/1310	1490	1550
EPON (IEEE 802.3AH) PX10 1,2	Channel attenuation (dB)	3.5	3	-
	Supportable distance m (ft)	10000 (32808)		
EPON (IEEE 802.3AH) PX20 1,2	Channel attenuation (dB)	7	6	-
	Supportable distance m (ft)	20000 (65616)		
10G EPON (IEEE 802.3AV) PR10 / PRX10 1,2	Channel attenuation (dB)	3.5	3	2.5
	Supportable distance m (ft)	10000 (32810)		
10G EPON (IEEE 802.3AV) PR20 / PRX20 1,2	Channel attenuation (dB)	7	6	5
	Supportable distance m (ft)	20000 (65616)		

10G EPON (IEEE 802.3AV) PR30 / PRX30 1,2	Channel attenuation (dB)	10.5	9	
	Supportable distance m (ft)	30000 (98424)		
GPON (ITU G.983) Class B+ 1,2	Channel attenuation (dB)	7	6	
	Supportable distance m (ft)	20000 (65616)		
GPON (ITU G.984) Class C+ 1,2	Channel attenuation (dB)	10.5	9	
	Supportable distance m (ft)	30000 (98424)		
10GPON (ITU G.987) Class N1 1,2	Channel attenuation (dB)	7		5
	Supportable distance m (ft)	20000 (65616)		
10GPON (ITU G.987) Class N2 1,2	Channel attenuation (dB)	10.5	9	
	Supportable distance m (ft)	30000 (98424)		
RFOG (SCTE IPS SP910) 1,2	Channel attenuation (dB)	7		5
	Supportable distance m (ft)	20000 (65616)		

PON Components
FTTH PONs use mostly conventional fiber optic components, some optimized for the application. The BPON use of analog video and higher bit rates in short singlemode links makes reflectance from connectors important, so many systems use APC (angled physical contact) connectors to reduce reflectance. Of course, the basis of a PON system is splitting the signal, so splitters are extremely important to PON systems.

PON Splitters
Splitters are passive optical branching devices which couple fibers in multiples, leading to their other name - couplers. They can be made from planar waveguides (flat pieces of optical material that geometrically divide the light as it passes through the material) or from fused fiber bundles (fused biconically tapered fiber couplers are made by wrapping fibers together and heating to melting temperatures in a controlled manner.)
Splitters are bidirectional. In the illustration above, light coming in one

direction will be split into four roughly equal outputs, while light coming from the other direction will be combined into the one fiber on the other side of the splitter - effectively becoming a combiner.

Splitters are available in 1:2, 1:4, 1:8, 1:16, 1:32 configurations. PON architectures are generally based on a maximum of 1:32 split. High split ratios are usually made by planar waveguide devices, while fused biconical tapered fiber couplers have smaller split ratios.

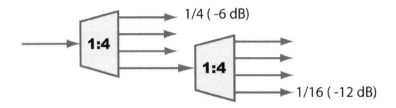

Splitters can be cascaded to achieve the desired split ratio, e.g. a 1:4 splitter then four 1:4 splitters is 1:16. Needless to say, if you split the light from one fiber into several fibers, the amount of light is divided, so the light in the several fibers is lower by the split ratio. In fact the loss is 3 dB per 2x split (3 dB is a 50% loss) plus a certain amount of "excess loss" caused by the inefficiency of the splitter - loss inside the splitter caused by the mechanism of the splitting.

Split Ratio	1:2	1:4	1:8	1:16	1:32
Ideal Loss (dB)	3	6	9	12	15
Actual Loss (dB)	4	7	11	15	19
Excess Loss (dB)	1	1	2	3	4

FTTx PON Testing

FTTx PON testing is similar to OSP testing but splitter and WDM add complexity as well as more loss to each link. FTTP PON networks can also be more complicated than simple OSP links, with WDM, splitters, etc. in a single link, so complete testing can include some components and installation issues not familiar to the usual OSP tech. In addition, once installed, adding users to a live network means testing cannot disrupt service. Thus testing may be as simple as checking power at the ONT on the subscriber's house with a power meter or just seeing if the ONT has a "green" connection light!

That ONT also has some intelligence that can be accessed from a remote location, allowing a service tech to initiate a loopback test to verify connections at any user. If only one user has a problem, a service tech is then sent there, while if all users are down, the tech is sent to the central office. Typical tests on a link include each coupler, and end-to-end link loss. Loss and reflectance are important if systems are using an AM video transmission system at 1550 nm, as it has a maximum tolerable loss and reflectance

before signals are noticeably affected. Tests may be necessary at all three wavelengths of operation: 1310 nm for upstream digital data, 1490 for downstream digital data and 1550 nm for AM video downstream.
Insertion loss is tested using an optical loss test set and OTDRs can be used if length is adequately long, to determine connection reflectance, fiber attenuation and troubleshoot problems. Many systems will take OTDR traces and store for troubleshooting.
The splitters confuse the OTDR so one must reverse OTDR test and shoot upstream toward the CO.

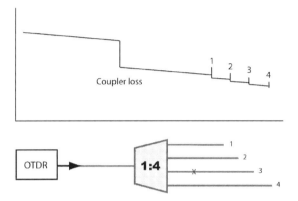

Using an OTDR to test every fiber in an OSP link is traditional, as the OTDR provides a picture of the losses in the fiber, locates loss events (connectors, splices and bending losses from improper installation), aids troubleshooting and provides a trace which can be stored for later troubleshooting and restoration. However, PON systems create problems for OTDRs. Shooting from the input of a PON splitter at the CO, the OTDR sees and adds together the backscatter traces from all the fibers. As a result, it becomes impossible to see individual fibers, and an event (connector, splice of bending loss) cannot be assigned to any individual fiber. Consider the "X" shown in fiber 3. If it was a loss or reflective event, it would show on the OTDR trace, but the operator would not know if were in fiber 1,2,3 or 4. The only unambiguous part of the OTDR trace shown is the end of fiber 4, the longest fiber, beyond the length of the next longest fiber, #3.

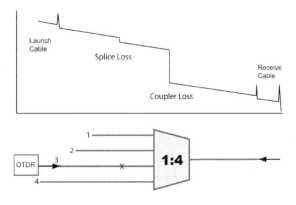

As a result, OTDRs are generally used on PONs from the subscriber end toward the CO to characterize the fiber path. However, the OTDR may also be used from the CO end, because, as you can see from the diagram above, it allows the operator to quickly characterize the length of each fiber link, providing actual fiber length to add to network diagrams for future troubleshooting. Special PON OTDRs will test at 1310, 1490 and 1550 nm. Some also test "out of band" at 1650 nm, which is more sensitive to bending losses and allows in-service testing with a filter to remove signal wavelengths. Since PONs are short, the OTDR needs very high resolution, usually obtained by having the shortest test pulse that will give adequate range.

Appendix C
Additional References For Training and Study
For FOA Certification or Additional Knowledge

As with any fast-moving technology, keeping abreast of the latest technology, techniques and products can be a daunting task. Here are some references which will assist you.

FOA Websites
The FOA website, www.thefoa.org, has a special section of the Online Fiber Optic Reference Guide (www.foaguide.org) with extensive pages on fiber optics and study guides for FOA Certifications as well as for those interested in refreshing or increasing their knowledge of fiber optics.
The FOA has also created an online learning site, Fiber U at www.fiberu.org, that offers online courses for self-study.
On the FOA website, you will also find links to other useful websites, including technical as well as product web sites, books, publications, etc.
The FOA has over 80 YouTube Videos including many lectures on fiber optics and premises cabling, demonstrations of how fiber actually works and directions for hands-on installation. The FOA YouTube channel is "thefoainc" and links to the videos are on the Table of Contents of the FOA Online Reference Guide.

FOA Textbooks
The FOA has published two other Reference Guides that are the references for FOA certifications.

The FOA Reference Guide to Fiber Optics is a general reference guide for fiber optics and the basic study guide for the CFOT certification.

The FOA Reference Guide to Premises Cabling is a reference guide for copper and fiber optic cabling and wireless as used in indoor applications and the basic study guide for the CPCT certification.

All FOA textbooks are available for purchase from most booksellers. Links to the FOA eStore are provided on the FOA home page and each individual book page.

FOA/NECA 301 Fiber Optic Installation Standard is a ANSI standard covering the installation of fiber optic cable networks written by the FOA in conjunction with the NECA NEIS standards series. It is available from NECA (www.

necanet.org). It is being revised for release late 2010.

Other Websites
Many organizations have websites with useful information. USAD/RUS has design and installation guides for OSP fiber optic cable installation. ITU has most telecom standards available online, for example, the international FTTx standards. TIA and some other standards groups charge for their standards but these are often explained on websites and in catalogs or papers by manufacturers who make products conforming to those standards. Since items on the web change continuously, giving exact references can be difficult, so we encourage you to search for appropriate terms.

Training Curriculum For Instructors
The FOA offers complete curriculum packages to simplify teaching fiber optic courses from this book. The curriculum packages include instructor guides, student manuals, PowerPoint slides, etc. Subjects available include basic fiber optics, advanced fiber optics and premises cabling. Details are available on the FOA website or by contacting the FOA.

Appendix D
Definitions of Terms

A
Absorption: That portion of fiber optic attenuation resulting of conversion of optical power to heat.

Analog: Signals that are continually changing, as opposed to being digitally encoded.

APC: Angled Physical Contact, APC Connector

Attenuation Coefficient: Characteristic of the attenuation of an optical fiber per unit length, in dB/km.

Attenuation: The reduction in optical power as it passes along a fiber, usually expressed in decibels (dB). See optical loss.

Attenuator: A device that reduces signal power in a fiber optic link by inducing loss.

Average power: The average over time of a modulated signal.

B
Back reflection, reflectance, optical return loss: Light reflected from the cleaved or polished end of a fiber caused by the difference of refractive indices of air and glass. Expressed in dB relative to incident power.

Backscattering: The scattering of light in a fiber back toward the source, used to make OTDR measurements.

Bandwidth: The range of signal frequencies or bit rate within which a fiber optic component, link or network will operate.

Bending loss, microbending loss: Loss in fiber caused by stress on the fiber bent around a restrictive radius.

Bit-error rate (BER): The fraction of data bits transmitted that are received in error.

Bit: An electrical or optical pulse that carries information.

Buffer: A protective coating applied directly on the fiber.

C
Cable: One or more fibers enclosed in protective coverings and strength members.

Cable Plant, Fiber Optic: The combination of fiber optic cable sections, connectors and splices forming the optical path between two terminal devices.

CATV: An abbreviation for Community Antenna Television or cable TV.

Chromatic dispersion: The temporal spreading of a pulse in an optical waveguide caused by the wavelength dependence of the velocities of light.

Cladding: The lower refractive index optical coating over the core of the fiber that "traps" light into the core. Connector: A device that provides for a demountable connection between two fibers or a fiber and an active device and provides protection for the fiber.

Connector: A device which terminates an optical fiber and allows temporary joining of fibers with like terminations.

Core: The center of the optical fiber through which light is transmitted.

Coupler: An optical device that splits or combines light from more than one fiber.

Cutback method: A technique for measuring the loss of bare fiber by measuring the optical power transmitted through a long length then cutting back to the source and measuring the initial coupled power.

Cutoff wavelength: The wavelength beyond which singlemode fiber only supports one mode of propagation.

CWDM: Coarse wavelength division multiplexing using lasers spaced widely over the range of 1260 to 1670 nm.

D

dBm: Optical power referenced to 1 milliwatt.

Decibel (dB): A unit of measurement of optical power which indicates relative power on a logarithmic scale, sometimes called dBr. dB=10 log (power ratio)

Detector: A photodiode that converts optical signals to electrical signals.

DFB laser: Distributed feedback laser used for high speed and long distance transmitters.

Digital: Signals encoded into discrete bits.

Dispersion: The temporal spreading of a pulse in an optical waveguide. May be caused by modal or chromatic effects.

E

EDFA: Erbium-doped fiber amplifier, an all optical amplifier for 1490-1650 nm SM transmission systems.

Edge-emitting diode (E-LED): A LED that emits from the edge of the semiconductor chip, producing higher power and narrower spectral width.

End finish: The quality of the end surface of a fiber prepared for splicing or terminated in a connector.

Equilibrium modal distribution (EMD): Steady state modal distribution in multimode fiber, achieved some distance from the source, where the relative power in the modes becomes stable with increasing distance.

ESCON: IBM standard for connecting peripherals to a computer over fiber optics. Acronym for Enterprise System Connection.

Excess loss: The amount of light lost in a coupler, beyond that inherent in the splitting to multiple output fibers.

F

Fiber Amplifier: an all optical amplifier using erbium or other doped fibers and pump lasers to increase signal output power without electronic conversion.

Ferrule: A precision tube which holds a fiber for alignment for interconnection or termination. A ferrule may be part of a connector or mechanical splice.

Fiber tracer: An instrument that couples visible light into the fiber to allow visual checking of continuity and tracing for correct connections.
Fiber identifier: A device that clamps onto a fiber and couples light from the fiber by bending, to identify the fiber and detect high speed traffic of an operating link or a 2 kHz tone injected by a test source.
Fiber optics: Light transmission through flexible optical fibers for communications or lighting.
FO: Common abbreviation for "fiber optic."
Fresnel reflection, back reflection, optical return loss: Light reflected from the cleaved or polished end of a fiber caused by the difference of refractive indices of air and glass. Typically 4% of the incident light.
FTTH: fiber to the home
Fusion splicer: An instrument that splices fibers by fusing or welding them, typically by electrical arc.

G
Graded index (GI): A type of multimode fiber which used a graded profile of refractive index in the core material to correct for dispersion.

I
Index of refraction: A measure of the speed of light in a material.
Index matching fluid: A liquid used of refractive index similar to glass used to match the materials at the ends of two fibers to reduce loss and back reflection.
Index profile: The refractive index of a fiber as a function of cross section.
Insertion loss: The loss caused by the insertion of a component such as a splice or connector in an optical fiber.

J
Jacket: The protective outer coating of the cable.
Jumper cable: A short single fiber cable with connectors on both ends used for interconnecting other cables or testing.

L
Laser diode, ILD: A semiconductor device that emits high powered, coherent light when stimulated by an electrical current. Used in transmitters for singlemode fiber links.
Launch cable: A known good fiber optic jumper cable attached to a source and calibrated for output power used used as a reference cable for loss testing. This cable must be made of fiber and connectors of a matching type to the cables to be tested.
Light-emitting diode, LED: A semiconductor device that emits light when stimulated by an electrical current. Used in transmitters for multimode fiber links.

Link, fiber optic: A combination of transmitter, receiver and fiber optic cable connecting them capable of transmitting data. May be analog or digital.
Long wavelength: A commonly used term for light in the 1300 and 1550 nm ranges.
Loss, optical: The amount of optical power lost as light is transmitted through fiber, splices, couplers, etc.
Loss budget: The amount of power lost in the link. Often used in terms of the maximum amount of loss that can be tolerated by a given link.

M
Margin: The additional amount of loss that can be tolerated in a link.
Mechanical splice: A semi-permanent connection between two fibers made with an alignment device and index matching fluid or adhesive.
Micron (*m): A unit of measure, 10-6 m, used to measure wavelength of light.
Microscope, fiber optic inspection: A microscope used to inspect the end surface of a connector for flaws or contamination or a fiber for cleave quality.
Modal dispersion: The temporal spreading of a pulse in an optical waveguide caused by modal effects.
Mode field diameter: A measure of the core size in singlemode fiber.
Mode filter: A device that removes optical power in higher order modes in fiber.
Mode scrambler: A device that mixes optical power in fiber to achieve equal power distribution in all modes. Mode stripper: A device that removes light in the cladding of an optical fiber.
Mode: A single electromagnetic field pattern that travels in fiber.
Multimode fiber: A fiber with core diameter much larger than the wavelength of light transmitted that allows many modes of light to propagate. Commonly used with LED sources for lower speed, short distance links.

N
Nanometer (nm): A unit of measure , 10-9 m, used to measure the wavelength of light.
Network: A system of cables, hardware and equipment used for communications.
Numerical aperture (NA): A measure of the light acceptance angle of the fiber.

O
Optical amplifier: A device that amplifies light without converting it to an electrical signal.
Optical fiber: An optical waveguide, comprised of a light carrying core and cladding which traps light in the core.
Optical loss test set (OLTS): An measurement instrument for optical loss that includes both a meter and source.
Optical power: The amount of radiant energy per unit time, expressed in linear

units of Watts or on a logarithmic scale, in dBm (where 0 dB = 1 mW) or dB* (where 0 dB*=1 microWatt).

Optical return loss, reflectance, back reflection: Light reflected from the cleaved or polished end of a fiber caused by the difference of refractive indices of air and glass. Expressed in dB relative to incident power.

Optical switch: A device that routes an optical signal from one or more input ports to one or more output ports.

Optical time domain reflectometer (OTDR): An instruments that used backscattered light to find faults in optical fiber and infer loss.

Overfilled launch: A condition for launching light into the fiber where the incoming light has a spot size and NA larger than accepted by the fiber, filling all modes in the fiber.

P

PC: Physical Contact, PC Connector

Photodiode: A semiconductor that converts light to an electrical signal, used in fiber optic receivers.

Pigtail: A short length of fiber attached to a fiber optic component such as a laser or coupler.

Plastic optical fiber (POF): An optical fiber made of plastic.

Plastic-clad silica (PCS) fiber: A fiber made with a glass core and plastic cladding.

PMD, polarization mode dispersion: Dispersion in singlemode fiber caused by the difference in speed of light of the polarization modes in the fiber.

Power budget: The difference (in dB) between the transmitted optical power (in dBm) and the receiver sensitivity (in dBm).

Power meter, fiber optic: An instrument that measures optical power emanating form the end of a fiber.

Preform: The large diameter glass rod from which fiber is drawn.

R

Receive cable: A known good fiber optic jumper cable attached to a power meter used as a reference cable for loss testing. This cable must be made of fiber and connectors of a matching type to the cables to be tested.

Receiver: A device containing a photodiode and signal conditioning circuitry that converts light to an electrical signal in fiber optic links.

Reference cable: A known good fiber optic jumper cable attached to a light source or power meter used as a reference cable for loss testing.

Reflectance: Light reflected from the cleaved or polished end of a fiber caused by the difference of refractive indices of air and glass.

Refractive index: A property of optical materials that relates to the velocity of light in the material.

Repeater, regenerator: A device that receives a fiber optic signal and regenerates it for retransmission, used in very long fiber optic links.

S

Scattering: The change of direction of light after striking small particles that causes loss in optical fibers.

Sheath: The term used for the outer protective layers of a cable consisting of jacket, armor and strength members.

Short wavelength: A commonly used term for light in the 665, 790, and 850 nm ranges.

Singlemode fiber: A fiber with a small core, only a few times the wavelength of light transmitted, that only allows one mode of light to propagate. Commonly used with laser sources for high speed, long distance links.

Source: A laser diode or LED used to inject an optical signal into fiber.

Splice (fusion or mechanical): A device that provides for a connection between two fibers, typically intended to be permanent.

Splitting ratio: The distribution of power among the output fibers of a coupler.

Steady state modal distribution: Equilibrium modal distribution (EMD) in multimode fiber, achieved some distance from the source, where the relative power in the modes becomes stable with increasing distance.

Step index fiber: A multimode fiber where the core is all the same index of refraction.

Surface emitter LED: A LED that emits light perpendicular to the semiconductor chip. Most LEDs used in datacommunications are surface emitters.

T

Talkset, fiber optic: A communication device that allows conversation over unused fibers.

Termination: Preparation of the end of a fiber to allow connection to another fiber or an active device, sometimes also called "connectorization".

Test cable: A short single fiber jumper cable with connectors on both ends used for testing. This cable must be made of fiber and connectors of a matching type to the cables to be tested.

Test kit: A kit of fiber optic instruments, typically including a power meter, source and test accessories used for measuring loss and power.

Test source: A laser diode or LED used to inject an optical signal into fiber for testing loss of the fiber or other components.

Total internal reflection: Confinement of light into the core of a fiber by the reflection off the core-cladding boundary.

Transmitter: A device which includes a LED or laser source and signal conditioning electronics that is used to inject a signal into fiber.

V

VCSEL: vertical cavity surface emitting laser, a type of laser that emits light vertically out of the chip, not out the edge, widely used in fast multimode networks.

Visual fault locator (VFL): A device that couples visible light into the fiber to allow visual tracing and testing of continuity. Some are bright enough to allow finding breaks in fiber through the cable jacket.

W
Watts: A linear measure of optical power, usually expressed in milliwatts (mW), microwatts (*W) or nanowatts (nW).
Wavelength: A measure of the color of light, usually expressed in nanometers (nm) or microns (*m).
Wavelength division multiplexing (WDM): A technique of sending signals of several different wavelengths of light into the fiber simultaneously.
Working margin: The difference (in dB) between the power budget and the loss budget (i.e. the excess power margin).

Index
Finding Things In This Book

This book is adopting a lot of new ideas in creating a more useful book for reference and training, so we thought we'd try a new approach to the index also. Often when trying to find something in an index, you end up looking at dozens of pages before you find what you want.

We're going to try another approach, closer to a detailed Table of Contents with comments, organized by topics we think will be most likely sought. Start with the area of interest, then look for the subjects below. Let us know what you think.

The FOA Online Reference Guide has a Google Custom Search function that can help find specific topics or terms on the FOA site.

Preface.. vii

Chapter 1
Introduction... 9
What is "Fiber Optics"?.. 9
   A Brief History 9
Which Fiber Optics? 11
   Outside Plant.. 11
   Premises Cabling 12
   The Installers.. 13
Fiber, Copper or Wireless ?.. 13
Standards Facilitate Fiber Applications 13
Two Important Issues When Working With Fiber 14
   Safety When Working With Fiber Optics............................... 14
   Zero Tolerance for Dirt 15

Chapter 2
Fiber Optic Jargon... 19
If you are looking for a definition of a term used in Premises Cabling, start here. If you are looking for a specific definition of a technical word, there is a Glossary in the FOA Online Reference Guide.
What Is Fiber Optics?... 19
The Metric System.. 19
   Meter 19
   Kilometer 20
   Micron 20
   Nanometer 20
Fiber 20
   Optical Fiber... 20
   Core 20

Cladding 20
Buffer 20
Mode 20
Multimode Fiber 20
Singlemode Fiber 21
Fiber Identification 21
Plastic Optical Fiber (POF) 21
Fiber Optic Cable 21
Cable 21
Jacket 22
Strength Members 22
Armor 22
Sheath 22
Outside Plant Installations 22
Underground 22
Direct Buried 22
Aerial 22
Submarine 22
Termination and Splicing 22
Connector 22
Splice 23
Mechanical Splice 23
Fusion Splice 23
Fusion Splicer 23
Hardware 23
Fiber Performance Specifications 23
Attenuation 23
Bandwidth 23
Decibels (dB) 23
dB 23
dBm 23
Loss, Optical Loss 23
Optical Power 24
Dispersion 24
Scattering 24
Wavelength 24
Tools 24
Jacket Slitter or Splitter 24
Fiber Stripper 24
Cleaver 25
Scribe 25
Polishing Puck 25
Polishing Film 25
Crimper 25

Fusion Splicer 25
Fiber Optic Test Equipment 25
Optical Power Meter... 25
Light Source... 25
Optical Loss Test Set (OLTS)... 25
Reference Test Cables.. 26
Mating Adapter 26
Fiber Tracer.. 26
Visual Fault Locator (VFL) 26
Inspection Microscope 26
Optical Time Domain Reflectometer (OTDR)..................................... 26
Specialized Testers 26

Chapter 3
Fiber Optic Communications 29

Why use fiber?... 29
Fiber Optic Communication Networks 30
Outside Plant Networks.. 30
Telephone Networks 30
The Internet 31
CATV 31
Security Systems.. 32
Metropolitan Networks.. 32
Utility Networks 33
Premises Networks 33
Optical LANs.. 34
Industrial Networks 34
Military and Platforms 35
Designing Fiber Optic Networks 35

Chapter 4
Fiber Optic Transmission Systems And Components.......................... 39

Fiber Optic Data Links.. 39
Analog or Digital.. 40
Packaging 40
Sources for Fiber Optic Transmitters.. 40
Typical Fiber Optic Source Specifications...................................... 41
Detectors for Fiber Optic Receivers 43
Specialty Fiber Optic Transmission Components 43
Wavelength Division Multiplexing 43
Repeaters And Fiber Amplifiers... 45
Fiber Optic Network Optical Wavelength Transmission Bands.............. 46
DWDM Band Wavelength Range 47
Data Link Performance And Link Power Budget 47

Measuring Data Transmission Quality 47
Link Power Budget 48
Typical Fiber optic link/system performance parameters 49
Long Distance Considerations 49

Chapter 5
Optical Fiber **53**
What is Optical Fiber? 53
Manufacturing Optical Fiber 54
Fiber Types 54
Multimode and Singlemode Types 54
Step Index Multimode 55
Graded Index Multimode 55
Singlemode 56
Specialty Fibers 56
Fiber Sizes and Types 56
Fiber Types and Typical Specifications 57
Mixing Fiber Types 58
Fiber Specifications 58
Attenuation 58
Bend-Insensitive Fibers 60
Low Water Peak Fibers 60
Modal Effects on Multimode Fiber Attenuation 60
Modal Effects on Singlemode Fiber Attenuation 62
Dispersion in Multimode and Singlemode Fiber 62
Modal Effects on Multimode Fiber Bandwidth 62
Chromatic Dispersion 63
Dispersion in Singlemode Fiber 63
What Causes Chromatic Dispersion 64
Waveguide Dispersion 64
Engineered Dispersion in Fibers 65
Dispersion Compensation 65
Chromatic Dispersion in the Cable Plant 65
Polarization Mode Dispersion 65
Waveguide Birefringence 66
Material Birefringence 66

Chapter 6
Fiber Optic Cable **71**
Fiber Optic Cable Design 71
Cable Construction 72
Tight Buffer Coating 73
Loose Tubes (loose tube cables) 73
Strength members 73

Cable Jacket 73
Protection Against Water and Moisture 74
Protection Against Crushing or Rodent Penetration 74
Fiber Optic Cable Types 74
Tight Buffer Cable Types 74
Simplex And Zip Cord 74
Distribution Cable 75
Breakout Cable 75
Loose Tube Cable Types 76
Loose Tube Cable 76
Ribbon Cable 76
Armored Cable 77
Aerial Cables 77
Underwater and Submarine Cables 78
Other Types of Cable 78
Air-Blown Cable 79
Air-Blown Fiber 79
Hybrid and Composite Cables 79
Choosing a Cable Design 80
Pulling Strength 80
Bending Radius Limits 80
Water Protection 80
Crush Loads or Rodent Penetration 80
Fire Code Ratings For Premises Cables 80
Grounding and Bonding 81
Cable Color Codes 81
Premises Cable Jacket Color Codes 82
Fiber Color Codes 82
Choosing Cables 83

Chapter 7
Splices and Connectors **87**
Splices or Connectors? 87
Performance Specifications 88
Optical Loss 88
Reflectance 90
Splicing Optical Fibers 90
Color Codes for Splicing 91
Fusion Splices 91
The Fusion Splicing Process 92
Preparing the Fibers 92
Running the splicer program 92
Mass (Ribbon) Fusion Splicing 92
Mechanical Splices 93

Mechanical Splicing Process 93
  Preparing the Fibers 93
  Making The Mechanical Splice 93
Making Good Splices, Fusion or Mechanical 93
Verifying Splice Loss 94
Choosing a Splice Type 94
Protecting Splices 95
Connectors 96
Styles of Fiber Optic Connectors 96
Connector Popularity 98
Connector Construction 99
Connector Ferrule Shapes & Polishes 99
Connector Color Codes: 100
Termination Procedures 101
Multimode Terminations 101
Singlemode Terminations 101
Adhesive Terminations 102
  Epoxy/Polish 102
  "Hot Melt" Adhesive/Polish 102
  Anaerobic Adhesive/Polish 103
The Termination Process 103
Crimp/Polish 104
Prepolished/splice (also called "cleave & crimp") 104
Do You Have To Terminate In The Field? 106
Managing and Protecting Terminations 106

Chapter 8
Fiber Optic Testing 111
Fiber Optic Tests 111
Visual Inspection 112
Visual Tracing 112
Visual Fault Location 112
Optical Power 114
Calibration of Power Measurements 115
Understanding FO Power Meter Measurement Uncertainty 116
Instrument Resolution vs. Measurement Uncertainty 117
Fiber Optic Power Meters 118
Optical Loss or Insertion Loss 118
Fiber Optic Test Sources 120
Reference Cables 121
Testing Loss 122
  One Cable Reference 123
  Two Cable Reference 124
  Three Cable Reference 125

Choosing a Reference Method 126
Modal Effect on Multimode Loss Measurements 126
What Loss Should You Get When Testing Cables? 127
Troubleshooting Hints 127
OTDR testing 127
How OTDRs Work 129
Making Measurements With The OTDR 130
Fiber Attenuation Coefficient 131
Splice or Connector Loss 131
Reflectance 131
Comparing Traces 132
OTDR Measurement Uncertainty 132
OTDR "Ghosts" 134
OTDR Limitations 134
Using The OTDR Correctly 134
Testing Long Haul, High Speed Fiber Optic Networks 135
Chromatic Dispersion in the Cable Plant 135
Testing Chromatic Dispersion 135
Phase Shift Method 136
Pulse Delay Method 136
OTDR Test Method 137
Polarization Mode Dispersion 137
Testing PMD 137
Spectral Attenuation 139
Other Testing 139

Chapter 9
Fiber Optic Network Design 145

What Is Fiber Optic Network Design? 145
Working With Others 145
Qualifications For Fiber Optic Network Designers 146
Copper, Fiber or Wireless? 146
The Communications System 146
Outside Plant Networks 147
Premises Networks 148
Cabling Design 148
Long Distance and Outside Plant Cabling 148
Premises Cabling 149
Use of Cabling Standards 150
Choosing Transmission Equipment 150
Planning The Route 152
Site Visits 153
Call Before You Dig 154
Choosing Components 154

Choosing Components For Outside Plant Installations............................ 154
Cables.. 155
Splicing And Termination Hardware 157
Choosing Components For Premises Installations 158
Creating A Materials List 159
Cable Plant Link Loss Budget Analysis 160
Cable Plant Passive Component Loss... 161
Step 1. Calculate fiber loss at the operating wavelengths................ 161
Step 2. Connector Loss 161
Step 3. Splice Loss.. 162
Step 4. Total Cable Plant Loss.. 162
Equipment Link Loss Budget Calculation... 163
Step 5. Data From Manufacturer's Specification for Active Components
163
Step 6. Loss Margin Calculation 163
Project Documentation 164
The Documentation Process... 164
Protecting Records... 165
Planning for the Installation 165
The Project Manager... 166
Design Checklist 166
Design process... 166
Contractor package for the install.. 166
Requirements for completion of cable plant installation 167
Developing A Project Checklist 167
Facilities and Power/Ground issues.. 168
Developing A Test Plan 168
Required vs. Optional Testing.. 169
Coordinating Testing and Documentation.. 169
Planning for Restoration 170
Documentation for Restoration 170
Equipment For Restoration 170
Testing and Troubleshooting.. 170
Tools and Components 171
Preparing Personnel... 171
Managing A Fiber Optic Project.. 172
On Site Management and Supervision 172
Contacts with Local Authorities 173
Continuous Inspection, Testing and Corrections................................. 173

Chapter 10
Fiber Optic Network Installation **177**
Preparing For Installation 177
The Role of the Contractor in an Installation.. 177

The Contract 179
Planning For The Project 179
Installation Checklist.. 180
Pre-install checklist: 180
Before starting the install:.. 181
During The Installation: 181
After completion of cable plant installation: 181
Preparing For Outside Plant Installations 182
Call Before You Dig.. 182
Pulling and Placing Cable.. 183
Underground Cables.. 183
Buried Cables 186
Aerial Cables 187
Submarine/Underwater Cabling....................................... 189
Hardware and Equipment 190
Splicing Cables 190
Midspan Entry.. 191
Termination.. 192
Preparing For Premises Fiber Optic Installations 193
Premises Support Structures 193
Fire Stopping... 194
Electrical Systems... 195
Grounding and Bonding 195
Marking and Identifying Cables.. 195
Removal of Abandoned Cables.. 196
Equipping Installation Personnel 196
Equipping The Installer With Tools....................................... 196
Equipping The Installer With Test Equipment 198
Training and Safety 199
Fiber Optic Training.. 199
Getting More Training... 199
Learning to install new components...................................... 200
Learning to use new equipment.. 201
Learning New Applications... 201
Finding Appropriate Training 201
Safety In Working With Optical Fiber 202
Safety.. 202
Eye Safety 203
Bare Fiber Safety.. 205
Other Considerations for Safety 206
Fiber Optic Installation Safety Rules................................. 206
Installing Fiber Optic Cable 207
Receipt.. 207
Handling Fiber Optic Cables 207

Storage.. 207
Installation Guidelines 208
Pulling Tension.. 208
Twisting Cable... 209
Installing Swivel Pulling Eyes on Fiber Optic Cable............................ 209
    Procedure For Installing Swivel Pulling Eyes: 210
How To "Figure 8" Cable for Intermediate Pulls in OSP Installations..... 210
Use this procedure for pulling from one end: 210
For a midspan pull, use these directions:..211
Bend Radius..211
Vertical Cable Runs...211
Installing Premises Cable in Cable Trays..211
Use of Innerduct..211
Use Of Cable Ties 212
Fire Stopping 212
Grounding and Bonding 212
Termination and Splicing 212
Splicing.. 213
Termination.. 213
Labeling and Documentation 214
Cleaning Up The Job Site 214
Saving Excess Components 214
Testing the Installed Fiber Optic Cable Plant 215
Continuity Testing 215
Insertion Loss 215
OTDR Testing.. 216
Administration, Management, and Documentation 216

Appendix A
KSAs for CFOT + CFospT.. 221

Appendix B
Fiber To The Home 225
Fiber To The Home Architectures... 227
    FTTC: Fiber To The Curb (or Node, FTTN) 227
    FTTH Active Star Network 228
    FTTH home run 228
    FTTH PON: Passive Optical Network.. 229
    Triple Play Systems 232
Fiber To The Home PON Types 232
    Standards for PON Triple Play Systems... 232
    RFOG: CATV's FTTH 233
    PONs in Premises Applications 234
    PON Components.. 235

PON Splitters 235
FTTx PON Testing 236

Appendix C
Additional References For Training and Study 239

Appendix D
Definitions of Terms 241

Index 249

44615970R00146

Made in the USA
San Bernardino, CA
19 January 2017